THE KILLING GAME

(An Alexa Chase Suspense Thriller—Book 1)

Kate Bold

Kate Bold

Debut author Kate Bold is author of the ALEXA CHASE SUSPENSE THRILLER series, comprising three books (and counting).

An avid reader and lifelong fan of the mystery and thriller genres, Kate loves to hear from you, so please feel free to visit www.kateboldauthor.com to learn more and stay in touch.

ISBN: 978-1-0943-9280-6

BOOKS BY KATE BOLD

ALEXA CHASE SUSPENSE THRILLER

THE KILLING GAME (Book #1)
THE KILLING TIDE (Book #2)
THE KILLING HOUR (Book #3)

CHAPTER ONE

Sonora Desert, 25 miles southwest of Tucson, Arizona
June 24, Noon

"What you have to remember, Alexa, is that there are three types of people—the strong, the weak, and those who think they're one but are really the other."

Deputy United States Marshal Alexa Chase ignored her prisoner and looked through the steel mesh of the prisoner transport bus at the beautiful Sonora Desert rolling by. The glaring spring sun had shot the temperature up to the high 90s, but it couldn't wash out the varied colors and subtle beauty of the desert.

Unlike the rolling sand dunes people typically associated with deserts, the Sonora Desert was alive with life. Prickly pear cacti and barrel cacti were interspersed with the low green domes of sweet bush. Here and there a majestic saguaro rose up twice the height of a man, looking like stationary sentinels against the clear blue sky. Birds flitted in the air, and a jackrabbit darted across the road. The rocks were varied hues of browns, oranges, and reds that would turn brilliant in the region's matchless sunsets.

A much nicer view than the one inside the prison bus she was riding. But she forced herself to look back at her prisoner. Only an idiot would take their eyes off Drake Logan for more than a few seconds.

He was a small man, barely five eight and slight of build, but Alexa knew he compensated for this with a surprising strength and coldblooded ruthlessness. Soft, intelligent brown eyes looked out from an angular, poorly shaven face beneath a shock of unruly brown hair.

Drake smiled a little, knowing she didn't want to hear what he said but also knowing she was a captive audience. Not that he needed much encouragement. Dad would have said he "could talk the spines off a cactus."

"You see," Drake said, raising one manacled hand to his thin lips as if to smoke a cigarette, an odd habit of his. "The duty of the strong isn't to crush the weak, like a lot of people think; it's to expose the weak who think they're strong. That's the only way to show society what true strength is. That's why I don't kill children, not even bratty ones. Too easy."

A slow clap came from the seat behind him. U.S. Marshal Robert Powers, still clapping, said, "Alexa, I never realized we were in the presence of a humanitarian."

"I am a humanitarian, in a way. Inspiration helps people far more than handouts."

"Humanitarian contains the word human," Robert said, studying the arm and leg manacles that kept Drake secure to the metal seat bolted to the bottom of the bus. "There's nothing human about you."

"On the contrary, my dear friend," Drake said, raising a forefinger like a university professor. "I'm more human than anyone on this bus."

Alexa snorted. The only other people on the bus besides the two U.S. Marshals transporting the prisoner to a new maximum security prison in the middle of the desert were the two prison guards up front. Usually this bus would have twenty prisoners packing the seats. But the prison Drake was being transferred from was full of murderers, rapists, meth dealers, and human traffickers. It wouldn't be right to subject that quality of people to the company of a scumbag like Drake.

The man had killed dozens of people across the Southwest in the most horrible, humiliating ways possible. He was a monster. A highly intelligent monster. It had taken Alexa and her partner more than a year to track him down, and even then, it had been as much luck as it was policework that nabbed him.

Going to prison hadn't stopped his killing spree, either.

Drake put his hands to his lips again. He was a chain smoker, and the five-hour drive without a single menthol must have been torture for him. Good.

"With one exception, of course," Drake said, his eyes lingering on her.

Even chained up that felt creepy. Alexa knew he was trying to draw her into the conversation. She didn't take the bait. She wanted to get this transfer over, go home, and take a long shower.

He looked out the window. Alexa watched his eyes. You could always tell a lot about a perp from the eyes. Drake's never stopped moving. Always searching. Always assessing. The few witnesses who had survived to testify said he always looked like a scientist who had just discovered something fascinating under a microscope, even when strangling someone with their own intestines.

Those eyes were especially watchful on this trip. They flicked a bit to one side as the bus sped past a mile marker.

"People like me are helping humanity," Drake declared.

"Yeah, sure you are," Powers said. He was a rugged man in his fifties with the deeply tanned, seamed face of someone who had spent a lifetime outdoors. His gray eyes, bright by contrast, never strayed from the prisoner, and his strong hand never strayed far from the Glock 9mm at his side.

Neither did Alexa's. She had learned a lot about law enforcement from Powers. A friend of her uncle's, it had been Powers who had noticed the aimless twenty-something with an urge to be something more than a rancher and convinced her to try her hand at law enforcement. It had been Powers who thought her deadly aim to be something more than cute, and besides one of her brothers, he was the only person to notice her brains at all.

"I am helping humanity," the prisoner continued. "Modern society crushes people down. Puts them in a position of powerlessness. They are dependent on the system for their food, electricity, livelihood, everything. The system keeps them from being independent, keeps them from being strong. Ted Kaczynski, the Unabomber, taught me that. Ever read his manifesto? Interesting stuff. So anyway, by killing the weak masking as the strong, I show society for what it is—a mirage. Society is weak, my friends. It can only enforce its will through its agents of law enforcement and sap the spirit through mass entertainment. But when a little runt like me strikes back, people's spines straighten a bit."

"You going to babble on like this for the entire trip?" Powers asked, rolling his eyes and looking at Alexa, who smiled but never took her eyes off Drake for long. You had to act professional at all times in a job like this. Otherwise you get distracted, and distracted agents ended up dead agents.

Powers had taught her that too. He had told her, in gruesome detail, how every U.S. Marshal who had died in the line of duty came to their end. Then he had given her pop quizzes.

"Elwin Hubbard?" he would ask.

"Failed to check the back seat of his car."

"Ricardo Gonzalez?"

"Walked into the suspect's bar alone."

"Robert Forsyth?"

"Didn't think a woman would shoot him in the back."

Drake laughed. "Why shouldn't I? You two caught me when no one else could. That makes you among the strong, although not as strong as me; and the strong need to stick together. It was nice of you to give me a solo ride. Most of the inmates back in Phoenix are boring as hell. Nothing to learn from those losers."

Alexa grimaced. The reason Drake was riding alone was that he had killed two inmates in the five years since he had been incarcerated, and seriously injured three more. Every time he got out of solitary he'd strike out at someone, usually the biggest, best connected gang member he could find. Bloods, Crips, Latin Kings, MS-13 … they were all terrified of him.

It was remarkable that such a small man could get away with it, but he had lightning fast reflexes, and always seemed to have access to a shiv, a couple of lookouts, and an accomplice to distract his victim. He had a whole network of followers on the inside, attracted like cult members to his sermons about personal liberation.

Drake kept staring out the window. Another mile marker flicked by.

He turned and looked directly at Alexa, studying her under those microscope eyes.

She tensed. She had never gotten used to that.

"Some people are naturally strong, as I said. Like your partner here. That man's got a will of cast iron, and I salute him for it. But he's not our kind. The two donut boys in the front sure aren't our kind either. Weak. Their badges and guns don't change that one bit. Took jobs bullying men locked in cages. Weak. You and I, on the other hand, we were strong and thought we were weak. We grew. And in growing, we became the strongest of the strong."

Alexa turned away, an unpleasant memory welling up inside of her.

Sixteen years old on her father's ranch. The new ranch hand, only a few years older and super cute, asked her to help him in the stable.

She had thought nothing of it, until Alexa discovered what he wanted help with.

She felt flattered, nervous, tempted. Then he got rough.

Teeth lying scattered amid the straw on the stable floor. He bled so much. Alexa running out to apologize to her dad before he even knew what she had done.

Training took over. Alexa shrugged the memory off and watched the prisoner. Shackled hand and foot, he was helpless, but you could never assume that, especially with someone like Drake Logan. The previous year, he had come one fence away from escaping a maximum security prison.

"I'm glad you volunteered for this assignment, Alexa," Drake said. "You too, Robert, despite what I just said. You're good company. I'm going to miss you."

"We won't miss you," Robert Powers grunted. "But we'll sure be happy knowing you're buried in Arizona's brand new maximum security prison."

"They're coming for me soon," Drake replied. "The strongest of the weak."

"Oh, that's right," Powers said, shooting a smile at Alexa. "All those gang members who you attacked have homies in this new place. You're going to have to prove yourself all over again, and this time they're ready for you. They've had time to prepare."

Powers had been frustrated that Drake didn't get the death penalty. Drake had pled guilty, which meant he could only face prison. That frustrated Alexa too. How could he plead anything else when he owned a trailer full of body parts?

"Nobody's ever ready for me," Drake said.

Suddenly he bent over, getting into the brace position like he was on an airplane in freefall.

Alexa stared at him for a second, confused.

Then she had a sudden shock of realization—followed instantly by terror.

She whirled around to look through the metal grill, past the two officers in the front seat, and out onto the road ahead.

They drove along an isolated stretch of two-lane highway, uninhabited desert stretching to the horizon on either side. Only one other vehicle was visible, an armored car with the Arizona Bank and Trust logo.

It was in the opposite lane, coming in their direction.

It was almost to them.

"Look out!" Alexa cried.

The driver of the prison truck and his partner both turned around to look at Drake.

"No! The armored car!"

They both turned back. Too late.

The armored car swerved into their lane just as it passed, slamming into the side of their bus with a screech of tortured metal.

Alexa felt an impact, her head slamming into something, her ribs feeling like they were being crushed in a gigantic vice.

Then her world spun.

Her ears filled with the sound of crumpling metal as the bus turned over and over, each turn hurting some other part of her body. She raised her arms, doing her best to protect her face and head.

Finally the rolling stopped as the bus crashed to a hard stop in a dry wash.

She tried to raise her head, but it hurt too much.

Then, only blackness.

CHAPTER TWO

Consciousness returned slowly. At first Alexa heard sounds—the buzz of a circular saw on metal, the groans of a man, the creak and screech of a bent door being forced open. All of these things registered on her already half-alert consciousness even before her vision returned.

At first, only hazy shapes in a bleary light.

Then, the pain.

Alexa hurt all over, a uniform ache that focused especially in her midsection. There she felt a tremendous weight that made every breath a jabbing agony. There was also a burning agony down the length of her left forearm.

Even as her vision began to clear, she lowered her hand to her holster, only to find jagged metal in the way. She fumbled for a moment, searching by feel as she blinked her eyes, trying to focus. The seat had twisted and pressed against her. That was what hurt her midsection and stopped her moving. The seat belt was still around her, digging painfully into flesh.

She managed to find her holster, and a jolt of fear ran through her as she realized it was empty. Her other hand went for the holster containing her bottle of pepper spray. That was gone too, as was the telescopic metal baton that hung next to it.

She blinked a couple more times, and the world came into focus.

The prison bus lay on its side. She lay crushed against one wall, now against the ground, pinned by the row of seating that had crumpled and twisted to wrap around her like a restraining arm.

Her entire side was soaked in blood, which flowed freely from a deep gash running from the heel of her left palm almost to her elbow.

A burly man wearing a ski mask stood above Alexa, her Glock in his hand.

The interior of the bus shook and clanged with the sound of hurried activity. Alexa looked around, neck aching in protest as she did so, and saw Drake above and a bit behind her, suspended in the air by his chains, grinning from ear to ear.

"You can't keep a good man down," he said, and gave her a wink.

Alexa's blood ran cold. She looked to Powers, and saw him stretched out, unconscious, a great gash to his head. His seatbelt and half the seat had been torn out with him on impact.

She wanted to call out to him, and yet didn't dare. She didn't want to bring any attention to her partner.

That was in vain. The man who had taken her gun bent over Powers and took his as well.

"He's alive," the masked man said with the trace of a Mexican accent. His skin, where it showed between gloves and sleeve, was that of a Caucasian. Strange.

Another man clambered through the open door in the back of bus. He was shorter, thinner, but moved with grace and strength, carrying a large pair of bolt cutters.

The buzz of a circular saw, the same sound that had woken her up, sounded from the front of the bus. Alexa looked in that direction and through a cracked window saw a masked woman kneeling on the side, now the top, of the bus, cutting through the metal door. Sparks flew in a great jet from the metal grinding at metal. A man stood beside her, a sawed-off shotgun in his hands. Both prison guards hung slack in their seats.

"Wake up!" Alexa shouted at them.

She felt the cold muzzle of her own gun pressed against her temple.

"Another word and you're dead," the masked man told her.

A loud snip made her turn her eyes, although she didn't dare move her head. The man with the bolt cutters cut through Drake's leg chains, freeing them so he could awkwardly support himself by standing on tiptoe on the wreckage beneath him. The masked man turned his attention to the chains on his wrists.

Desperately, Alexa looked back at the woman working with the circular saw. She finished the work, set the saw to one side, and hauled open the door. Her companion with the shotgun aimed down at the two helpless prison guards.

Just at that moment, one of the guards stopped pretending to be unconscious, yanked out a pistol, and fired.

The man with the shotgun jerked back, blood gushing from his chest, and toppled off the bus. The woman with the buzz saw leaped off.

Shouting and confusion from two masked men in the back of the bus, cut off short by Drake's commanding voice.

"Do what you came here to do!"

The guy with the bolt cutters got back to work on Drake's chains. His companion, wielding a U.S. Marshal Service gun in each hand, stood a bit back, covering both Alexa and Robert.

The sound of someone clambering onto the bus up front made Alexa turn again. The woman was back, now gripping the shotgun. Keeping out of sight of the open doorway, she reached around with her gun, ducked back as the guard fired at her hands, missing, then reached around again and blasted the shotgun at point blank range.

A spray of blood against the window at the back of the cab made Alexa cry out. While she could barely see through it, she did see the guard still moving. His gun barked again, but to no effect. The woman fired a second time, pumped another shell into the chamber, and fired again.

She fired three more times before she finally stopped. By then the entire window was a mass of dripping gore.

Alexa slumped, all feeling gone. She knew she would die in the next few moments.

Die a painful, humiliating death.

"Well, now," Drake said as if he had spotted an especially pretty girl at a square dance.

Alexa forced herself to look at him. He stood in the overturned bus hunched somewhat under a hanging seat. He smiled and rubbed his wrists.

"Get it over with," Alexa grumbled.

Drake put on an innocent face. "Get what over with?"

"Shut up and do it. After I'm dead, you're going to set off the biggest manhunt in American history."

Drake waggled a finger at her. "Wrong on several accounts. First, they're not catching me. Not with as many friends as I got." He slapped the gunman on the back. "Second, I'm not a rabid dog. I'm a shining light to oppressed humanity." Alexa snorted. He said this without any irony whatsoever. "And third, I'm not going to kill you."

A little spark of hope flickered in her. Alexa dismissed it. She would die in the next couple of minutes, in the horrible, demeaning way he killed all his victims.

Drake turned to the man with the bolt cutters, who handed him a Bowie knife.

Alexa took a deep breath and prepared herself.

I did some good in the world. Was kind to my family and friends. Caught a lot of bad guys. So I die at 31. I did a lot more than most people who live twice as long.

All that reasoning couldn't dampen her terror, but it did give her the strength to hide it. She wouldn't give him the pleasure of seeing her tremble, hearing her beg.

"Prison gives you a lot of time to read," Drake said, testing the blade with his thumb. "I've read a lot about these Islamic radicals that seem to pop up everywhere these days. They're my kind of people. Oh, I don't like their religion. Too oppressive to women. I believe a strong spirit can be found in either a man or a woman." At that he made a little bow toward Alexa, and in the direction of the woman who had murdered two prison guards. "What I *do* like about them is how they find strength from a position of weakness. Here they are, squaring up against the world's biggest superpower, and fighting it to a standstill. And how do they do it? They're outnumbered and way outgunned, but they have more savagery than all the United States armed forces and all its allies put together. Terror. That's their weapon, and it's a weapon the entire West can't beat."

Drake leaned over Robert Powers, lifted him up by the hair, and put the knife to his neck.

"Stop!" Alexa shouted.

Drake grinned at her. "What? You think I'm going to cut his head off and trail his DNA all across the state? Come on, Alexa. I'm smarter than that. I'm just going to kill him."

Alexa struggled against the cordon of steel wrapped around her, panicked at seeing her friend and mentor helpless in a psychopath's hands.

"Drake, wait! Take me as a hostage. You can get away. I won't try to fight. Just leave him be."

Drake tut-tutted.

"You haven't learned a single thing I've tried to teach you. If I take you as a hostage, you can't play the game. You can't grow."

Robert Powers's eyes flicked open, bleary and unfocused. For a second they met Alexa's own.

And focused on her.

Alexa looked into those eyes, those eyes that were always confident, always reassuring and wise. Those eyes that always told her she could do more than she thought she could.

And despite the fear and resignation she saw in them now, they still told her the same thing.

Then Drake drew the knife across his throat and a great gush of blood burst forth.

"No!" Alexa screamed, feeling like that knife was cutting her own throat, her own soul.

Powers choked and flailed for a moment, then gradually went slack. Drake tossed him aside like an empty wrapper.

Alexa's gut wrenched, bile rising in her throat. The horrible vision was thankfully blurred by her own tears.

"I'm going to kill you," Alexa sobbed, tears blurring her vision. "I swear to God I'm going to hunt you down and kill you."

"Good," Drake said in a cheerful voice. "Now you're learning."

He snapped his fingers and he and his men clambered out of the van, leaving Alexa to sob all alone, trapped with the dead bodies of three of her colleagues.

CHAPTER THREE

Alexa woke up. The haze from the painkillers the EMTs had given her had begun to wear off. Dull pain laced down her left arm and her ribs were a constant ache. Several lesser pains reminded her of just how much abuse she had taken.

At least the painkillers still dulled it some. She should rest while she still could …

No!

Alexa's eyes snapped open. She lay in a hospital bed of starched white linen, staring at the equally blank white wall. A clock on the wall said three p.m.

Drake had been on the loose for three hours. She had to help hunt him down!

She sat up, wincing at the pain in her side. An IV drip was attached to her arm. She began to fiddle with it.

"And what the hell do you think you're doing?" A hefty Black nurse demanded, stomping into the room. She had a tray of food in her hands, which she set on the bedside table before slapping Alexa's hands away from the IV.

"Don't touch that!" she said.

"I need to get out of here," Alexa said.

"You need to lie back and rest. I brought you some lunch. Now that you're awake you should eat something.

"I don't have time to eat, I—"

"Relax," the nurse ordered as she gently but firmly pushed Alexa back into the pillows.

Alexa lay there, the fight momentarily taken out of her. Even the little effort she had expended had tired her out. The painkillers hadn't worn off as much as she had thought, and her head was still fuzzy.

She would get out of here, but she needed to gather her strength first.

The nurse checked her vitals, plumped up her pillows, and swung the little table on the side of the bed around so the lunch tray was in front of Alexa.

"Do you want something for the pain?" she asked.

"No. I can take it."

"All right, honey. Just push this red button here if you need me. Try to eat something."

"I'm not hungry," Alexa said without emotion. She hadn't felt any emotion for a few hours. She felt like an empty shell. Gutted.

"Your body has been through some rough treatment. You need to keep up your strength."

The image of Robert's neck getting slashed open like a slaughtered hog's flashed through her mind. It had been the same movement—a quick, strong slice.

Back on the ranch, she'd made the same movement on animals countless times.

But Robert wasn't an animal. He had been her mentor, her guide, her partner, and one of the best friends she ever had.

If I tried to eat right now, I'd puke all over these nice clean sheets.

Alexa didn't bother telling the nurse that. She was unstoppable. A bit like her.

The nurse swung the side table on its moveable arm to put it in front of Alexa.

"Eat. Doctor's orders."

"You're not a doctor," Alexa grumbled.

"Fine. Nurse's orders. Don't you know nurses really run things in hospitals? Doctors are too busy examining people's insides and flirting with interns."

"I'm not hungry."

The nurse put her hands on her hips. "I didn't believe that the first time. Eat."

Alexa grunted and picked up her plastic fork, pushing around some peas in one of the little containers on the tray. Besides the peas there was a mass of lumpy mashed potatoes, something that looked like a pork chop that made Alexa's stomach roil, and a miniscule brownie.

She looked away.

"Eat." The nurse ordered, then in a softer tone added, "Look, honey, I know you've been through a lot. This isn't the way to react to it. You need to keep up your strength and move on."

A little flare of anger burst through her numbness.

Move on? How the hell am I supposed to move on from seeing Robert killed?

Just then, Marshal Juan Hernandez, Alexa's commander at the U.S. Marshal Service, walked in.

"Deputy Marshal Chase, I came as fast as I could," he said in a breathless voice.

Marshal Hernandez was a stocky Mexican-American with a thick moustache that was going gray just like his close-cropped hair. Deep worry lines were permanently etched into his weathered face, courtesy of thirty years chasing down some of the region's worst criminals. He was one of the toughest people Alexa had ever met in law enforcement, but he had a kind and supportive side too, especially with his younger officers.

"How are you?" he asked.

"Not eating," the nurse interjected.

"Could you leave us for a moment please?" Marshal Hernandez asked.

"All right. But get her to eat."

The nurse walked out. Alexa's boss turned back to her.

"Deputy Marshal Powers. Alexa. I am so sorry. Robert was a good man. We've got every available person on this case."

Alexa nodded. Of course he did.

Clearing her throat, she said, "The doctor said besides the bruised ribs and some cuts and bruises, I'm fine. They're letting me out this afternoon."

"That's great. You go home and rest for a few days. Take all the time you need."

Alexa sat up in bed, feeling like she had just been struck by lightning. "Go home and rest? I have to help with the manhunt!"

Marshal Hernandez shook his head. "No, Alexa. You were injured in the line of duty and your partner was killed in front of you. You need time to recuperate."

"Drake is out there with a whole team of followers! He's probably killed again already! He may have even crossed the border."

"We have every available marshal on the case, plus the state troopers, local police departments, and we're calling in the FBI. He won't stay free for long."

"Unless he gets to Mexico."

"Border Patrol is keeping an eye out, and we have men posted at the usual coyote paths."

"That won't be good enough for a man like Drake," Alexa grumbled.

There were countless secret routes through the desert, where the men known as coyotes guided illegals across the border. It was impossible to watch them all, or even know about them all.

And there was no reason those routes couldn't run south as well as north.

"We'll get him," her boss repeated. "You have my word on that."

And your word is gold. You won't sleep until you get him. And you will get him. Maybe. And how many innocent people will die between then and now?

"Check the files we assembled from the case," Alexa said, wincing when she said "we." There was no longer a "we." Robert was gone. They'd never work together or talk together or laugh together again. "We have a list of all his known associates."

Hernandez nodded. "We're already on that. That was the first thing we did."

"CSI find anything in the prison van?"

"A couple of hairs that might be from the suspects. We're running a match on all prisoners and staff who have used the van recently to cut out anyone not associated with the attack."

"Check out the back-road compounds in the area. He might have gone to ground in one of them. Although he's probably shifted to another by now."

"We're doing all that, Deputy Marshal Chase."

The switch back to her title showed that her boss was losing patience. She had been telling him to do things that were standard procedure, like she was lecturing a rookie.

Alexa paused, then said, "Sorry. I just feel helpless here."

"It's all right. I got shot in the line of duty back in '98. Threw me for a loop. It happens to all of us."

Alexa looked up at him. She'd heard about that fight, an epic shootout between two U.S. Marshals and five narcotraffickers armed with AK-47s. Hernandez and his partner had won. The fight had made national headlines, and made their careers.

But while that story had taken on the nature of a legend among the U.S. Marshals, told to every rookie and repeated often on long trips or at staff barbeques, she had never heard him mention it.

He looked her in the eye. “It’s tough sitting around doing nothing when the bad guys have hurt you. I know that. But you’re injured and you’re traumatized and you need to take some time off. After I got out of the hospital I went and saw my cousins in Juarez. Smartest thing I could have done.”

“I need to get back on the case.”

“No you don’t,” Hernandez said patiently. “You need to rest.” His face cracked into a weak imitation of a smile. “And you need to eat, or that nurse will kick your ass. Mine too. Take as much time as you need. I have to go now. The office is a madhouse, as you can imagine.”

“All right,” Alexa said.

“Take care. You need to work through what happened. We all do. For you, the best thing to do is to take some time off.”

He moved to the door, then hesitated.

“Do you have any idea why Drake let you live?” he said this in an almost apologetic tone, then quickly added. “It just seems strange, considering his history.”

Alexa shook her head, guilt washing over her as the images of her partner and the two dead prison guards flashed through her mind.

“I don’t know,” she whispered.

“Did he say anything to you? Give any indication why you were spared?”

“I offered myself as a hostage if he spared Rob. He said no, saying if he took me as a hostage, I couldn’t play the game. I couldn’t grow.”

“What the hell is that supposed to mean?” Marshal Hernandez said, shaking his head. “What a nut. I’ll keep you posted.”

Marshal Hernandez tipped his hat to her and walked out of the room.

We’ll see about that, Alexa thought.

Alexa started counting to a hundred, knowing that her boss would be out of the building by then. She could imagine him hurrying down to his vehicle and speeding off to get back into the manhunt.

A good man, and a good officer of the law, but nobody knew more about Drake than her. She needed to be leading this case, not him.

And she would, once she got to a hundred.

* * *

Alexa made her way painfully down to her car, which a fellow agent had brought to the hospital in Tucson where she had been recovering, and headed north on Interstate 10. She managed to dodge the bossy nurse and the security guards, who didn't think anything of a bandaged woman as long as she was wearing civilian clothes. They must have assumed she had just been released.

Alexa had been released. She had released herself.

Usually she hated driving the Interstate. It was no way to see the desert she loved, lined as it was with towns and truck stops and billboards, which she and her friends not-so-affectionately called "garbage on a stick."

She had to get to her files in her home office. She had several boxes of information on Drake piled up in her office closet, including a long list of all known associates.

Maybe among them she could find the men and women who helped set him free.

Plus she felt an urge to get the hell out of Tucson and back home. Away from the city. Away from people. Peace.

Peace eluded her the entire two hours up the highway as she risked an awkward chat with the Highway Patrol as she floored it at 80 mph, weaving in between commuters and eighteen-wheelers.

Robert Powers was dead, and Drake Logan was on the loose.

Even though she had seen it all with her own eyes, the images seared into her memory forever, she had trouble grasping it.

Still weaving through traffic, she cursed Hernandez for not letting her get back on the job. She and Powers were the ones who had caught Drake, after all. They'd spent months poring over the evidence, interviewing witnesses, associates, and the rare survivor of his killing spree.

If anyone could track that animal down, it was her.

In fact, she and Powers had been the best U.S. Marshals team in the region. Over the past eight years since he had recruited her, they had tracked down escaped prisoners, drug traffickers, arms dealers, and white supremacists. And they had always got their man.

And women. She'll never forget the case of Martha Lawrence—a graying, bespectacled schoolteacher who lived a double life of trafficking underage girls for prostitution. Human evil knew no gender, no race, and no age. Powers had told her that on her first day on the job and, later, experience sure taught Alexa that was true.

Thankfully, Martha Lawrence was now serving life in prison and her victims were receiving much-needed counseling.

That perp had worked out of an inconspicuous suburban home, her neighbors never realizing that the boring, quiet woman who went to church and neighborhood watch meetings was actually a monster.

Other perps had been tracked down in the middle of the desert, hiding in caves or remote compounds. There was no area in the Southwest, no matter how remote, that she and Powers hadn't scoured for criminal elements.

Drake would be hiding out somewhere like that. He had created a cult following for himself in the margins of society through the nature of his murders. That line about "there are three types of people—the strong, the weak, and those who think they're one but are really the other" had really resonated with some people. Now every misfit and antisocial element in the region thought of themselves as a hidden superman.

What resonated even more was the kind of victims he picked—the barroom brawler, the local thug everyone feared, the cyberbully. If someone was feared or hated, if someone caused unnecessary harm to everyone around them, Drake killed them in the most painful, demeaning way possible.

In every single case, the people he targeted were bad people, people no one would miss. But that didn't mean they deserved to be staked out in the sun in the middle of the desert until they died of thirst, or have their skin peeled off like some rabbit caught on a hunting trip, or be doused in just enough gasoline to be lit on fire but not killed and *then* staked out in the desert to die of thirst.

There were no limits to his meticulous cruelty.

And then there was his causal cruelty. Because if anyone got in his way, no matter how innocent, he'd kill them too.

Like U.S. Marshal Robert Powers and those two prison guards.

She had to get back on the job.

Damn you, Hernandez. Just because I'm hurt doesn't mean I'm useless.

Traffic increased and slowed. Alexa blinked and realized she had already entered the sprawl of Phoenix. Where had the past hour gone?

She drove through Phoenix, looking with distaste at the high rises and the overpasses and the vast spread of concrete and glass marring the beauty of the desert. She took the turn for U.S. Route 60 north and west, leaving the worst of the ugliness behind her and driving into suburbs patched with forlorn bits of surviving desert.

The suburbs gradually grew smaller, set apart by wider spaces of open land.

Not wide enough, Alexa thought bitterly. Tucson and Phoenix were spreading like cancers over some of America's most beautiful land.

While most people would agree with her about Tucson, nestled as it was in the lush Sonora Desert with all its variety of plant and animal life, many would laugh to call the flat, gritty land northwest of Phoenix with its patchy bushes and withered clumps of grass "beautiful," but it was beautiful to her.

It was open. Quiet. Peaceful.

Ten miles outside Phoenix, as the desert finally took over. Traffic dwindled to almost nothing. Alexa breathed easier.

Another ten miles and a line of hills grew closer; the land took a dip and the desert became a bit greener. She passed through Morristown (population two-hundred-something) and took a turn off to get out of it. Even that little town, with its windblown old houses and boarded up businesses speaking of better days, was too populated for her.

Another mile on cracked asphalt took her to her little ranch house. A stable and corral stood in back. A girl's bicycle leaned on the wire mesh fence. Stacy was home.

Alexa parked her car under the corrugated steel awning she had built with her own hands—essential if you wanted your paint to survive under Arizona's blazing sun—and got out, breathing the clean air of the desert.

She looked out over the broad vista of the surrounding land and could only see two other ranch houses and a trailer home. She could hear no traffic, and the only sign of movement was a lizard darting over a nearby rock and the distant contrail of a high flying jet.

There was an old saying on the frontier, "when you can see the smoke from your neighbor's chimney, it's time to move." She hadn't made it out that far, but this was pretty good.

Alexa walked past Stacy's bicycle, unlocked the front door and went inside.

Her house was small. A living room had a lumpy old sofa, recliner, and TV. Pictures on the walls of friends and family. Alexa winced as she saw one of Powers at her acceptance ceremony into the U.S. Marshals—him looking fatherly, her looking so proud she could burst.

Going down the hallway, she passed the laundry room and looked at her bedroom. Her bed had been slept in. Stacy had had another bad night at home. She always came over when that happened. She must be out back. Alexa would check on her later. First she had to get to those files.

She hurried into her home office, a crowded room with a computer and police radio and scanner. One wall was covered with a detailed topo map of Arizona. Another was lined with filing cabinets. The walk-in closet was floor to ceiling boxes.

Drake's files were on top, thank God. She pulled the top box off the stack, hissing with pain as the cut along her arm jabbed with pain.

The box of files landed on the floor with a thump. She rummaged through them, flipping through file folders bearing the names of some of the worst criminals and strangest loners in the whole Southwest. She ignored the ones she knew were either dead or in jail, and pulled out any that she thought might be a fit.

She ended up with a stack of about thirty.

Damn. She needed to narrow this down more.

She got up, rubbing her arm and pacing back and forth. Alexa flicked on the police scanner. While she doubted any of the chatter from the local P.D. and Highway Patrol would be about Drake, the noise helped her think.

There had been at least four people helping Drake—the white-skinned man with the Mexican accent who had taken her gun, the smaller man who had used bolt cutters to free Drake, and the man and woman who had dealt with the prison guards up front.

That stolen armored car was probably driven by a fifth person. Drake was a careful planner, and he wouldn't want to leave the armored car idling. He would want a driver ready to peel out once he was on board. He wouldn't want to waste a moment.

So five. Maybe more. And they were all hardened to violence. That woman hadn't panicked at all when the guy next to her got shot.

And all had worked as a team. None of them had hesitated in the slightest. The attack had been well planned and had worked flawlessly.

This wasn't just a group of loners and crazies like Drake had always gathered around him. This was a criminal gang. They had worked together before.

That narrowed it down, but not enough.

Better to search for the woman. Most of the files were about men. She flipped through the files—a survivalist, a woman who ran safe houses for the cartels, the leader of a millennial cult. None fit.

None of the men really fit either. None were in a criminal gang. Drake preferred to work with loners. That way he could be in charge. With a gang you had to usurp authority. Even that cult leader wasn't a close contact. Drake had just used her to get to some of the woman's female followers. A bit of easy sex in exchange for drugs and illegal firearms.

Alexa stood. She was missing something. It would come to her, though. She just needed to let her subconscious mind work on it.

Remember that your subconscious is always working even when your conscious mind draws a blank, Robert Powers always used to tell her. *Just let it do its work.*

Alexa stopped pacing, her eyes brimming with tears.

When you're stuck, go do something else. Everyone with a life has at least two important things they need to get done. Go do the other thing and let your subconscious work on the first thing.

Alexa wiped her eyes and left the office, the police scanner still crackling behind her with news of drunk drivers, speeding tickets, and an attempted break-in.

Passing into the kitchen, Alexa found a mound of dirty dishes in the sink. Alexa grunted. She still hadn't taught the neighbor girl to clean up after herself.

Through the sliding glass door, she could see out to the stable and pasture. Smith and Wesson, her two geldings, stood in the pasture. Smith ate from the food trough while Wesson calmly stood nearby while getting groomed by a petite thirteen-year-old girl in jeans and a pink top, straight blonde hair reaching past her shoulders. Stacy Carpenter.

For a moment Alexa simply watched the girl and the two horses, so at peace and content with the world.

Well, that was true for the horses. Not so true for the girl. When she was here she could at least pretend, though.

Alexa took a deep breath and slid open the glass door.

Stacy waved. "Hi! I heard you come up." Then her pert, freckled features grew long with shock. "What happened?"

Alexa grimaced. Her long-sleeved shirt hid her bandages, but the big bruises down one side of her face were plainly visible even from a hundred yards.

"I … got in a car accident."

"You OK?" Stacy hurried toward her. Even in her worried state, she had the presence of mind to place the curry comb carefully on top of a fence post. She was always meticulous around the horses. Not so much with making the bed or cleaning the kitchen.

"A couple of bruised ribs," Alexa said. She didn't want to worry the girl, but she didn't want one of her usual tight hugs either. That would hurt like hell, no matter how much she needed a hug at the moment.

"What happened?" the girl said, coming up to her and reaching up to place a gentle hand on her shoulder.

"Collision. We ended up in a ditch."

"Anyone else hurt?"

"I'm fine," Alexa said, dodging the question.

"Want some coffee?"

Alexa smiled. Stacy had been making herself breakfast and brewing coffee for her parents since she was tall enough to reach the kitchen counter. They were usually too hung over in the mornings to make her breakfast or themselves coffee.

They lived in that trailer half a mile away. At night Alexa sometimes got woken up by their drunken arguing. The mornings after, she'd usually find Stacy asleep on her couch.

The parents complained sometimes, confronting Alexa and saying, "The girl's place is with us." or "You think we're bad parents or something? We provide for her, don't we?" or even better "We could charge you with kidnapping." As funny/sad as that last one was and some of their other outbursts, Alexa took it all in with stony-faced reserve. It wasn't like those complaints would go anywhere.

What were they going to do, call the cops?

Stacy went in and starting fussing with the coffee maker.

"Once you get that going, you can clean the dishes and make the bed," Alexa said.

The girl needed some discipline. Alexa had been inside the Carpenter home. Piles of dirty dishes in the sink. Beds that looked like they had never been made. As much as the kid hated being bossed around, she needed structure.

"Um, OK."

Alexa smiled and gave the girl's shoulder a reassuring squeeze. Although the kid would never put it into words, she knew she needed structure too, and never complained about Alexa's regular reminders to clean up after herself. Much.

"You said I could use the bed if you weren't going to be in at night," Stacy said, "and you told me you wouldn't be in last night."

"Impeccable logic, but I also told you that you need to make it afterwards."

"I was going to make it before you got back."

"Isn't it easier just to make it when you get up?"

Stacy ignored that question, as usual. "So you broke your ribs?"

"Bruised them. They hurt a bit but not too bad."

"You're lucky. Someone could have been killed."

Tears welled up in Alexa's eyes, and she felt grateful the girl's back was turned. Stacy had enough troubles. She didn't need to hear about Alexa's.

Alexa wiped her eyes before Stacy turned around, cleared her throat, and asked, "Want to talk about it?"

The girl shrugged her shoulders, switching on the coffeemaker and putting soap on a sponge by the side of the sink.

"Same old shit," Stacy said.

"Language."

"Same old crap," Stacy corrected.

"Language."

"Dad puked on the floor and Mom fell through the screen door."

Alexa rolled her eyes. Just another night at the Carpenter household.

For the hundredth time she wondered if she should call Child Protective Services and decided against it. A pretty young girl would be in serious danger in a foster home, so Alexa would make damn sure she'd never go to one. At least at her parents' home she wasn't abused. Just ignored.

Alexa went up to the girl as she washed the dishes, put her hands on her narrow shoulders, and kissed her on the top of the head. From the smell she could tell Stacy had used her shampoo. The Carpenters had probably run out again.

"It's not your fault," Alexa told her.

"Duh. Want me to scramble you some eggs?"

Alexa's stomach growled. She hadn't managed to eat much of lunch. Maybe she could get through some food now. Having the kid here helped.

"Sure, if you can scrape off all the gunk you left on there for the last twelve hours."

"Annoying."

Stacy scrambled her a couple of eggs while Alexa sat at the kitchen table sipping coffee and listening to all the local middle school gossip. The details of who liked who, and who wasn't talking to who, and how the math teacher still had bad breath. It washed over her unheard. All she could think of was Powers getting his throat slit, and Drake out there. Somewhere.

"Will you be all right here alone?" Alexa asked. "I have something pretty urgent at work."

Stacy looked dumbfounded. "You have to work right after a car wreck?"

"Crime doesn't take a holiday."

"Isn't that a commercial or something?"

"Highway Patrol recruitment commercial. Yep." Alexa tried to smile and couldn't quite manage it.

"Can't they get someone else? You're all beat up."

My inside worse than my outside, thought Alexa.

"There's food in the fridge. Here's a twenty in case you need to go to the store. We need some milk and probably a few other things."

Alexa had tried to pay her for taking care of Smith and Wesson during her numerous absences, but the girl loved the horses as much as she did. She'd take money if it was for "our" groceries.

"All right. Will you be back soon?"

"I hope so. Maybe a couple of days. You can always call me. You have credit on your phone?"

"Yeah."

Stacy didn't look happy about being left so soon, but Alexa didn't have a choice. Drake would be killing again soon, assuming he hadn't already. He thrived on it.

And Alexa's subconscious had finally thrown up an idea, a lead that might help her narrow down where Drake had hidden out.

The problem was, the person she needed to talk to lived where she least wanted to go right now.

Her family's ranch.

CHAPTER FOUR

Her destination was sixty miles to the northeast, a little ranch outside Bumble Bee that had been in her family for three generations. The person she needed to talk to would be there.

She knew he would be, because there was nowhere else for him to go.

State Route 74, a quiet two-lane road, skirted some low mountains and the recreation area of Lake Pleasant, which she couldn't see from the road. That was fine by her. She'd rather see saguaros than boaters any day.

Unfortunately she had to get onto I-17 for the last stretch. More asphalt and billboards. She felt much more comfortable in the vast silence of the desert.

So did Drake. He was hiding out there somewhere, waiting to strike like a scorpion from under a rock.

Scorpions. Ugh.

She remembered the time when she and Powers found the body of one of Drake's victims, staked to the ground with a sack full of scorpions tied around his head. The man's face was so bloated from venom, they had to take fingerprints to ID him.

To the west the sun dipped low, turning the clouds a deep crimson in one of Arizona's breathtaking sunsets.

She picked up her phone and called Hernandez. He answered on the fifth ring.

"Hello, Alexa. How are you doing?" the concern she could hear in his voice sounded genuine. She pitied her many friends who always complained about tyrannical and uncaring bosses. Hernandez was more like a rather strict but loving uncle.

"Ribs are sore. Otherwise I'm fine. Look, I was thinking about Drake—"

"Try to take your mind off it."

"You know he had those friends down near Tubac. The survivalists."

"We're already checking on them."

"Sure, but one member, Bob McBriar, split into a different cell early this year. We lost track of him, remember? Might be good to chase up."

"Good tip, Alexa. I'll have someone check it out."

"I can do that." The words just spilled out of her mouth. Alexa knew she shouldn't have said that, because she knew the reaction she'd get.

"You've been through a lot. I understand you want to get him, but you're off the case. You need to recover. Call me in a couple of days."

"Drake will have killed someone by then, perhaps several people!"

"We've got a huge dragnet out. All the different branches of law enforcement are in on this and cooperating well. The governor is on board and giving us everything we need."

"The governor can't get inside Drake's head. I can."

My partner could too, even better than I could. But now he's gone. It's up to me.

"We'll get him. Take some time off and deal with what happened."

"I can do that after we catch him."

"The answer is no, Deputy Marshal Chase. Now get some rest and report for duty when you're feeling better. That's an order."

Alexa cursed and hung up on him. She fumed for the next few miles until she saw the sign for Bumble Bee.

A sign for a ghost town. While still on the map, its only residents were RV campers in the winter attracted to the quiet desert and the interesting atmosphere of an abandoned town dating back to the early days of the Arizona Territory.

What many of those winter visitors from the northern states (called "snowbirds" by Arizonans) didn't know was that the dilapidated saloon, general store, post office, and stagecoach stop weren't vintage 1860s, but vintage 1930s. Bumble Bee had already been a ghost town for a generation by that time, when a promoter breezed in, built some western-looking buildings, and tried to market it as a genuine Wild West ghost town and tourist attraction.

It failed, and the ghost town that was supposed to draw in people by the thousands was abandoned a second time.

Bumble Bee was silent as Alexa passed through, the window open to the clean desert air now that she was off the highway.

She drove along a gravel road west of town, not a light visible until, after a few miles, some twinkled up ahead. The family ranch.

Alexa had grown up out here, around the coyotes and jackrabbits and rattlesnakes. She had learned to shoot and milk cows and slaughter chickens before she started middle school, helping her parents and two older brothers. She had never known her grandparents, who first founded the ranch back in the 1940s, Grandpa just out of the war and married to his high school sweetheart.

They were buried in the family plot out just beyond the north forty. So was mom. She had died when Alexa was only fifteen and she still missed her terribly.

She got to the gate, unhitched it, and drove her truck through as a chorus of barks rose from the night, moving closer.

Those barks turned to happy pants and wagging tails as three German Shepherds danced around the truck, catching the scent of a long-awaited member of the family.

She pulled in behind three pickups as the porch light came on.

Wayne, her oldest brother, a lanky rancher approaching forty, came out first.

"Alexa, are you OK? We saw it on the news."

Before she could reply, Alexa felt his strong arms around him.

"Ouch! Don't squeeze too hard. I got a pair of bruised ribs."

Wayne immediately let go. "I am so sorry about Robert. Melanie told me as soon as the story broke."

Melanie was his wife, a reporter for Action News down in Phoenix. She only stayed at the ranch on her days off. That was fine by Alexa. She didn't want to talk to her on a normal day and she sure didn't want to talk to her today.

"My boss wants me to take a few days off," Alexa said, wiping her eyes.

"How about a whole lifetime off?" her father growled, stomping out onto the porch.

Dad was a broad, powerful man whose presence and physical strength made him seem far taller than his actual 5 foot 8. He sported a white handlebar moustache and the leathery face of someone who had spent a lifetime outdoors, dismissing modern conveniences such as sunblock as something for "city sissies."

He put a powerful hand on her shoulder. "Come inside. I'll fix you a steak."

Dad's cure for everything was a thick, juicy steak.

"I'm not hungry."

"You had dinner already?"

"No."

"Then you're hungry. Come on in."

"Where's Malcolm?" Alexa asked of her other older brother, the middle child. She needed to talk to him.

"Doing that meditation crap on the back porch," Dad replied.

"It helps him," Wayne objected.

"Load of hooey if you ask me," Dad grumbled. "Proper diet and a lot of hard work is all that boy ever needed."

"Is he staying clean?" Alexa asked as she came to the familiar living room. It was paneled in wood the same as it had been in the seventies. Family portraits adorned the walls, Mom and Dad and the kids at all stages of their lives. She and Wayne took a seat on the sofa. The TV was switched to some old war movie. Explosions and gunshots remained as a background to their conversation.

"Yeah, he's keeping clean," Wayne said. "Having a tough time of it, though."

"Boy needs more work. Needs a woman too," Dad announced.

Malcolm was 32, a year older than Alexa, but Dad still referred to him as a boy. In many ways he was.

As Dad went off to the kitchen to cook up a steak, Wayne turned to her and put a gentle hand on her shoulder.

"He was a good man. You stay here as long as you like. This is your home too, you know."

No, my home is down near Phoenix.

"Thanks."

A hurried step made them both turn. Malcolm rushed into the living room. He would have looked like the splitting image of his father, even down to the handlebar moustache, if he wasn't so thin and wasted away. In many ways he looked older than Dad. A year of meth addiction, and abuse of other drugs and alcohol for many years before that, will do terrible things to a body. As a teen he had been radiant with health, and now it killed her to see him looking so bad.

"Oh, Alexa, I heard the news. I am so sorry!"

Malcolm wrapped his arms around her neck and immediately burst into tears. He had always been quick to cry, something Dad and Wayne had teased him about mercilessly when he was young. After Malcolm had fallen into a spiral of self-abuse, Wayne had stopped. Dad hadn't.

Dad couldn't understand that there was something more wrong with Malcolm than simple weakness. Just what that was, no social worker or court psychologist had yet to be able to figure out.

"It's all right," Alexa said, comforting her brother. "I'll get through it. I've heard you've stayed clean and sober. Good for you."

Malcolm grinned, suddenly radiant, dug into his pocket and pulled out two tokens. One was an Alcoholics Anonymous token for three months. The other was a Narcotics Anonymous token for six months.

"That's great, Malcolm. Really great."

"I've been doing meditation and yoga too. It helps align my chakras and release energy blockage."

A loud snort came from the kitchen.

"So tell me how things have been around here," Alexa said before they could turn the conversation back to Drake's escape.

Alexa listened as Wayne talked about the horses and cattle, complained about the price of feed, and how the neighbors' cat had just had a litter. Malcolm talked excitedly about a Native American site he had found a few miles away on one of his frequent wanderings in the desert.

All this day to day chatter soothed her a little. While it didn't quite take away the pain, it was nice to hear about regular life every now and then. In her line of work, she tended to forget that most people actually had quite uneventful lives. Sometimes she envied them.

Dad came out with a plate with a steak and potatoes. Vegetables had never made it into his cooking repertoire.

"Want it on the porch as usual?"

"Thanks, Dad," she said, rising and taking the plate.

When she visited the ranch, she always wanted to have her dinners on the porch with the lights off so she could commune with the night.

Her brothers stayed in the living room. Dad switched off the porch light and joined her on one of the old wooden chairs arrayed on the front porch. The night was quiet except for the distant howl of a coyote. Alexa picked at her food. One of the dogs lay curled at her feet, gazing mournfully at the steak on her plate.

She looked at her father out of the corner of her eye. He turned to look at her and quickly looked away. In the dim light filtering through the screen door she could see his lips moving silently. Dad had never been good with emotional stuff. Too old school.

“He was a damn good man,” he said at last. “I hope they kill the son of a bitch that got him.”

“I should be on the case.”

“Why aren’t you? You’re not that banged up.”

“I asked, but they said I had to take some time off,” Alexa replied, still picking at her food.

Her father snorted and shook his head. “Since when did you take no for an answer. You sure as hell never listened to me.”

Alexa laughed a little.

“You didn’t even want me to be a U.S. Marshal.”

“No I did not. You’re a damn good rancher and Wayne could sure use your help. I can’t do a day’s work like I used to, and Malcolm’s useless.”

“He’s troubled, Dad.”

“I should have never let him go to university. All those rich kids are what got him down the wrong path.”

“He had problems way before he ever went to ASU.”

Her father sighed. “I suppose so. Losing his mom sure didn’t help. But those college kids are what really knocked him sideways. But enough about him. You got enough to worry about.”

They sat in silence for a while. Alexa managed to eat a few potatoes but couldn’t touch the meat.

“Lose your appetite?” Dad asked.

“You could say that.”

“Got to keep your strength up. Well, I got to go check on the stable and lock the gates. It’s getting late. You take care.”

Dad rose, hesitated, then put a hand on her shoulder and squeezed.

Once he was gone, Alexa started dropping slices of the steak onto the porch floor for the dog.

Her phone buzzed. Hernandez with a change of heart? She scrambled to get it.

No. A text from Stacy. She opened it and smiled. It was a selfie of the girl standing between Smith and Wesson, her arms around both their necks in a heart-shaped frame. The caption said, “Feel better!” along with several heart emojis.

Alexa smiled.

I won’t feel better for a long time, but this helps.

Briefly she wondered how long it took the kid to get that selfie. She envisioned Stacy propping the phone on top of a fence post, steering the horses into position, setting the timer to the camera, and the trying to keep the horses still for the shot.

She probably had to try twenty times to get it right. Smith and Wesson didn't like to stay still. One or the other would have tried to wander off, or look away, or bend their head to search the ground for anything interesting. Alexa estimated that this little selfie probably took the kid half an hour to do.

Well, those horses and her phone are her two favorite things.

Alexa put her phone away and looked out into the desert night.

It was nice that at least someone was rooting for her. Stacy must not have heard the news yet. At the Carpenter home, the TV was always set to game shows, and it wasn't like there were many teenagers scouring the news sites every evening.

Good. That kid had enough to worry about.

And Alexa felt awkward getting sympathy. Wayne's gruff concern, the teary emoting of Malcolm, and the gruff lectures of her dad didn't exactly help.

But, Alexa realized with a sudden shock, Dad was right.

"Malcolm," she called. "Could you come out here? I need to talk with you for a minute."

CHAPTER FIVE

The next morning, Alexa strode into the Phoenix office of the U.S. Marshals Service in full uniform—blue slacks, blue shirt with "Deputy US Marshal" emblazoned in white across the back, a Glock automatic pistol in the holster at her belt, and of course the pride and joy of every man and woman in the US Marshals Service—the six pointed star badge. Like most Marshals in the Southwest, Alexa added cowboy boots and a ten-gallon hat to the ensemble.

With barely a nod to the secretary, and ignoring whatever the woman said to her quickly receding back, Alexa burst into Hernandez's office.

She was going to get a yes whether her boss liked it or not. And with what she had learned, he'd be an idiot to refuse her.

As soon as she stepped in the room, she stopped. Hernandez sat behind his desk, the wall behind him arrayed with awards for valor and service and photos of him with two presidents and six governors.

But it wasn't the surprised look on his face, quickly replaced with anger, that stopped her in the tracks.

It was the five men in dark suits sitting in a half circle in front of his desk.

Feds. They practically smelled like Feds.

They all turned to her, five nearly identical faces. Of course they weren't identical; each had its own features and of the five one was Hispanic and another was African-American, but they all had the such similar conservative haircuts and poker faces that they looked like quintuplets.

"Gentlemen, this is Deputy Marshal Alexa Chase."

If her boss said this with so much tension, his voice would have turned into a screech.

"We're sorry for your loss, deputy," one of the feds said. He was the oldest and Alexa guessed he was in charge.

"Thank you," she said, nodding at him, then turned to Hernandez.

Before she could speak, Hernandez continued. "Deputy Marshal Chase is on recuperative leave."

Alexa flushed. She was being obliquely dressed down in front of these strangers.

All men, as usual. That bothered some women. Alexa had been dealing with it all her life. Being the only woman in the room did not faze her.

Although feds of either gender generally spelled trouble.

She struggled to find words, the impassioned speech she had practiced on the way down here now forgotten.

All she could manage to do was stammer out, "I think I have a lead on the female perp."

Her boss studied her. All the feds studied her. She gulped.

"Well?" Hernandez asked.

"There's a female meth dealer in Phoenix who's linked with the Glory of the Sun cult."

"The one whose leader had a fling with Drake?" Hernandez asked, a little less dismissive than before.

"That's right. Fiona something. No known last name. She supplied meth to the cult for some of their rituals, and she matches the same general description as the woman I saw. Of course she wore a mask, but the height, build, and hair color all matches.

"Drake never used drugs," her boss objected.

"Yes he did, he just didn't take them. He used drugs to bribe people, or seduce them. The opiate of the masses, he always used to say. That's from Marx. He likes quoting famous people. It makes him sound educated. We should try and track this woman down. She dealt around the university area; at least she did a year ago."

"And how did you come across this lead?" Hernandez asked.

"An informant."

She wasn't about to mention that informant was her brother Malcolm. While Hernandez wouldn't hold having a brother in recovery against her, there were people in the U.S. Marshals Service—the ladder climbers, the backstabbers you get in any organization—who would use that to push her down.

"Thank you for the tip Deputy Marshal Chase. We'll look into it."

"But I—"

"I said we'll look into it, Deputy Marshal Chase."

The tension in his voice was back. Big time.

A sudden thought came to her mind.

"Remember the Gutierrez case?" she asked Hernandez.

A wary note came into her commanding officer's voice. "Yes."

"Remember what you said to me after I cracked that?"

Gutierrez had been a hit man for one of the cartels, one of the most ruthless in a ruthless business. He specialized in killing off people's families as a way to intimidate everyone else. Powers had been on leave for a fractured elbow after tackling a perp and Chase had run Gutierrez down on her own. When she had hauled Gutierrez in, gunshot wound to his thigh and a heap of evidence in her truck, Hernandez had been ecstatic and had broken into a litany of flowery praise quite unlike him. He had promised her the sun, the moon, the stars, a personal photo op with the governor.

She had gotten that photo op. The picture hung in her office. Now it was time to collect the rest of it.

Hernandez must have realized that too. While his face did not soften, Alexa thought she detected a sparkle in his eye. "I said I owed you one."

"Yes. A favor. I'm calling it in."

"Chasing a serial killer through the desert with two bruised ribs counts as a favor?" one of the suits asked with obvious amusement.

Alexa looked him in the eye.

"Yes it does," she told him. He looked away. Feds weren't nearly as confident without their regulation sunglasses.

The oldest suit looked at Hernandez and raised his eyebrows slightly.

"You sure?" Alexa's boss asked.

"The CV certainly is a good fit," the fed replied, then made a tiny motion with his hand.

The other four suits rose in unison and walked in a file out the door. The last one shut the door behind him.

Who's in charge here? Alexa wondered.

Hernandez gestured to one of the vacated seats.

"You might as well sit, Deputy Marshal Chase."

Alexa sat, looking first from one man to the other.

"This is Deputy Director Sandford of the FBI. He's down here helping up with the Drake Logan case."

"Glad to have you on board, Deputy Director Sandford," Alexa said, deliberately speaking as if she was on the case too.

I won't leave this room until I am.

"It just so happens that the FBI reached out to us recently about a new joint task force," Hernandez said. "Their Behavioral Affairs Unit has been seeing a growing number of serial killer cases that spill over into US Marshals Service and other federal jurisdictions. They are thinking of an experiment: a joint task force to deal with this issue. And it just so happens that the U.S. Marshals Service was also interested in testing a unit dedicated to serial killers."

The FBI man spoke up. "We're anxious not to step on any toes, so Marshal Hernandez and I would like to set up this joint task force as a one-time test. We've been discussing it over email for some time and now, sadly, we have the opportunity to put it into practice. This could be a worthy tool in the fight against crime. Ever since 9/11, the folks in Washington are anxious to have more interagency cooperation."

We're an awful long way from Washington, Chase thought.

She had never trusted the FBI or CIA, the few times she had to work with them. Big city slicks working out of air-conditioned offices coming to what they considered the flyover states to tell people how to do their jobs.

But she kept it polite. She wanted back in.

"The various law enforcement agencies have made great strides in interagency cooperation in the past two decades," she said diplomatically.

"There's always room for improvement," Deputy Director Sandford said.

"And thus the test program," Hernandez said. "We'd like to bring in a serial killer specialist into the manhunt, someone who has experience getting into the minds of serial killers and tracking them down. He has a great track record and I think his expertise will mesh well with your personal experience with the case."

Alexa's heart lifted when she realized that meant she was back on the case. That elation was mixed with a bit of reserve. She was about to be saddled with a new partner, a fed, less than forty-eight hours after her old partner got killed in the line of duty.

"And who would this FBI agent be?" she asked.

Hernandez hit an intercom switch on his desk. "Grace, would you send in Agent Barrett please?"

The door opened, and a broad-shouldered, somewhat short man came in. He had short blonde hair, blue eyes, and a round, youthful face. If Alexa didn't know he was a full agent at the FBI, she would have guessed he was in his twenties. He had to be at least a decade older, though, to be in his position.

Still, he looked more like a university football star than an FBI agent. Ex-military too, judging from the good posture.

Alexa stood and extended a hand.

"Deputy Marshal Chase," Hernandez said, "I'd like you to meet Special Agent Stuart Barrett."

Alexa looked into Barrett's eyes. You could tell a lot from the eyes. His were blue and set a bit too close together. She saw arrogance there, and a flash of hostility when he saw his new partner.

Hostility that I'm a woman or hostility because he doesn't want to be stuck working with some cowgirl in the sticks?

Probably both.

"Pleased to meet you, Special Agent Barrett," Alexa said.

Actually, I'm not pleased at all. I think you're going to be one giant pain in the ass.

The last thing I need is some fed tagging along while I hunt down my brother's old drug connections. Not only will he be useless in the street scene, but if he finds out about Malcolm, my career could be toast.

CHAPTER SIX

Alexa turned to her boss, trying to formulate an objection that would keep her on the case while getting away from this Neanderthal. Before she could say anything, Hernandez spoke.

"You two will have our full support and full independence. Take any avenue of investigation you want. In the meantime, we and the FBI and the regular police will continue our investigations. You'll have full access to what we find, of course, and if you need any backup manpower, that can be arranged as well."

Alexa glanced at Agent Stuart Barrett.

I have too much backup manpower as it is. Are they saying I'm not capable of doing this myself?

Hernandez went on.

"Let me get you up to speed on what we know so far. The armored car was stolen from the Arizona Bank and Trust depot the night before the attack on the prison van. It was an expert job. The security guard was knocked out from behind and never saw a thing, the alarm was cut, the cameras destroyed, and the hard drive with the recording stolen. The thieves didn't leave any fingerprints or other evidence we could find."

"What about the tracker in the armored car?" Agent Barrett asked.

Alexa nodded. Maybe this guy wasn't a total moron. All armored cars have a tracking device attached inside the engine so the company can monitor its progress and the police can follow it if it gets highjacked. It's a basic security precaution that has been in place for years.

"They removed it," Hernandez said. "Knew right where to look."

"But the location of an armored car's tracker is kept secret," the FBI man said. "It must have been an inside job."

"Or by someone who has worked with armored cars before," Alexa said.

Agent Barrett gave her an annoyed look. Alexa ignored it and asked, "Any clue to where it was hidden for the time between it being stolen and being used in the heist?"

“Not a clue,” Hernandez replied. “No one saw it. Most likely the thieves drove it on some back desert road with the lights off and kept it in a safe house until it was time to bring it out.”

“They were pretty bold not to even change the logo,” Alexa replied. “The Highway Patrol must have had an APB out for it.”

“They did. We think they came onto the highway just before you met them. There’s a little-used county road leading to the highway just a couple of miles beyond the spot where you met them.”

“So they timed it perfectly,” Alexa mused.

“Maybe one of the prison guards was in on it and alerted them,” Agent Barrett said.

“You wouldn’t say that if you saw how they fought,” Alexa grumbled.

The FBI agent shrugged. “Could have been a double cross.”

“More likely they had a lookout in the desert with binoculars who radioed in to the armored car,” Alexa said. “Drake seemed to know it was coming. He was looking at mile markers and sure didn’t seem surprised when they sprung him. He had probably arranged it all ahead of time, and they had told him at what mile marker they’d make the escape attempt.”

“Has the vehicle been found?” Agent Barrett asked.

Hernandez nodded. “On that same county road I mentioned, just over a ridge and out of sight of the highway. It had been torched. No evidence could be recovered from it.”

“Another dead end,” Agent Barrett grumbled.

“I’m sure you’ll find a way forward,” his boss at the FBI, Deputy Director Sandford, said. He had been silent for much of this conversation. Being an outsider to the case and the state, Alexa figured he didn’t have much to say besides bland encouragement.

Hernandez gestured to the door. “Now I’m sure you are both eager to get busy. At the end of the hall you’ll find a work room where we’ve assembled all the files for the Drake Logan case, from the original evidence you used to track him down and catch him, to witness testimony and prison records. It’s all there, and there’s a computer in the room that’s fed with every report by all agencies working on the case the instant it’s filed.”

“I’ll get to work, sir,” Agent Barrett said, springing from his chair.

“*We’ll* get to work, sir,” Alexa said, rising and following the FBI guy out the door.

He was already halfway down the hall as she closed the door on the bigwigs who had just saddled her with this guy. She paused in the hallway for a second, trying to get her composure.

At least I'm back on the case. I can get Powers some justice.

Time to get to work.

By the time she got to the work room, her temporary partner had already hogged the lone computer and was banging away with his thick fingers on the keyboard. Alexa ignored him and went to the stacks of file boxes taking up much of the room. She rummaged around until she found his prison correspondence. It took up no fewer than four large boxes.

Drake had kept up a massive correspondence from behind bars. Having become an underground hero for the dispossessed and maladjusted, he received mountains of mail and responded to every letter. The prison had photocopied everything and filed it by the correspondent's name and the date it was sent.

Alexa paused. The sheer size of it all stunned her. While she knew he was well-connected, she had no idea just how extensive his fringe-y following had become. How was she supposed to sort through all this?

One box at a time. How else?

She lifted up a box, heavy with paper, and felt a sharp twinge from her injured ribs. This thing weighed a ton! She waddled over to a work table as fast as she could.

"Need help carrying that?" Agent Barrett asked.

"No," she said, gritting her teeth and hoping he couldn't see the pain on her face.

Alexa thumped it on the table, sat down, and got to work.

First she took a pad and paper and began to note down the names of any correspondent from the Southwest. Drake had received letters from all over the country and even abroad. Alexa figured the people who had helped him were probably from the region, however. Those would have been familiar with the territory and would have had an easier time organizing in Arizona. This breakout had obviously been well planned.

"What are you doing?" Agent Barrett asked, still pounding away on the keyboard with those meaty fingers like he was in a fight with it.

"Checking his prison correspondence," Alexa said, not looking up. "Trying to find who might have been on his team."

"Waste of time," he grunted.

They were sitting with their backs to each other. Nether turned around as they continued to talk.

"Why do you say that?" Alexa asked, allowing a bit of her annoyance to leak through into her tone.

"Look how much there is! You'll never find anything in there."

"I will if I narrow it down."

Agent Barrett typed louder. Alexa was already getting annoyed with his typing. She decided not to ask what he was looking into. No point in feeding his ego.

The first thing to check was if Fiona, the female meth dealer in Phoenix who was linked with the Glory of the Sun cult, was in the correspondence. She wasn't.

Next she looked at the file for Re-Hotep, the leader's name, and found a big wad of letters going back years.

Re-Hotep wasn't her actual name, of course, although it was her legal one. Had it changed in 2007 from Fran Smith. Not nearly as catchy for the leader of a sun cult.

She started going through the letters, which also included a lot of birthday and Valentine's Day cards, scanning for Fiona's name.

That took some time. Re-Hotep had a flowery style of handwriting that was hard to read. She sent a text to the Phoenix police department asking if they had any cons with the first name Fiona. While she waited for a response, she continued to go through the cult leader's letters to Drake Logan.

She didn't read, only scanned. She had read enough of the Glory of the Sun's literature while hunting down Drake, and it was a bunch of mind-numbing stupidity, a mixture of New Age babble with some Egyptology thrown in to make it sound ancient and mysterious. An Egyptologist at the University of Arizona, who she had consulted on the case, had almost died laughing at how inaccurate it all was.

"I've met grade schoolers who had a better grasp of ancient Egyptian mythology," the professor had said.

But there was nothing grade school about Re-Hotep. She used mind control, bullying, and drugs to keep a couple of hundred cultists emotionally enslaved and peddled them out for sex parties.

Alexa went from the most recent correspondence on back, growing increasingly frustrated as she did not come across the meth dealer's name. Perhaps she was Inner Circle. The Inner Circle members all got bogus Egyptian names like Ptah and Khnum. There were plenty of those mentioned in the letters. The Outer Circle members had to keep their regular names.

"Bingo," Agent Barrett said.

Alexa turned around to look at him. Maybe the big lug managed to find something useful.

"What?" she asked.

Agent Barrett turned to look at her.

"I've been looking at the police report for the break in at Arizona Bank and Trust. When they stole the armored car they didn't steal the key. It's kept in a safe inside a locked building. I guess they didn't want to waste time breaking in and dealing with the safe. Maybe they didn't even know the location of the safe."

Alexa shrugged. "So they hot-wired it."

"You can't hot-wire an armored car," Agent Barrett said and laughed, making Alexa grit her teeth. "They're designed specifically so you can't do that."

"So they used a key. Where's the spare?"

"That's the thing. There were only two other keys besides the one in the safe. One was with the regional manager, and the other is in the safe at the Arizona Bank and Trust's headquarters in Scottsdale. All are accounted for."

Alexa cocked her head. "So someone made a duplicate. Interesting."

"Yeah. The keys are stamped with 'Do Not Duplicate.' No reputable key maker would do that."

"There are plenty of disreputable key makers."

"True. Or they could have gotten a duplicate from the manufacturer."

"Were any of the keys reported missing for any time? Lost and supposedly found again?" Alexa asked, her interest rising.

"Nope."

Alexa didn't like the smug look on his face. But at least he had found a lead.

"Sounds like it's worth following up," she conceded.

"I'm going to make some calls."

"All right." Alexa got back to Drake and Re-Hotep's correspondence. She flipped through letter after letter, scanning all the names, and found nothing about any Fiona there.

Cursing silently to herself, she put them back. Agent Barrett kept talking in the background, hunting down information about the key to the armored car. While the FBI man had made an interesting point, Alexa didn't think that would be the most fruitful line of inquiry. It's not like finding out how a key went missing and got copied would give them a name and address, not like Drake's prison correspondence.

Because with these letters, he might have let his guard down a little. He was in jail for life, with little chance of escape, and had been there for years. Prisoners got lonely. Even Drake couldn't keep up a façade for all that time.

Alexa opened another box of correspondence and paused. The entire box was filled with letters to and from only one man—someone named Charles Farley. His name had never come up in any investigations into Drake's dealings; otherwise Alexa would have remembered it. Who was this guy and why had he and Drake written literally hundreds of letters to each other?

She began to leaf through the correspondence. All the letters she checked to or from Chuck Farley were labeled with the same address in Tucson. The latest letters dated to only a week before that group of killers sprung him from custody.

Alexa edged forward in her seat and began to read.

"Dear Chuck,

"Good to hear from you again. Double plus good, as they'd like us to say in this Orwellian nightmare. The sparrows have been flying around my cage and tweeting up a storm. The pigeons have been strutting around too, but luckily none of them have taken a sump on me. Lucky for them!

"I've noticed that you're in the train district. Ride off the rails yet? Reminds me of that song. Thanks for offering the lyrics. Cheers me up in here."

Her brow furrowed. She leafed through some of the other correspondence. All the letters to this Chuck Farley were the same, strange statements that didn't seem to mean much and oblique references to things she didn't catch.

"Hey, Agent Barrett, take a look at this."

The FBI man let out a sigh, quiet but not quiet enough for Alexa not to catch, and moved over to her table. He took a couple of the letters in her hand and read through them.

"Huh. Looks like Drake Logan was on something when he wrote these."

"No. Drake never took drugs."

Agent Barrett waved the letters around. "Come on, they all take drugs, especially once they get to prison. What else are they going to do all day? Well, a few other things, but I'm not going to mention them. Might offend you and get me in trouble."

Alexa gave him a cold look. "I know what happens in men's prisons. I also know my suspect. He's a control freak. He'd never take drugs because that would mean losing control. No, these are some sort of code."

The FBI guy laughed. "Well, the name sure is."

"What do you mean?"

"Come on, Charles Farley? It's the oldest one in the book."

Alexa stared at him impatiently, waiting for him to get to the point.

He rolled his eyes and said in a tone like he was explaining something to a child. "Charley. Chuck. Chuck U. Farley. Fuck you Charley."

"Never heard of it."

"Guess it's not Cowtown humor," he said with a shrug.

She cocked her head and gave him a withering look. "Har har. You mean it's not high school boy humor."

This guy was getting more and more annoying. Maybe she should shoot him instead of Drake.

But Agent Barrett did have a point. If this was a common joke, Drake was making fun of his captors. Typical behavior for him. He always wanted to prove he was smarter than everyone around him.

The problem was, he was pretty much right.

"So this is a code," Alexa said, looking at the letters again.

"Maybe. A lot of prisoners do that. It's usually pretty easy to figure out. But there's a mountain of stuff here. We don't have time to wade through it all."

"This could be important. He's got hundreds of correspondents, many of whom look at him as a sort of guru. He could have organized them into a network to help him get away."

"You're reading too much into this. Drake Logan is a psychotic thug with delusions of grandeur. He doesn't lead an army of helpers from behind bars. The guys who sprung him were a small group of nutcases like him. Sure, they're capable, and they're obviously armed and dangerous, but don't start seeing conspiracies everywhere. He's not Lex Luthor."

"I know my suspect. I've been in his damn head for years."

"And that technique caught him once. Fine. But it took ages, and we're rushed for time. The best way to catch him is to find the people who sprung him, and the best way to do that is to follow up on this key."

"You go do that," Alexa said, standing. "I'm going to check out this address."

Agent Barrett looked worried. "Alone?"

"I can take care of myself."

"Wait, I'll go with you."

Alexa turned and frowned at him. "I thought it was a waste of time."

He looked her in the eye. This time he wasn't being condescending, but deadly serious. "It is, but you might need backup. We don't go anywhere alone, not with this maniac on the loose."

Alexa grunted and picked up the box of correspondence she had been studying.

"You're taking that with you?" Agent Barrett asked.

"That's right. Take that one over there. You'll drive. I'll read."

At least you'll be good for something.

"You OK for carrying that?"

"Yes."

"I mean because of your injuries and everything."

Alexa walked out to the parking lot, the FBI agent tagging along and her ribs and arm burning from the strain of carrying the heavy box.

"If we run into trouble," Agent Barrett said, "just know I got a marksmanship medal in the Army. Served two tours of duty in Iraq and Afghanistan."

Oh, what a hero. So this guy is going to be shadowing me all the time? Wonderful. It's obvious he doesn't respect my ideas or my background. He just thinks I need protection. The delicate little girl being saved by the musclebound hero. How many times have I had to deal with idiots like this? They always get in the way more than help.

And now I have to deal with one on the most important case of my life.

CHAPTER SEVEN

Drake Logan sucked on a menthol cigarette and let out a long, easy breath. He looked out over the nighttime desert from the porch of an isolated cabin a good five miles from the nearest paved road. It was quiet here. Peaceful. Nothing but the brilliant stars above and the occasional howl of a coyote.

The worst thing about prison was the constant noise. You never got a chance to be by yourself, never got a chance to be alone with your own genius.

Most guys in the pen were afraid of getting shanked or bent over. Drake had never worried about that. He could take care of himself. All he had to do was set a few examples and he could take a shower in peace. The few times someone came at him with a shiv, his followers always gave him plenty of warning, and he was armed and ready.

But the *noise*. That never ended. Clanking on the bars, the echo of slamming doors through the concrete and metal halls, shouts from one cell to the other, cries of pain and humiliation from the weak … a man couldn't get any peace.

He took another drag, his feet up against the rail of the porch, the old wooden chair on which he sat leaning way back. It was good to be free again.

A hefty man with greasy black hair came bustling out. "Sure is an honor to have you here in my place, Mr. Logan."

Drake grunted. So much for peace.

"It's mighty kind of you to allow me to stay," Drake said in as polite a tone as he could manage.

The man let out a nervous, stupid laugh. "The honor is all mine, and don't you worry none. It's real quiet and private around here. That's why I'm out here. No one round for miles. You won't have no one bothering you."

Except you.

Drake took another drag of his cigarette and stubbed it out on the bottom of his boot, a nice pair of tooled leather cowboy boots his people had brought him. In prison he would simply flick the cigarette butt on the floor. That was against prison rules, but he always had some flunky nearby who would pick it up.

He didn't trust this particular flunky to be smart enough, and they were deep in the dry season. A careless scrub fire wasn't something he could afford right now.

The flunky—Drake hadn't bothered to learn his name—stood nearby, looking like he wanted to speak but unsure how to proceed. The coyote yipped out in the night.

"Need anything, sir?"

"Just need to think. Got to plan my next move."

The flunky's face lit up. "I'll help any way I can, sir. I'll do whatever you want."

Except take a hint.

"What guns you got in the house?" Drake asked.

His team had plenty of weapons, but it never hurt to have more.

"I got a twelve-gauge double barreled and a .357 Magnum."

"Can I see them?"

"Sure!"

The guy rushed back into the cabin like a kid about to fetch a favorite toy. Drake shook his head. What a weakling. Eager to please. A sure sign of a weak man.

Women, on the other hand, generally acted eager to please, but that wasn't a sign they were weak. Society made them that way, but the smart ones, the strong ones, played that to their advantage. Like Fiona. That chick was just plain dangerous. All smiles and snuggles and a knife in your back.

Well, not Drake's back. The little minx was too smart to try anything like that.

The flunky came out again. In the brief time between the front door opening and closing Drake heard the crackle of a police radio.

"Any news?" Drake asked.

"No, sir."

It was Harry's shift to monitor the police radio. He was the best man for the job, a real techy nut. He had set up a special antenna on a pole on the cabin roof to pull in signals from far and wide, and his scanner was the best model money could buy.

Police communications were scrambled, but Harry had bought a descrambler off the Dark Web that took care of that. Ever since they had set up here, Harry or one of the others had been listening in to the manhunt's progress.

The other two members of his core team, Quincy and Fiona, were positioned out in the desert, keeping watch.

The flunky handed over the shotgun and .357. Drake looked them over.

"You keep good care of your weapons," Drake said, noting how clean and free of dust they were. A real challenge in the desert.

"Yes, sir. Never know when you have to protect your liberty."

Drake patted the Bowie knife on a sheath on his belt. "I prefer to use one of these."

The flunky grinned. "Oh, I know, sir. I've seen the pictures."

Drake let out a tight smile. "Chuck show them to you?"

"Sure. I've seen plenty on the Internet too, but he's got some real good ones, ones the police don't show."

"Some the police never even took," Drake said, lighting another menthol and looking out into the night. It was good practice to take photos of his killings. Made for nice gifts to inspire the strong, and reward those too weak to kill for themselves.

Like this joker.

"Your four by four all gassed up?" Drake asked.

"Sure. And it's got twenty gallons in jerry cans in the back. We got plenty of range."

"Let me see that map of yours," Drake said. "Can't risk using a GPS."

"Sure thing."

The flunky hurried back inside, the crackle of the police radio audible when he opened the door.

That made Drake think of Deputy United States Marshal Alexa Chase, formerly FBI Special Agent Alexa Chase. Most people didn't know about her brief stint in the FBI's Behavioral Affairs Unit, even most people in the U.S. Marshals Service.

Drake Logan made it his business to know. A country girl with dreams of something bigger, she had decided to go into law enforcement and see a bit of the world beyond her ranch. And not just as some local cop checking license plates and giving tickets to drunk drivers, but the most specialized unit in the most important law enforcement agency in the country.

Yes, Drake knew a lot about Alexa Chase. That was a smart move. You needed to know about your enemies.

And there was no more dangerous enemy than Alexa Chase. Fiona was a kitten next to her.

"Sir?"

"Hmm?" Drake looked up. That idiot was back, holding out a map.

Drake cursed himself. He had wandered off in his head and hadn't even noticed the loser had returned. He had to be careful. That kind of daydreaming could get him killed.

Alexa had that effect on him. She was the only person who did.

"Thinking about your next kill?" the guy said, all eager.

Drake took the map. "Nope. Thinking about that Deputy U.S. Marshal we left behind in the armored car."

The man hesitated a moment, as if unsure what to say, then in a submissive voice said, "Gee, sir. I don't understand why you let her live." He hurried to continue. "I mean, I'm sure you got your reasons. Don't get me wrong. It's just I can't think of what they might be."

Drake took a drag and scanned the brilliant night sky. The nights were clear in the desert, the stars looking like brilliant pinpoints, the Milky Way a cloudy arch high overhead. He saw the silent white dot of a satellite making its slow progress across the sky.

"Alexa Chase is one of the real people," Drake said.

"She's the law!" the flunky growled.

"Makes no difference. It ain't about law vs. crime or black vs. white or Christian vs. Muslim or any of the other divisions people set up for themselves. It's about the strong vs. the weak."

"Law of the jungle."

Drake rolled his eyes, the movement lost on the flunky since Drake still faced away from him. *Law of the Jungle* was one of the essays he had written in prison. Those essays were like porn for losers like this guy. Drake went on. He had to explain. For some reason, he felt a need to explain to people who would never truly understand. His one weakness.

"She's one of the strong who thought she was weak, and then realized she was strong. Sad to say, she got to thinking she was weak again. Now I want to make her strong, really strong. I want to make her one of us."

"One of us?"

I wasn't including you, dumbass.

Drake didn't let his feeling show. He was good at that.

"That Deputy U.S. Marshal used to be an FBI agent. Worked at the Behavioral Analysis Unit."

"The what?"

"They hunt serial killers," Drake explained, trying to be patient. "They get inside their heads and figure out how they tick, then hunt them down. Even though Alexa Chase was a new recruit, she was one of the best. Caught the Grappler and the Cincinnati Child Killer in record time."

The flunky's face lit up. "I've heard of the Cincinnati Child Killer. He used to tie up little girls and boys and make movies."

The guy snickered. Drake's hand moved to his Bowie knife.

"Killing children is a waste of potential," Drake snapped. "You can't know if they'll grow up strong or weak. They need a chance to grow into what they are. Anyone who kills kids deserves to be flayed alive."

The flunky's face fell. "Sorry."

You will be.

Drake went on.

"Anyway, Alexa—I like to call her by her first name because we know each other better than most married couples—was a rising star in the BAU. But she turned out to be too good at her job. She really got into those killers' heads. So much that she started uncovering her true nature. You see, Alexa thinks she's a law enforcement officer. But what she really is, is a predator. She knows the minds of predators so well because she is one. She learned that from an early age but tried to ignore it. Pretended she was really one of the so-called good people. Wouldn't see the truth. She went into law enforcement to prove it to herself."

"So why did she change from the FBI to being a U.S. Marshal?"

"She claimed it was so she could be closer to home. That was a lie. She's never been all that close to her family. Too restless of a spirit to be a rancher. Never fit into the life, although she always wanted to. So she said she wanted to move back to Arizona. Alexa really left the FBI because she got scared. She was afraid she was turning. She felt she'd be safer with more straight-up law enforcement with the U.S. Marshal Service."

The flunky gaped. "How do you know all this?"

Drake shrugged. "I read her psych files from the FBI."

The flunky stared then burst out laughing. "Dang, Drake. You got contacts everywhere!"

Drake nodded. "I do at that. There are strong people hidden in the most unlikely places."

The flunky stood a little straighter. "Darn right. But I don't understand something. You let her live so you can turn her. But how are you going to do that? And why would she even want to become one of us?"

Drake still had the shotgun and .357 on his lap. The flunky stood a little to his left, close to the door. Drake set the guns down on the floor to his right and stood. He turned to face this idiot who was so quickly outliving his usefulness.

"Alexa is hunting me right now, and she's smart enough that, despite all the care I've taken, she stands an even chance of actually catching me. I've got to string her along as much as I can and leave a trail of bodies to build up the pressure." Drake took a couple of steps toward the man, coming up close. The man looked to the porch floor, then uncertainly up at his hero. "A whole string of bodies. Horrible bodies. Pretty soon she'll realize there's only one way to stop the killing, and that's to join me. Her weak side, the side whose stomach turns at the death of a so-called innocent, will prompt her to become strong, to become what she truly is. Ironic, isn't it?"

The guy laughed nervously. "Yeah. Ironic."

Drake took a step closer, looking him in those weak, evasive eyes. "How's it ironic?"

"Well, um, it just is, you know?"

"How?" Drake snapped.

"Because … it's like … her weak side is helping her be strong, like you said."

Drake let out a slow breath and leaned forward, shaking his head. The flunky took half a step back, jerking a little as he bumped into the wall.

Drake took another draw from his cigarette and blew smoke in his face. The guy gave out a nervous laugh.

"Wh-what are you doing, Drake?"

Drake took the cigarette and stubbed it out on the wall next to the guy's head.

"Wh-what are you doing?" the guy asked again.

Drake ignored him and opened the door. Through the living room he could see through to a back room where Harry sat at the police scanner. He was a nondescript man of medium build and unremarkable features. Only his eyes marked him out. They were dead. Flat. Like a shark's.

"Harry, could you come here for a minute?" Drake asked.

The flunky started to babble. "I'm sorry if I said anything to offend you, sir all I was trying to do was—"

"Shut up," Drake snapped.

The man shut up.

Without a word, he strolled through the living room to the doorway.

"Turn off the porch light and come back in five minutes with the camera."

Harry leaned over to the light switch inside the front door and flicked off the porch light. Then he closed the door, leaving Drake and the flunky in darkness.

"Wh-what you doing, Drake?" the man's voice had taken on a high-pitched whine.

"Getting rid of the weak."

While the porch light had been switched off, the stars and the light filtering around the blinds gave enough illumination for the owner of the cabin to see Drake pull out the Bowie knife.

"What do you mean? I've helped you. I'm an individual. I've always stood up for myself."

Drake gripped him by the throat. The man didn't even try to resist. Drake could smell the sweat, the fear, cut with the sharp smell of the man's piss as he soiled himself.

"You're not an individual. You're a follower. A sheep."

"But I'm one of the strong! One of the elite!"

"You?" Drake chuckled, raising the Bowie knife to the man's face. "If you were in the Special Olympics, you'd come in last."

Drake began to carve.

CHAPTER EIGHT

Agent Stuart Barrett drove down Interstate 10 toward Tucson, admiring the northern slopes of the Catalina Mountains, a jagged brown line jutting into a clear blue sky. On the slopes he could see tall saguaro clinging to almost impossibly sheer slopes, and the entrances to old mines like dark eyes against the lighter stone.

At least the scenery is pleasant. I wish I could say the same about my temporary partner. She hasn't said a word to me for the past hour.

Stuart was not happy with his new partner. Barrett had done a lot of work in the flyover states, and Alexa Chase was a classic case of a small-town law officer who couldn't stand having a federal agent on their turf. They didn't know how to do teamwork with anyone they hadn't gone to high school with and they had a superstitious fear of big government, as if the federal government was some evil monster that wanted to oppress them and control their every move.

These hicks should go to the Middle East and see what a real oppressive regime looked like.

The deputy marshal had been leafing through photocopies of letters written to and from that psychopath. She hadn't even shared anything with him about what she'd found.

Probably because she hasn't found anything. This is a waste of time, but I can't let her go running off on her own.

Stuart knew the dangers of people going off on their own.

He shuddered and gripped the wheel harder. A bit of sweat glistened on his brow. He wiped it off, giving the Deputy Marshal a sidelong glance to make sure she didn't notice.

No need to worry. She was lost in her reading. She was so obsessed with reading those damn letters, he could have driven off the road and taken out half a dozen cacti and she wouldn't have stopped reading.

Unobservant. Perhaps overconfident. Certainly territorial and not a team player. All bad signs.

Maybe that overconfidence and lack of team spirit had helped Drake escape. Sure, it had been the most professionally planned and timed breakout he'd ever heard of, but she should have seen it coming.

If she'd really been in this guy's head all this time, she should have seen warning signs that he was planning an escape. Maybe those poor dead prison guards had even said something and she had ignored them, figuring she knew better.

Stuart glanced at her again, taking in the bruises on the face and the bandage poking out the sleeve of the long shirt she wore in an attempt to hide her injured arm.

OK, it wasn't entirely fair to judge her. Those guys had been real pros. And once the hit happened, she'd been pinned down by twisted metal. He'd read the report. The highway patrol had to use the jaws of life to get her out. It was a miracle she lived, and a second miracle that she was back on duty. She had willpower; he had to give her that.

But she was so focused that Stuart bet she couldn't see anything except what was right in front of her.

And then there was the other question, the one no one on the investigation seemed willing to ask.

Why was Alexa still alive? Why did Drake Logan not cut her head off too?

Not having an answer to that question, Stuart pulled out his phone and brought up Google Maps. After checking no cops were in view—it would be just his luck for some good old boy to stop him for using his phone while driving—he typed in the address used in the Logan correspondence.

It came up on the south side of the city, near some train tracks. He switched to street view and saw it was the warehouse district.

"Huh," Stuart grunted.

Alexa flicked to another page of letters. Was she ignoring him or so much in her own little world she hadn't heard?

"Drake Logan's pen pal was writing from a warehouse," he said.

That got her attention. For the first time in an hour, she looked up from her work and paid him some attention. Stuart turned the phone in her direction, only to have it snatched from his grasp.

Stuart shrugged and focused on driving. "Check the neighborhood. See the tactical situation."

"That's what I'm doing," Alexa grumbled.

"Do you know Tucson?"

"I know Arizona like the back of my hand. I've even been to this neighborhood."

"What's it like?"

"During the day, pretty quiet. Not many trains stop in Tucson anymore. You're likely only to see a few semis and delivery vans. Plus homeless people and drug users. No real threats."

"And during the night?"

"Prostitution, dealing, illegal raves. Some of these warehouses are derelict and haven't been used in years. DJs slip the owners some cash to look the other way and have raves there. Heaps of drugs. The owners, since there's no record of a rental, claim they didn't know. That hides them from liability. And there's a lot of liability. Besides the drugs inside the venue, there are all the muggings and sexual assaults outside the venue."

"Pleasant neighborhood."

"Where are you from?"

"New York."

Via Anbar, Mosul, and Kandahar.

"Yeah, it's all safe, secure neighborhoods in the Big Apple."

Stuart clicked his tongue. Her sarcasm was obvious.

"Actually I'm from Cortland. Upstate. And New York City is pretty gentrified these days. It's not like in the old movies."

"I've never heard of Cortland."

"Not much to hear about. Small city. Second-rate state university. Not much crime other than meth and opioids. But we weren't in the sticks. We were halfway between Syracuse and Binghamton, two kind-of bigger cities. No cowboys or cattle."

"You see any cowboys or cattle around here?" Alexa asked, gesturing at the cookie-cutter housing developments half hidden behind an endless succession of billboards.

"We're on the interstate," Stuart said with a grin. "I'm sure there's plenty of that once we get into the desert."

Stuart stopped himself from saying more. He had to work with this woman, even though he didn't want to. He quickly changed tone.

"So what are you seeing on Street View?"

"I've found a place to park that will be out of sight and we'll be able to approach the entrance without being seen from any windows."

"Good. Want to call the local P.D. for backup?"

Alexa actually looked surprised by the question.

"No. Why?"

Stuart shrugged. "Well, you know, serial killers and all that."

“He’s not going to be there. He won’t hide out in a big city when his face is on every newspaper and TV station.”

“I didn’t mean that,” Stuart said, irritated. “I mean his helpers are going to be armed and dangerous too.”

For a moment Alexa did not respond, and when she did the defiance had fled her voice.

“I know,” she said softly, then a hardness returned. “But I can handle them.”

“*We* can handle them.”

They took the highway along Tucson’s western edge before getting off it and driving along a business loop of cheap motels and liquor stores and into a nearly abandoned area of windowless warehouses. In three blocks Stuart saw only a couple of people—a grizzled old homeless guy pushing a shopping cart full of empty bottles and cans, and a cocky young man in jeans and a t-shirt standing in the shade. He gave Stuart a cocky look as he made eye contact. Stuart ignored him and kept on driving.

“Take a right and park,” Alexa said, looking at his phone, which she still hadn’t returned. “It’s another block. We’ll walk.”

“All right.”

Stuart parked, got out, and locked the car. No one around. Then he started checking the rooftops.

There aren’t any snipers in Tucson, you idiot.

He checked all the same.

“It’s just a bit down that street,” Alexa said, pointing to a side street branching off to the left, half a block ahead.

They began to walk. Stuart loosened the gun inside his jacket. It was midafternoon and the sun beat down hard. It had to be in the high nineties, maybe even a hundred. Stuart wished he was back somewhere civilized.

They came to the corner, peeked around. The street was empty, lined on both sides by warehouses. In the distance, an eighteen-wheeler rumbled across an intersection.

They rounded the corner.

“Hold on,” Stuart said. Alexa stopped, hand going to her pistol.

“No trouble,” he told her. “At least not yet.”

He ducked back around the corner to find the young man he’d made eye contact with approaching the car.

The young man stopped, his cockiness suddenly vanished. Stuart opened his jacket to reveal the Glock in the holster inside. The guy turned and bolted.

"Nice public outreach," Alexa said.

"Better than having to walk back to the office."

They turned and headed for the warehouse.

It was a long concrete structure, featureless, and only one story. Stuart was unpleasantly reminded of Iraq. This building looked like a larger version of the peasants' compounds, minus the courtyards. Hopefully there weren't any bombs inside either.

From what I've read about Drake, I wouldn't put it past him.

They came to the loading dock, the metal shutters down on the large entrance, the concrete platform that the trucks would back up to empty except for a few discarded beer cans. The place smelled of stale urine and neglect.

"The entrance is around the corner," Alexa said.

A delivery van rushing by made Stuart tense. He stopped and glanced all around the roofs, resisting the urge to pull out his gun.

"Why are you looking up there?" Alexa asked.

"No reason. Habit."

"Well, look at the street. That's where trouble is going to come from."

You may wear a uniform, but you're still a civilian.

"Don't go anywhere alone," Stuart said.

"You're not my babysitter."

"We're safe if we stick together."

Alexa gave him an odd, searching look. Stuart flushed and looked away, moving toward the corner of the warehouse.

He got to the corner and peeked around. This was the long end of the warehouse, and close to him was a door and a sign saying "office." A larger sign, which had once borne the name of the company, had hung above this but it had been removed. Only its steel frame remained, glinting sharply in the hard sun.

No one was in sight except for a couple of Hispanic workers a block away, walking away from them.

"Let's go," Stuart said.

They came to the office door, a blank steel rectangle. A mail slot next to it was stuffed to overflowing with supermarket circulars and other junk mail.

Before he could say anything, Alexa tried the door. Stuart almost leapt back into the street.

It's not going to blow up, you idiot.

"Locked," Alexa said. She studied the door. Even though it was metal, the wooden frame was dried out and cracked from years in the fierce sun. "Can you break it down? I got some cracked ribs and a bad arm, otherwise I'd do it."

The look on her face made Stuart realize that having to ask for help hurt her more than her actual injuries.

"We don't have a warrant," Stuart said.

"We don't have any time, either. Hernandez will take care of it."

"Who?" Alexa glowered, which prompted Stuart's memory. "Oh, your boss. Right. You sure?"

"The governor is breathing down his neck. The whole state is in a panic. Not even the press will complain about searching some old warehouse without a warrant."

Stuart shrugged and, before he could chicken out, rushed the door, hitting it square with his shoulder.

A jarring pain and the door burst open, the cheap, old wooden frame splintering under the force of impact.

He stumbled into the front office. A dusty metal table and chair were the only furnishings. A three-year-old calendar hung above them. One wall was entirely windows. Stuart raised his gun and looked through just as Alexa came up to his side.

The interior of the warehouse was one vast empty space, dimly illuminated by a series of dirty skylights. There was nothing inside. Stuart shook his head. He knew this would be a dead end …

… until he saw what was hanging from the ceiling.

CHAPTER NINE

It was a doll, hanging from a rafter not far from the office window, placed so that anyone coming into the office would clearly see it.

Alexa stared at it for a second, feeling a prickling all over her flesh. Even from this distance she could see the note pinned on it.

A note for her. She felt sure of it.

Drake had always had a strange focus on her, ever since they had caught him. It was unsettling, sickening even.

And, in a strange way she didn't really like to delve into, flattering. This was a man who thought most of the human race was inferior. He actually admired her.

He had admired Powers too, she reminded herself. *And look what happened to him.*

They opened the interior door, Agent Barrett ducking around the corner, leading with his gun and ready to fire at anyone hiding beside the door. There was no one. Alexa knew that now. They were too late.

Nevertheless she didn't venture far out of the office before stopping and taking a long look around the single large space. She didn't see anywhere for someone to hide except behind the steel pillars that ran down the center of the warehouse. She kept an eye on those pillars as she moved to the doll.

It was a Barbie doll, stripped of its clothes. A piece of paper had been stuck to the doll's chest with a large needle. Two other needles were stuck through the eyes just above Barbie's pert little nose and wide smile. The Barbie hung at eye level from a noose of string around the neck. Without touching it, they read the note.

"Too late to see me here but it's never too late for a reunion. You'll have to work faster than this, Alexa. Hope you have a speedy recovery! I sure won't. Sans Bombo"

"What's that supposed to mean?" Alexa wondered out loud.

"No idea," Stuart said. He moved across the warehouse, gun leveled, to get a different angle on all the pillars. When he got halfway to the far wall, he ducked back the way he came at a jog.

"You see something?" Alexa asked, raising her gun.

"No. It's an old army trick. Someone knows you're moving across the room so they creep around the pillar. You make a sudden move and you can catch them at it. There's no one here."

Despite his reassurance he moved the other direction and did the same trick.

Well, at least he's thorough. Maybe obsessively so.

Alexa went back to studying the note. Why would he not have a speedy recovery? He didn't get hurt in the escape, did he? She didn't remember him getting hurt and there was no evidence for that. Perhaps he got injured later? And why did he sign with that weird name?

"Does Sans Bombo mean anything to you?" Alexa asked.

Stuart came back to where she stood in front of the dangling Barbie doll. His eyes never rested. Even though he had cleared the room, he kept checking.

"'Sans' is French for 'without' and 'bombo' is Spanish for 'bomb'. Without bomb? No idea what that's supposed to mean."

Alexa cocked her head. "Nice try, but the Spanish word for bomb is bomba, not bombo."

"Oh. He could have gotten it wrong too."

Alexa looked at the note again. Drake never got anything wrong. That was the trouble.

The two of them kept staring at the enigmatic message in silence. Alexa grew increasingly frustrated. Drake was taunting them. He had even come to a major city right after the breakout instead of running into the desert as she had anticipated.

Or had he? While the note was in his handwriting, that didn't mean he wrote it after the breakout. He could have sent the note to one of his followers to be placed here along with the Barbie. Maybe he never came here. If so, a photocopy of that note would be among his correspondence.

All those boxes …

She didn't have time to check that theory. The clock was ticking. Sooner or later Drake would commit another murder. He couldn't help himself. Even though lying low would be the best thing for him, sooner or later, probably sooner, the urge would come over him to cull one of the "weak." It was what he lived for.

"It's an anagram!" Stuart cried.

Alexa jerked at the sound and turned to him.

"What?"

"An anagram. I used to love them." He holstered his Glock and pulled out a pad and a pen. "Keep an eye out while I work on this."

Alexa kept watch as Agent Barrett wrote down Sans Bombo and then, with remarkable speed, began trying various combinations.

Alexa fidgeted, looking around the empty warehouse. He had been here, not too long ago …

"Got it!" Agent Barrett shouted, making her jump. "If you unscramble Sans Bombo, you get Bob Samson."

Alexa looked back at the note. "Could be."

Stuart snapped his fingers. "The key! Maybe this Bob Samson got a copy of the key from the manufacturer or the armored car company. We have to check if there's a Bob Samson working at either of those companies."

Alexa nodded. Maybe this FBI guy wasn't so useless after all. "Sounds like a plan. I'll call the Tucson P.D. and get them to bring their CSI team. I doubt Drake and his people left any traces, but it's worth a check."

* * *

Three hours later as the sun sloped low in the west, turning the desert gold, they bounced along a rough dirt road, the bottom occasionally scraping the mound between the two ruts made by previous vehicles. Every now and then a sharp clank told them the wheels had kicked up a stone against the undercarriage. No homes were in sight, but they knew they would soon come to one.

The isolated cabin of Bob Samson.

Alexa was impressed. It turned out Agent Barrett's hunch had been correct. While the key manufacturer had never heard of Bob Samson, the armored car service had. In fact, he was a security guard at the facility who happened to be in the middle of a two-week vacation. He had told his supervisor he was going down to fish in Baja. Alexa suspected he had been up to something a little closer to home.

She glanced to the west, where the sun was a shimmering red ball hovering above a distant line of hills. The shadows of the saguaro cut dark lines across the landscape.

"Step on it," she said. "We don't want to do this after dark."

"Almost there," Agent Barrett said. "We should have taken a U.S. Marshals Service four by four instead of an FBI Lexus."

"We'll grab one when we get back to the office."

Alexa's statement was followed by an awkward silence. Her gut feeling told her they would not catch Drake at this place, that this was just another breadcrumb on the trail. Agent Barrett apparently felt the same. They hadn't even called for backup.

Alexa had a couple more reasons for not calling for backup. Every available officer needed to be running the dragnet and chasing up the dozens of leads and sightings that came pouring into the operations center. Drake Logan's murders and capture had been headline news several years ago, and his bloody escape had once again captured the attention of a news cycle ever hungry for sensation. Now civilians as far away as Alaska were calling in panicked reports of seeing him in their local supermarket produce section.

Of course most of these reports were nonsense, but you could never tell. You had to follow up each one, and that took manpower.

A lot of manpower.

And there was the final, most important reason why Alexa didn't want anyone else on this job.

She wanted to catch Drake herself. He needed to pay for what he had done to Robert Powers.

Alexa teared up just thinking about him. She turned to look out the window so Agent Barrett wouldn't see. It was these lulls she hated the most. When she was looking through the police reports, or scouring Drake's prison correspondence, she could take her mind off that terrible scene in the prison bus. But sitting here in the passenger seat with nothing to do, it all came back to her.

Yeah, we'll get a four by four and I'll drive. Maybe that will help. This city boy probably doesn't know how to drive one anyway.

"GPS says it's half a mile beyond this ridge," Agent Barrett said. "Living way out here he's probably a gun nut. I suggest we stop here and proceed on foot."

"He's probably seen our dust trail already. You can see those miles off."

"Probably. But there's no use making a bigger target."

"All right."

Alexa reached into the back seat and pulled out a pair 12-gauge pump action shotguns. Both she and Agent Barrett wore Kevlar.

"Wish I had my M16," the FBI agent said as he stopped the car and took one of the shotguns.

"You miss the Army?"

"Hell, no. I'll take a serial killer over an Al-Qaeda or Taliban operative any day. Less dangerous and easier to spot."

"He's plenty dangerous."

"Is he willing to blow himself up?"

"No."

"Then he's less dangerous."

"Just be careful," Alexa warned. The last thing she needed was some gung-ho veteran underestimating the fugitive.

The warmth of the desert afternoon after the chill of the car interior felt embracing and reassuring. Alexa had never liked air conditioning. She thought it was unhealthy and, for someone acclimatized to Arizona's dry heat, unnecessary. The land was silent except for the buzzing of insects. She and Agent Barrett moved a hundred yards off from the road and then spread out to put about twenty feet between them. Then they walked toward the cabin hidden behind the rise. Each gripped their shotgun and kept silent, watchful.

They climbed the gentle slope, wending their way around prickly pear cactus and jagged rocks until the cabin came into view.

It stood at the end of the dirt track, a small, one-story place with a front porch. No cars were parked out front and no lights shone inside. The setting sun glinted off solar panels on the sloping roof. In the yard were some old tires, what looked like a rusted engine block, and various bits of trash.

Alexa stopped and crouched, pulling out a compact pair of binoculars from her vest pocket. She scanned the house and the surrounding area. No sign of movement.

Alexa kept watching. The light was fading quickly now, but it paid to be careful. Agent Barrett, crouching behind a rock outcropping to her left, kept silent.

Either nobody's home or someone's in there waiting to snipe at us.

Only one way to find out.

Alexa signaled to the FBI man and they continued toward the cabin, crouching low, eyes and ears alert for any sign of movement.

A sharp rattle cut the still air between herself and Agent Barrett. The FBI man jumped back, looking around and pointing his shotgun at the rattlesnake that slithered on a sandy stretch between them.

"A rattler," she said. "It won't bother you if you don't get close."

Agent Barrett cursed. "What's next? Scorpions?"

“We’ve probably passed a dozen already.” *City boy.*

Alexa got moving again, her temporary partner getting underway a moment later. The poisonous denizens of the Sonora Desert were the least of her worries right now. They drew closer to the cabin. Still no sign of movement. She kept her shotgun trained on the front door. To either side were windows, the blinds drawn.

As they approached, she could make out something in the half-light of dusk. There was a large, dark stain on the front porch right in front of the door. Agent Barrett angled off to the left, using whatever cover he could find, and did a circuit of the house. He came back to a point about ten yards to her right and shook his head.

Steeling her resolve and trying to ignore the sweat trickling down her front and back from the confining heat of the Kevlar vest, she advanced.

It did not take her long before she could see that the black area was a large bloodstain soaked into the wood.

Alexa paused, and when she heard no sound from inside the cabin, she glanced over her shoulder at Agent Barrett. He was covering her, down on one knee to make less of a target.

She rushed up the two steps and kicked the flimsy wooden door in.

Just inside the door lay the body.

CHAPTER TEN

The body hadn't just been killed, it had been carved.

Alexa stared at the body lying on a rug in the middle of the living room. The rug and the body's clothing were caked in dried blood. Judging from the spatter on the front wall outside and the trail from the porch over the threshold, the man had been killed on the front porch and dragged inside.

She could not tell who it was. The face had been carved up so badly there wasn't a face left. Or ears. Or a nose. Bits of flesh lay all over the rug.

But she didn't need an ID, because daubed in blood on the faded wallpaper were the words, "Sans Bombo = Bob Samson. Good Luck Alexa!"

Agent Barrett came into the room, his face grim.

"Nothing and no one. I've searched this whole place. The bed is unmade and looks like it had been slept in. Also in one room all the furniture was pushed to the side. I think Drake and his buddies slept on the floor. Heap of dirty dishes and empty cans in the kitchen."

Alexa only nodded, not able to tear her eyes from the carnage on the floor. This was her fault. She should have caught Drake by now. Hell, she should have never let him get away in the first place. It didn't matter that this guy had probably helped the serial killer. Nobody deserved this. It was one more death on her conscience.

"I noticed a cell phone booster on the roof," Agent Barrett said. "It's the only way this poor bastard could have used his phone this far out in the sticks. I'm getting a signal. I'll call it in."

"All right." Alexa's voice came out harsh, her throat dry.

She agreed with Agent Barrett's assumption that the hunk of meat on the floor was Bob Samson. Not only did the bloody graffiti hint at that, but his general build and description matched what the armored car company had told them. Six-two, hefty body, black hair.

Samson's supervisor had described the face too, but there was no longer a face. And the hair color they could only tell from bits of the scalp scattered across the carpet.

What Alexa did know was that his description did not match any of the attackers she had seen. Perhaps he had been sitting behind the wheel of the armored car, but she had briefly seen the driver through the windshield just before the impact. She had trouble bringing up a clear memory considering what came afterward, but she had the impression that the driver had been a slim blonde man.

Alexa cursed. Another dead end. She made a slow circuit of the living room, looking for anything that might give her a lead. She saw an empty gun rack on the wall. A TV and a threadbare old sofa and recliner. Not much more. No family pictures or birthday cards. The guy seemed like a loner. The armored car company had given them two addresses—a studio apartment in the city and this place in the middle of nowhere. The local police were checking out the apartment. She doubted they'd find anything.

Dimly she became aware of Agent Barrett's voice calling in the crime scene. He stood outside, wanting to distance himself from the horror on the floor.

He must have seen worse if he served overseas in the armed forces, Alexa thought. *But that doesn't mean he wants to see it again.*

She moved to the back of the house where the kitchen was. Nothing of note, except there were dirty dishes piled in the sink and strewn across the counter, and oddly the kitchen table was bare. The oilcloth on it showed the impression of four little rectangles, as of some piece of heavy equipment had rested on it. A few short bits of copper wire and stripped insulation from a wire lay on the table and on the floor by the open window.

Some sort of electronics setup? Alexa had no idea what that could be for. She stepped out the back door, taking care to use a cloth when she touched the knob. Dusk was gathering quickly. She pulled out her mini mag light and shone it on the window and the nearby wall. She thought she discerned a couple of new scrapes on the eave.

She couldn't tell what that signified. Maybe the CSI guys would figure it out.

Reluctantly returning to the interior of the house, she checked out the two bedrooms. One was used as a storeroom with boxes of junk, some furniture, and a stack of old porno mags. It didn't look like the room was used much, except recently. Everything had been pushed to the side to leave an open space on the carpet. She couldn't make out any impression on the carpet, but guessed Drake and his followers had slept there in sleeping bags.

The other room was Samson's bedroom, a simple place with a couple of hunting posters and an unmade bed, bedside table, and an antique rolltop desk. It must have been an heirloom. The rest of Samson's cabin didn't show any taste or expense.

Using a handkerchief, she opened the rolltop desk.

And hit the jackpot.

Inside was a stack of letters. The top one was in Drake Logan's handwriting. She looked through several more and saw they were all from him. While the envelopes were missing, they were all in the same oblique style as the others sent to the warehouse, so unlike Drake's usual boasting lectures to his other followers.

A code? But where were the translations?

She checked the little pigeonholes in the desktop, finding more normal correspondence and legal records. Nothing of value. Next she checked the desk's three drawers. Two were packed with letters from Drake, bringing the total up to at least a hundred. The third contained a well-thumbed spiral notebook.

She opened it and found another jackpot.

The first page had two columns of text.

"Cigarettes = guns

Tobacco = ammo

Shopping mall = desert"

And so on. It was a translation of the code he had been using for his letters in prison.

Alexa read eagerly through the list. This was it. This was the key to catching him. Drake, or one of his henchmen, had made a fatal mistake. She'd make them pay for that.

"Find anything?"

Alexa spun around, her heel hitting the rolltop desk with a bang. Agent Barrett stood in the doorway.

"Don't sneak up on me like that," Alexa gasped.

The FBI man looked contrite. "Sorry. I hate it when people do that too. I just assumed you heard me come in. The Highway Patrol is on its way, along with a CSI team."

"Good." She held up the notebook. "This is even better."

"What is it?"

“A codebook for the letters Drake sent to the warehouse. We can translate them now.”

Agent Barrett let out a low whistle. “We scored big time!”

“I’m thinking Samson acted as a liaison,” Alexa explained, “translating the letters and sending them to Drake’s other followers. Now do you think the letters are a valid line of inquiry?”

The FBI agent grinned. “Hell, yeah.” Then his face grew worried. “But there are so many letters. Translating them is going to take a big team and way too long.”

“We can get the manpower. The code is pretty straightforward. We can pull in janitors and secretaries to help, keep the frontline officers out working the dragnet.”

She turned the page to look at more of the code, and her heart fell.

It was blank.

She flipped through the rest of the notebook and found all the pages were blank.

When she turned back to the first page, the only one with writing on it, she found it loose.

It had been pulled from a different notebook and the frayed edges carefully pushed between the metal rings. Alexa had been too eager to notice.

“He’s mocking us,” Alexa grumbled. “Damn it! I bet the words on this page don’t add up to enough to translate anything of value.”

Agent Barrett shook his head. “He’s a clever bastard, I’ll give him that. How the hell did they catch him in the first place?”

Alexa looked him in the eye, suddenly annoyed. “I caught him. Me and Robert Powers.”

“I didn’t know that,” the FBI agent replied softly. He looked at her, and the arrogance was gone in his eyes, replaced with sympathy. “And I never got the chance to tell you how sorry I am that your partner got killed.”

“Thank you.” Alexa felt awkward. Just talking about it threatened to bring on tears.

“It’s always tough when you lose someone you work with in the field.”

Alexa’s anger subsided. The way he said it made her know that wherever he had served, he had probably lost people in his unit. She’d met a lot of veterans in the force, and many of them had a haunted look about them. Agent Barrett didn't, but it came out in some of the things he said.

"Now what?" he asked.

Alexa looked around helplessly.

"I don't know," she said, and it hurt her to admit that.

"How did you catch him last time?"

Alexa sighed and threw the probably useless notebook back on the desk next to the indecipherable correspondence.

"I got into his head. *We* got into his head."

"We'll have to do that again," Agent Barrett said. "You know him best, so you can get back into his head a second time."

Not again.

It had been a dark, ugly search to track down Drake Logan, and it had brought up a lot of the dark, ugly parts of her own past.

She and Robert Powers had started by reading through Drake's proclamations. Unlike later, when he was in prison and sending his missives out to the world proudly under his own name, back then he posted anonymously on Internet forums. The tech guys had figured out it was him by his writing style, content, and tracing the posts to the anonymous library computers he favored. They had made a collection of his writings that she and Powers had read and reread to figure out more about their man.

Alexa, in her first year as a Deputy Marshal, had just come from the BAU, just come from tracking down a serial killer called the Grappler, and didn't want to deal with that sort of psychological toxic waste ever again. But her first big case ended up being one of the worst serial killers of them all.

Just her luck. She would have rather been assigned to clean the toilets.

But orders were orders, and the man needed to be caught. She and Powers had sat down and studied printouts of his online essays, posted in various Yahoo and America Online forums in the days when the Internet was just beginning to become mainstream.

She had read them with disgust that turned to interest that turned to obsession. There was one essay especially, "The Greater Strength of the Physically Weak," that she ended up reading five times.

"Those who lack physical strength," a portion of it read, "either due to being naturally born small, or as a woman, or because of some disability, have the opportunity to show their strength more than any barroom bully or street thug. Your average musclebound brawler can always prove his strength in a physical way, but will often be a coward on the inside. They will pick on people they know they can beat, and if they get in a fight with someone stronger and lose, the victor is often so obviously powerful that the loser doesn't need to feel much shame in losing.

"This is not the case with the physically weak. Knowing they can't win in a confrontation, they will often avoid confrontation. That is a mistake. They should seek it out. Even if they get beat, like the strong man getting beaten by the stronger, they should not take it as a defeat. They have stood their ground, and that is what is important.

"But there is no need to be defeated. Society is infected with the ridiculous concept of fair play, born of rule-bound high school sports that are a poor imitation of real life. In real life, in the dog eat dog world that adults actually live in, there is no such thing as fair play. If a weak person finds themselves facing a stronger person in a fight, either physical or mental, fairness has already gone out the window and the weaker person is within their rights as an individual to even the playing field as much as possible and by any means necessary. Then the weaker person might win, and gather more inner strength. Only by seeking out and beating stronger opponents can the weak become strong."

Those lines, for all their pseudoscientific babble and half-baked, almost fascistic statements, had nevertheless hit home to her.

They jolted her back to when she was sixteen, alone in the barn with that new ranch hand she had a crush on. He had come on to her too strong. Looking back on it, if he had come on to her subtly, playing on her teenaged romanticism and acted all sweet, he might have been given what he wanted. Instead he decided to take it.

He had pushed her down, and in her panic she had picked up a horseshoe discarded on the floor and smacked him across the jaw in a spray of blood and shattered teeth.

Her own strength had startled her, as well as the damage she had done. She had rushed to her father, begging forgiveness without really knowing why. When he had finally gotten a coherent explanation from her, he had grabbed his shotgun and gone after the ranch hand himself, but the guy had already jumped into his pickup and driven off.

No charges were ever filed on either side. Alexa's father had patiently explained to her that it would be hard to prove her side of the story, and the young man would be too embarrassed at being hurt by a girl to report it to the emergency room as anything other than an accident.

Dad had been right. He had also been proud. "That's my girl," he said with a grin, giving her one of his rare hugs. Then he had spoiled it by giving her a lecture about how to act around men that, while not absolving the ranch hand, put the bulk of the blame on her.

While that had enraged her, what really angered her the most was the fact that her first reaction was to go to her father for help, and to apologize.

She had seen that as weakness even before she had read Drake's essay.

The essay had more lines that resonated with her.

"If a weaker person wants to become strong, it's important to seek out confrontation. Bully the bully. Pick fights with those who are accustomed to winning, and beat them. There is nothing more liberating than cutting a bigger man down to size. Women, weak men, and the physically disabled should do everything they can to start confrontations with their physical superiors and use whatever means at their disposal to defeat them. This is not cheating. This is evolution. This is personal awakening."

That brought her back to a later time, when she had come back to the ranch at the age of nineteen for summer vacation from university. She had gone into town one night to pick a few things up from the supermarket when she saw him.

She was driving down the main drag. He was coming out of a liquor store with a six pack and heading for that same old pickup he had used to make his escape three years before. In the passenger's seat was a high school girl with a stupid grin on her face, all happy at the attentions of an older man and the prospect of getting to drink.

The shock of seeing him again was bad enough, but it was that girl's grin that really got her. That trusting, little-girl grin. That weakness. Alexa realized she must have looked the same way when the ranch hand had asked her to help him in the barn.

That guy was going to get that stupid, weak girl drunk and have his way with her.

Alexa saw red. She turned off the main drag, parked next to the pickup, and hopped out, wielding a tire iron.

The ranch hand turned around just as she came up to him. He had enough time for a spark of recognition to come into his eyes, followed immediately by fear.

Seeing that fear from a muscular man who stood a foot taller than her was one of the best feelings of her life.

Almost as good as the feeling of the tire iron taking out his knee.

The high school girl screamed. Alexa ignored her as she hopped back in her car and went on with her shopping.

For the next few days she was terrified the police would show up. They never did, and that taught her something. It taught her that cowards like that, no matter what kind of advantage they thought they had, could be defeated with a show of strength and willpower.

And then, years later, she had read that very same lesson in an online essay written by a serial killer.

Yes, Agent Barrett was right. She did know Drake well. Too well.

CHAPTER ELEVEN

Yvette Ramirez jogged through the quiet residential area of Marana, just off I-10 to the north of Tucson. It was dark, but she didn't worry. This was a safe neighborhood, the streets were well lit, and it was too darn hot to jog in the daytime anyway.

A thirty-two-year-old radiologist at the University Hospital, Yvette loved her evening jog. She kept fit, with jogging every night, swimming twice a week, and self-defense classes four nights a week. Moshe, her instructor, said she was the best in the class. And he should know. He used to be an unarmed combat instructor in the Israeli Defense Force. He had a perfect physique and was a brilliant teacher. Too bad he was married with two darling children. But at least Moshe had given her another reason not feel worried about being a lone woman jogging at night. She could take down a man twice her size. She'd done it in class plenty of times.

Not that she'd ever need to in real life. No one bothered her here in this sleepy bedroom district of Tucson.

Yvette gave a friendly wave to an older woman walking her dog. Jane something. They had met at a neighborhood meeting a few months back. Half a block later she waved to the Garretsons, a young couple just getting out of their car with bags from the supermarket.

She took a turn down a quieter avenue, picking up speed before entering the park. Legs pumping, blood flowing through her veins, lungs sucking in the clean, dry Arizona air, she didn't think about anything now except running.

The park was quiet. As Moshe had trained her, she checked out the area and saw no one. No threats. He called that situational awareness. In a place like this, a woman alone, or even a man alone, had to keep an eye out for any possible threats.

But the park was empty and she was a fast runner. Besides, a residential neighborhood was close by, within easy shouting distance.

Not that she consciously thought of any of these things. She just ran with a quiet, confident alertness along one edge of the park, past the baseball diamond with a chain link fence to her left.

She felt safe, until she ran past a tool shed and the man jumped out from behind it to block her path.

Yvette stopped short, momentarily paralyzed. It was only when the man moved toward her, arms outstretched, that the training Moshe had given her kicked in.

"No!" she shouted, and lashed out with her foot, landing a front kick right in his stomach. She had been aiming for the groin but in her panic had misjudged the distance.

Still, the attacker let out a satisfying "oof" and took half a step back.

"No!" she shouted again, punching with her right hand and clocking him on the side of the head.

The attacker brought up his hands in defense, blocking another punch, and tried to grab her.

That was a mistake, because getting in closer allowed Yvette to bring up her knee against his groin.

At least that was the plan. The man turned at the last instant and her knee glanced off the inside of his thigh.

The man grabbed her, spun her around with a terrible strength, and clapped a hand on her mouth. Yvette bit him, hard, and tasted the coppery tang of his blood. He hissed in pain but did not let go as he dragged her into the shadows behind the shed. On the other side of the chain link fence were some bushes. No one would see them back there.

Yvette kept fighting, more desperate now. Keeping her teeth clamped on his bleeding palm, she landed several hard kicks to his shins that made him stumble and fall, bringing her down with him.

They landed side by side. The man recovered first, grappling with her again. Yvette brought up her elbow and cracked him in the jaw. The blow came from an awkward position and didn't have enough strength, but it froze him for a moment.

Long enough for her to scramble to her feet.

Only to have them yanked out from under her.

She landed hard on her face, the wind getting knocked out of her lungs. Yvette felt a knee land hard on the small of her back, then the cold steel of a pair of handcuffs clamping around one wrist.

Panic gave her extra strength. She wrenched her body around, ignoring the pain of the knee grinding into her back and her shoulder almost getting dislocated. She got halfway around and jammed the heel of her free hand up into the attacker's jaw. His head jerked back and he landed on his ass. Yvette flailed around, righting herself and scrambling away.

The attacker laughed.

"Good one," he said, then landed a punch that laid her flat.

Yvette saw stars. Blackness tugged her down. She fought for consciousness. Fought for her life.

But it was no use. She felt a gag go in her mouth. Felt both hands get cuffed together in front of her. She shook her head to clear it and looked at the man who had captured her.

He chuckled softly.

Yvette tried to say something around the gag.

"What was that?" he asked.

She tried to speak again.

"You're a fighter. I like that. One of the strong. And that makes me want to hear what you have to say. If I take this gag off, do you promise not to scream?"

Yvette nodded.

"You agreed too quick. Let me put it this way. If you scream, I'll cut your tongue out. Now do you promise not to scream?"

A coldness Yvette had never known took over her body.

Survive. What's important is that you survive.

Yvette forced herself to nod.

Her attacker studied her for a moment, then removed the gag.

Yvette tried to speak, found her throat to dry, cleared it, then rasped, "I have my period."

The man kneeling above her chuckled. "Is that what some self-defense instructor told you to say? Make me not want to rape you? Well, I wasn't going to rape you anyway."

He put the gag back on and continued.

"I was planning on killing you, because we need to cull the weak. But that fight you put up, and the defiance I can see in you even now, shows you're one of the strong. So I'm not going to kill you. I'm going to make you stronger."

He pulled out a Bowie knife from a sheath at his side.

CHAPTER TWELVE

Alexa sat in the passenger's seat as Agent Barrett drove them back to Tucson, his headlights cutting the darkness along a deserted county road. The scene back at the isolated cabin went round and round in her head—not the carnage in the living room, but the location of the cabin itself. Isolated. Quiet. At the end of a dirt track at the end of a gravel track off this little-used county road. If that was the kind of place Drake's helpers were holing him up in, how the hell was she going to track him down?

She had to think like he did, much as she hated to. Go back through his previous behavior. When he had first been doing his killings, before she and Powers hunted him down, he had favored the Southwest's out-of-the-way places, the little towns and isolated ranches, the dusty trailer parks and the remote compounds of cults and survivalists. This had been his sort of people, the marginal and misfits. He had been a bit of a hero to them even before they knew of his killing spree. After he got arrested and became international news, he had been raised to cult status.

He would have even more followers now. More people willing to help or hide him. Alexa bet that if he showed up at some loner's house, or some fringe group's settlement out in the desert, whether an end of the world cult or a meth den or a bunch of gun-toting white supremacists, nine times out of ten he'd be able to find shelter.

And there were so many places like that in Arizona, New Mexico, and Nevada. Or further afield if he managed to get that far. The vast open spaces of the desert seemed to attract people like that. So how to narrow it down?

First off, there was the Glory of the Sun cult and all its associates. And Fiona. And any meth dealers and producers she was associated with.

Alexa knew the police were already investigating everyone in the cult. Fiona, assuming that was her real name, would be harder to track down. Things had been going so fast that Alexa hadn't even had the chance to try. And finding meth producers? Good luck. They brewed up their noxious product in little trailers out in the desert, or in the bathrooms of cheap motels in small towns, paying in cash and leaving after a couple of days. The police hardly ever caught them unless they got a tipoff or, as often happened, one of their labs went up in flames with them in it.

So who else? Alexa gritted her teeth in frustration, looking at the empty county road as Stuart sped down it, in a hurry to get back to Tucson.

Better to think about who he had already met up with. The only one they knew about was Bob Samson. While Drake's team had lost a man in the attack on the prison van, they had taken the body with them, and no doubt buried it in some remote spot or left it to the coyotes.

So Bob Samson had to be the key, and they knew damn little about him. According to his employer he was a loner, like so many of Drake's followers. He did not seem to be an especially offbeat one, though. He owned guns but there was no sign he was a gun nut. No known memberships in any fringe organizations. No criminal record except for an arrest for drunk driving from five years ago. His real name was not in Drake Logan's correspondence file. He had never been in contact with Drake before the killer started sending coded messages to him at the warehouse address.

That suggested one of Drake's other followers had recruited him, no doubt because Samson worked for an armored car company. The cabin in the desert was probably just a lucky bonus.

The warehouse was not owned by the armored car company, but by a shipping firm in California that hadn't used it for almost two years. Someone in Drake's group must have known it was a safe place to use and had obtained a key. They'd have to investigate that line. Maybe trace a clue to another flunky.

Hopefully this one wouldn't turn up carved like a Thanksgiving turkey.

Where else? Where else? She couldn't think. Those mocking notes from Drake distracted her.

She tried to focus, closing her eyes and pushing away those notes and that horrible body on the floor and the wretched scenes in the stable and the liquor store parking lot. Focus. That was what Robert Powers had trained her to do. Push away the terrible things this job entailed and focus. And yet all she could come up with were places she knew had already been checked.

There had to be more.

Just as she got an inkling of a place, something emerging from the depths of her memory, Agent Barrett's phone rang.

He identified himself, then listened, his face growing increasingly grim. Alexa watched him. Obviously this had something to do with the case, so why hadn't they called her? She checked her phone. Nope. No call. She was the expert. While this FBI agent had proven to be somewhat useful, she was the one who had the best chance of catching Drake Logan.

Or any chance at all.

After a couple of minutes, Agent Barrett hung up.

"There's been an attack in Marana, wherever that is."

"It's off I-10 just a little northwest of Tucson. We've already passed it. What happened?"

"Nasty stuff. Some woman out jogging got attacked. The guy beat her up, raped her, and then tied her up and wrote all sorts of insulting words on her body. He filmed the whole thing too."

Alexa's stomach turned.

"It's him," she whispered.

Agent Barrett shook his head. "No way Drake Logan would be so close to a major city. And think about it. He always killed his victims. He never raped and he never left anyone alive. Someone called 911 to tell them where to find her, but no one was with her when the cops and EMTs showed up. So it was probably the attacker who tipped them off. Drake wouldn't attack someone and then risk his freedom to make sure they'd be discovered."

That did seem unlike him. Or was it?

"Any witnesses?"

"The EMTs got there before the cops, and saw a burly Caucasian man running from the park as they entered it. They got the impression he had been waiting by the victim and took off as soon as their lights appeared."

"A burly man. They said a burly man."

"Yeah. At least six feet but they didn't get a good look at him. It was dark and he was at a distance."

"Drake Logan isn't burly. He's actually rather small."

"As I said, they didn't get a good look. You know how most witnesses are."

"Did the victim give any description of her attacker?"

“You kidding?”

Alexa grimaced. Yeah, that was too much to hope for, at least at this early stage.

“The 911 woman said the guy who called in had a Hispanic accent.”

That caught Alexa’s attention. “Really? One of the men who attacked the prison bus was a burly Caucasian with a Hispanic accent.”

“Why would a white dude have a Hispanic accent?”

“If you lived down here you’d know. A lot of the high-class Mexicans have very light skin. They’re descended from the Spanish and never mixed with Native Americans or Black people.”

“Oh. Then I guess this proves it isn’t Drake. Not the right M.O. or description. So once we get back to Tucson I suggest—”

“Wait a minute. Just because it isn’t Drake doesn’t mean it isn’t the guy from the prison break.”

“But why would it be? Wouldn’t he kill like Drake does? And Drake always went for tough guys. Barroom bullies or drug dealers who terrorized neighborhoods. That’s one of the reasons he got an underground following. He wouldn’t go after some woman out jogging and I don’t think one of his followers would either. It doesn’t make sense. Too much of a risk and it doesn’t follow Drake’s philosophy.”

“I’m not so sure. Humiliating someone but letting them live? It could be a new thing for his ideology.”

“He’s a killer, Deputy Marshal Chase. He doesn’t have an ideology. His only ideology is to kill people.”

That’s not entirely true.

But Alexa didn’t try to explain. She wasn’t even sure how to explain it to herself. Drake didn’t kill for the sake of killing. He killed for the power and to prove a point, and that wasn’t quite the same thing. But beyond that? Just what psychology it took to get to that mental place? She couldn’t understand.

No. She *wouldn’t* understand.

But you need to.

Alexa shuddered.

Clearing her throat, she asked, “What else do we know about the victim?”

“Unclear at this point. She just made it to the hospital. The Marana Police Department is out there now asking questions.”

“Where is the victim now?”

"University Hospital."

Alexa nodded. That was the best in the city. "Let's go."

Agent Barrett looked at her. "Go to the hospital? You're not going to get to talk to her. Not so soon."

"I need a better description of the attacker. See if he matches up with the man I saw."

"You're not going to get a description out of her. Not now. Maybe not ever. She's been through some serious trauma. She'll be in shock for days."

Alexa didn't say anything. He was right, of course. It would be pointless trying to interview her. Even cruel.

And unnecessary. She knew it was the same guy from the prison break, carrying out Drake's orders or trying to impress him. She didn't know how she knew; she just did.

But why so soon after the break? And why so close to Tucson? He didn't have a hideout around here.

She pulled a topo map out of the glove compartment. While most people used Google Maps, a proper topo map showed so much more and was essential for anyone spending time in the wilderness, or hunting someone in the wilderness.

Alexa turned on the interior light of the car, no doubt annoying the other drivers on the highway, and studied the map, looking for possibilities. They drove in silence, the FBI agent lost in his thoughts and Alexa lost in her perusal of the all the little ranches and hidden box canyons in the Tucson valley and just beyond.

If one of his men was striking in Marana, Drake would probably be close. He wouldn't want to risk a long drive, not with the Tucson P.D. and Arizona Highway Patrol stopping and searching so many vehicles.

Meticulously she searched all through the area, wracking her brain to think of where he might have gone to lay low. The topo map didn't show impermanent settlements like homeless camps or trailers that have simply been parked by the side of the road, or even trailer parks that had cropped up in the past couple of years since the map was a bit old. It was missing a lot, but then again he would most likely be in someplace familiar, someplace that was around the last time he was free a few years before.

Where? Where? Her frustration grew as the lights of Tucson shone over the Interstate ahead of them. They had already passed Marana, the scene of that horrible mutilation, and Alexa hadn't noticed. She needed to figure this out. Now. If he was sending his minions out to hurt people, he could be planning an attack right this moment.

It wasn't until they had gotten off the interstate and onto Speedway that it struck her.

"The access road just five miles north of here!" she shouted.

"What about it?"

"There's an abandoned building up there next to an old racetrack. He could be hiding there."

Alexa lifted up the map and showed it to him. Agent Barrett took his eyes off the road for a second to check out where she was pointing.

"Oh, come on! That's within the city limits. No way he'd be there."

"It's on the northern edge of town, and you can drive on access roads and back country roads to get to Marana. I've been there. It's out of sight of any building developments or major roads, and it's in good enough condition to act as shelter. It's perfect as a base of operations."

"As are a million other places within a twenty mile radius," the FBI man said in a dismissive tone as he turned back to watch the road. "Why do you think he'd pick this one?"

"The racetrack was used back in the thirties and forties to race cars. Drake loves racing and vintage cars. He loves how people risk their lives to prove they're strong. And the old races, before they put in all the safety measures, were even more dangerous. It's one of his passions. He loves vintage racing."

"He also loves his freedom. He's not going to hang out in some abandoned building where they haven't raced cars since Truman was president."

Alexa fell silent for a moment, looking out at the strip malls and apartment complexes, at the bars and restaurants full of happy, contented people with their little problems. People who never had to think about murderers except when they watched the news or a movie. They were so placid, so much in a dream state. Sometimes Alexa couldn't decide if she hated them or envied them.

This guy's in a dream state too, Alexa thought, *if he thinks regular police procedure is going to catch Drake before he attacks again.*

On the surface, Agent Barrett was right. It made no logical sense for Drake to be there, even though he had mentioned the place once in one of his essays as an example of brave men daring to be different. Racing was considered a bit suspect back in the thirties, attracting the "wrong" crowd that gambled and drank, especially on little country tracks like that one had been. To Drake the old building was a museum of the strong.

They pulled into the parking lot of the Tucson base of operations. It was evening and there were just a few cars in the lot. Most of the detectives had gone home for the night or were checking up on leads. Alexa guessed just a few of the computer guys and the people handling the phone bank were still in the office.

Agent Barrett parked. "Let's go inside and review the day's reports. Even being gone a few hours puts us behind in a big manhunt like this."

"I think we should check out the racetrack," Alexa insisted.

"It's a waste of time. He's not going to be that close. Remember how far out Samson's cabin was? And we know he was there. That's the kind of place he's going to hide. The desert is huge. It stretches across several states and there's a million places to hide. He's going to go deeper into the wilderness, not move closer to the city."

Alexa got out and slammed the door. "Well, if you don't want to come, don't."

"You can't go alone!"

"I won't. I'll call the local P.D."

At least they're cooperative. Most of the time.

She headed for the U.S. Marshals vehicle she had been assigned, parked just a few yards away.

"Come on, Deputy Marshal Chase, be reasonable."

"I am being reasonable," she said, unlocking the door.

"You're wasting your time."

The only waste of my time is trying to make you see sense.

CHAPTER THIRTEEN

The old racing building and track stood in a dead area. Alexa saw no sign of anyone living anywhere close. The Interstate and its access road stood half a mile off to the east. To the north stood another road, less used but well lit. To the south ran a drainage canal to siphon off the torrential rains that swept up from Mexico and dumped onto southern Arizona in the summer monsoon season. To the west was a narrow unpaved access road and a landfill.

In between stretched several hundred acres of dusty, bare soil of no use to anyone. It was unattractive to real estate developers, useless for businesses, and too out of the way for light industry. Alexa guessed that even homeless people probably didn't come here. It was too far of a walk from anything else.

Alexa drove on the unpaved access road with her lights off. The highway to the east and the paved road to the north were both brilliantly lit, leaving this unused area in relative shadow. From those two roads, anything inside this space would be invisible at night.

But within that space, the light from the distant roads gave her enough illumination to see as she drove with the headlights off. A low mound of spoil with a few scrubs clinging to it covered her approach, probably earth piled up when they flattened the desert to make the track all those years ago.

She drove as far as the mound could hide her and then parked, not bothering to pull off onto the shoulder. This old track didn't look like it got any traffic, certainly not at night. And if Drake tried to make a getaway, having a car parked in the middle of the road might slow him down a bit.

Alexa had changed back into her Kevlar and still had her shotgun. With that and her Glock she should have felt safe, but her heart still pounded and her mouth had gone dry. She told herself that there was little chance of Drake being here, that this was just a hunch she had to put to rest so she could sleep at night. She couldn't even make out any fresh tire tracks.

Even so, when she got out of the car she gripped her shotgun hard.

She stopped, looking around and listening. Silence, save for the distant whoosh of cars on the highway, punctuated by the occasional horn. Crouching low, she moved to the edge of the mound and peeked around.

The racetrack was visible as a flat area with a faint oval trackway. It had been nothing but packed earth back in the day. One of Alexa's friends, a bookish guy at the Arizona Historical Society, loved to regale her with tales of the old Arizona. Besides all the prospectors and gunfighters, he told her stories about the lesser-known aspects of the state's past, and that had included showing her pictures of this very track. She remembered the black and white images of vintage cars—then the latest thing—racing around the dirt track and kicking up clouds of dust into the faces of the crowd.

Her friend would never have guessed that his historical trivia would one day be used to hunt a serial killer. She'd have to tell him.

If she lived.

On the near side of the track stood a low concrete building with a corrugated iron roof that looked ready to fall down. There were only a couple of windows on this side, black rectangles through which no light shone. The glass had long since been broken, probably by the same people who had covered the walls in graffiti, and the windows were now empty cavities.

The front, which she couldn't see, was more open. She had come here once long ago and remembered it had a long window that had once been for a restaurant where richer patrons could dine and watch the races out of the heat and dust. There was also another long window for a food stand, and the remains of some bleachers.

She watched, and waited. No sign of life from within.

Alexa began to doubt herself. It was a slim chance Drake would be here. If anyone was here, it would more likely be some partying kids, judging from all the graffiti on the walls. But she didn't hear any sign of them either.

Wait. What was that? She thought she had seen a brief gleam of light in one of the windows.

There it was again! Someone was checking their phone in there.

Ducking out of sight, Alexa pulled out her own phone to call for backup. Actually she texted for backup, a habit many law officers had gotten into because it was silent. She gave her identity and location and requested a squad car. She got a text back within thirty seconds that one was on its way, with an e.t.a. of five minutes.

She hunkered down to wait, keeping watch on the building.

The gleam passed by the window. Someone was pacing around in there looking at their phone. She strained her ears to hear any talking, but whoever was on their phone wasn't using it for that.

The person passed out of sight. Alexa waited. Where the hell was that squad car?

Come to think of it, where was this person's car? This spot wasn't exactly walkable, and she didn't see any vehicle. Maybe it was parked around the other side of the building, but she hadn't seen any fresh tracks when she came in. She had looked.

Alexa let out a long, slow breath and tried to have some patience. A lot of policework required patience. Powers had taught her that. Well, re-taught her that. She had learned it and lost it in the FBI. If it hadn't been for Powers, she would probably have stayed burned out and would have ended up in some awful retail job.

Her eyes teared up again at the thought of Powers being gone. She still hadn't come to terms with it. She might never come to terms with it.

Seeing Drake and his buddies behind bars would sure help.

A soft sound from the building caught her attention. The sound stopped. Alexa, her senses on high alert, strained to hear.

It came again, very softly. Was that a woman's voice? She didn't see a gleam at the windows anymore, but she could pick out a very faint light inside, like that phone was still lit up but not right at the window for her to see directly.

The woman's voice returned. It sounded like it was pleading.

Alexa tensed. What was going on in there?

Then a scream launched her into action.

She bolted across the open field, her shotgun at the ready. No time to wait for backup. Drake was in there getting ready to kill someone. The scream came again.

It sounded strange, too quiet. Alexa tried to remember the building's layout and realized that on her one visit all those years ago she had never actually gone inside. Perhaps the victim was in an interior room, her screams muffled by the walls and corridors.

Alexa would find out soon enough. She got to the wall without anyone taking a potshot at her from one of the windows, put her back against it, shotgun sloped, and paused.

There came that scream again, longer, higher pitched, yet strangely distant at the same time.

She peeked in the window, leading with her shotgun.

Just inside was a large, empty room, its floor littered with trash. She couldn't see much because of the dim light, but she could see no one was inside. Just ahead and to her left was an open doorway. She could see some light, probably from that phone, shining from just beyond it.

Another scream, more panicked this time. Alexa leaped onto the windowsill and vaulted inside, gritting her teeth as her foot hit an old beer can and sent it rattling across the concrete floor.

She crouched so her body wouldn't make a silhouette against the window. The gleam of light winked off.

Well, he knows I'm here.

"Drake Logan! This is the U.S. Marshals Service. We have the building surrounded. Come out with your hands up."

Yeah, right. More like he'll come out shooting.

Fine by me. At this range, this 12-gauge will cut him in half.

Alexa waited, looking down the barrel of her gun at the doorway. Not a sound.

She glanced around the room. Another door stood open at the far corner.

Damn. He knows the layout and I don't.

Alexa knew the smartest thing to do would be to wait for backup, but with a hostage in danger, she couldn't afford to.

She rushed for the doorway, angling to the right so that she'd stay out of sight. When she got to the wall beside it, and paused again like she had at the window, listening, waiting, sweat trickling down the inside of her Kevlar. She heard no sound of movement, which meant Drake was listening and waiting for her too.

And he must be just as well armed as she was.

She peeked around the doorway, only exposing herself for a moment. It was darker in there, a short, interior hallway with no windows leading to another, slightly brighter room.

Damn. He could be anywhere, and he knows right where I am.

"Ma'am, if you can speak, identify your location!"

No response. She crept down the hallway, wincing every time her boots crushed broken glass or crinkled candy wrappers under her feet.

At the doorway she paused. Something told her he was just beyond it. She could not say how she knew—a little sound just beneath the level of conscious hearing, the warmth given off by a nearby body barely felt by the skin, or even some strange sixth sense that few people believe in except those who got in danger for a living. All she knew was that she knew he was close.

She ducked around the corner to the left and, not seeing him, immediately turned to the right.

For a moment she stood confused. He was nowhere in the room.

Then a heavy weight falling on top of her from above told her she had made a fatal mistake.

CHAPTER FOURTEEN

Alexa fell hard on the floor, crying out as pain lanced through her injured ribs.

She had no time for pain. Lashing out with her elbow, she managed to connect with the man who had fallen on her. She hit him in the hip, probably causing little pain, but the force was enough for him to half fall off of her and making him put one hand on the floor to steady himself.

That gave her enough time to turn over and see the man's other hand held a knife. In a holster on his belt was a pistol.

It was not Drake. It was some other, bigger, man.

She grabbed his knife hand by the wrist and slammed a punch into his armpit. From her awkward angle she wasn't able to get enough force to put the shoulder out of joint or even make him drop the knife, but it did make him waver for a moment.

Long enough to hit him again. This time he did drop the knife.

But the fight was far from over. He yanked himself free and tried to stand. Alexa was dimly aware of the woman pleading in the background but there was nothing to do about that now.

The man stumbled backwards, trying to get his balance and draw his gun.

Alexa was faster. She whipped out her Glock and leveled it at him.

He froze, his pistol half out of its holster.

"Drop it on the floor." Alexa was still prone at his feet, but her own gun did not waver.

The man hesitated.

"NOW!"

Slowly, reluctantly, he pulled out his gun and bent over. Alexa watched him, ready to pull the trigger if he made any move for her.

He chuckled and set it down.

"You should have shot me. Drake said you were one of the strong. I'm thinking maybe he's wrong about you."

While her attacker looked Anglo, his voice carried an upper class Mexican accent.

I know who you are.

An image of Powers getting decapitated rose up in her mind's eye. Her finger tightened on the trigger.

"Back up," Alexa ordered.

The man slowly raised his hands, his eyes never leaving Alexa.

As soon as I try to stand, he's going to make a move.

"Face down on the floor with your hands behind your head," she ordered.

"Help me! Somebody please help me!" the woman's muffled voice cried.

"I've captured your abductor!" Alexa shouted. "I'll free you in a minute."

The Mexican man chuckled.

"On the floor," she ordered. "I won't say it again."

"What are you going to do, shoot me? Not in cold blood. Drake is wrong. You don't have it in you."

Nevertheless, he did as he was told.

Once he had assumed the position, Alexa got up, kicked his gun and knife further away, and cuffed him. She put a second set of cuffs around his ankles, just in case.

She stood above the now-helpless man, her gun still in her hand. Alexa half raised it in the direction of his head, then let her hand fall.

The woman's voice had stopped, replaced with a low sobbing. That reminded her of her duty.

Now that Alexa had a chance to look around, she noticed a dull, flickering glow coming from a doorway not too far off. Leveling her gun, she crossed the room and ducked around the corner.

The room was empty except for a battered old wooden table. On the table, propped upright against a brick, was a phone showing a video. It showed a woman tied to a tree, completely naked. Several slashes to her arms and legs bled freely. A hand reached from around the camera holding a magic marker. The cameraman wrote "weak" across the woman's bare chest as she sobbed. The words "victim" and "useless" and "nothing" already adorned her body.

Curling her lip in disgust, she left the phone where it was. CSI would need to dust it for prints, although it was obvious who had taken the images.

She strode back to the prisoner, only to find he had wormed his way ten yards down the hall.

She gave him a kick in the ribs. "Stay where you are."

The man grunted at the impact of her boot, then laughed.

"She was a good target. A real proud woman humiliated. The bigger they are, the harder they fall. Isn't that the old saying? Hey, you see the video? I already uploaded it to a ton of sites. It's going to go viral."

The wail of police sirens in the distance told her that backup was finally coming.

About time.

She studied the piece of human garbage at her feet.

"Where's Drake?"

"Who?"

"Don't give me that! He sent you here."

"Oh, you men that serial killer? Yeah, I've seen him on the news. The news says he's smart. I guess with all the cops in the state looking for him he must move around constantly. And if he's as smart as they say, he's too smart to tell anyone where he is unless they need to know."

Alexa growled in frustration. That was probably true.

"You raped that poor woman and tied her to a tree but didn't kill her. Why?"

He gave a sly little smile. "I didn't rape her. Too predictable. She was expecting it after I grabbed her, and she sure expected it when I stripped her and tied her to a tree. That's part of the fun. Making the victim confused. Helps them along their path."

"I suppose Drake thought this up. What's his game?"

He looked up at her. "Who's Drake?"

"Don't act smart with me. You were part of his breakout. I recognize you."

Again her gun hand moved to aim at the prisoner's head before stopping halfway. He noticed the movement but did not appear intimidated. The horrible memory of her partner getting decapitated came back to her. This scum had a part in that.

She should just put a bullet through his head. It would be so easy.

"The news says they all wore masks," he said. "You won't be able to make that stick in court."

Her finger tightened on the trigger, then she eased up.

No, she couldn't become like this guy. He had hurt someone who was helpless. Now he was helpless. She couldn't do it.

"Maybe not. We'll just send you down for assault, kidnapping, and distribution of illegal pornography. And assaulting an officer of the law. That will get you twenty, twenty-five years once we have a word with the judge. Or you can tell me where Drake is and we'll have a different word with the judge."

Not that she had any intention of letting this guy walk. But she'd be willing to get his sentence reduced a little to catch somebody far worse.

Her job had forced her into that kind of thinking. She hated it, but it was all too necessary.

"I'm not saying anything," he grunted.

Alexa glared down at him. "We'll see about that."

"Why don't you kick me again?"

"I would if I thought it would help," she growled. "Hell with it."

She kicked him again, harder this time. He gasped.

"That's the spirit," he said, his voice coming out choked.

Alexa flushed with shame at the approval in his voice.

She heard a squad car pull up beside the building. Going to a window, she flagged them down. Two male officers jumped out of the car, pistols drawn. Another squad car was just coming up the road.

The first two officers rushed into the building. Alexa faced them.

"You, take this guy to the car. You, check out the building. There's a phone playing a video in that room over there. Don't touch it. Let CSI handle that. Check the rest of the building, though."

The two cops hesitated, torn between her gender and her uniform.

"MOVE!" she shouted.

They got to work.

Alexa walked out of the building, trying to suppress the shaking that threatened to take over her entire body. Now that the danger was over, the fear, the disgust, threatened to overwhelm her. She didn't want those two officers to see that.

Maybe some air would help. As she stepped out, she was almost blinded by the flashing lights of the two patrol cars. The approaching wail of an ambulance told her the perp would soon get the medical attention he didn't deserve.

Alexa walked around to the other side of the building to get away from the lights. She passed along the old frontage, the windows to the restaurant all boarded up, the wood covered with graffiti. The old track, lit crazily with alternating blue and red, looked surreal.

And dead. No one had raced here in a long time. Cacti and scrub had partially reclaimed the track, plastic and bits of paper were scattered across it, the detritus of the nearby city blown by the wind to litter this empty place.

It was the same with the desert at the edges of any major settlement in the Southwest, the once-pristine desert marred by the trash of consumer culture.

Alexa leaned against the cold concrete wall and let out a long, slow breath. Why did mankind always wreck everything beautiful? Was there a deep destructive streak in people that compelled them to wreck anything beautiful? Or was it an anomaly for individuals like Drake and that monster inside?

She hoped the latter was true. She didn't want to think everyone was capable of evil. But considering world history, she wouldn't want to be humanity's defense attorney in some celestial court.

At least she had captured one of Powers's murderers. That balanced the scales a little bit.

You should have killed him when you had the chance.

That made Alexa feel guilty, but not for thinking about killing him. What made her feel guilty was *not* feeling guilty about it. It told her something about herself she didn't want to face.

Why didn't you kill him? No one would have suspected it was anything but self-defense.

Stop. You did your duty. That's enough.

And you have a lot more justice to mete out before you're done.

Yes, but how? Drake had set another trap for her, one she had blundered into all too predictably. He had stayed one step ahead of her for this entire investigation.

Her phone rang. Stacy.

"You picked a hell of a time," Alexa muttered.

She answered anyway. There might be some drama in the Carpenter home. Alexa feared those arguments her parents had might one day turn to violence, or that Stacy might decide enough was enough and run away for good. Phoenix was the most likely place to go, and Alexa didn't want Stacy to fall prey to the dangers of a young girl on the streets.

"Hello, Stacy. What's up?" Alexa said.

"Are my boobs too small?" Stacy asked.

Alexa blinked. "I'm sorry, what?"

"Cheryl Tyler says my boobs are too small, and so does Hannah Lennon. She says they look funny too, and that I look like I'm eleven. I don't, do I? Rachel Gardener is like almost fourteen and she's as flat as a board. Of course, Luella Martinez has huge ones, but I think she stayed back a year. And I—"

"Your boobs are fine," Alexa said with a smile. From the girl's tone Alexa could tell nothing was wrong at the moment beyond a bit of adolescent insecurity.

"You think so? They don't look funny or anything?"

"To be honest, I've never really taken any time to study them."

"Well, you must have noticed *something*. You're a cop; it's your job to notice stuff like that."

"Breast size? Not really." Alexa heard the siren of the ambulance stop. It had arrived. "I focus on more important stuff."

"This is important! None of the guys look at me!"

"I thought you weren't interested in anyone in your class. You said they were all immature dorks."

"They *are* immature dorks. But I still want them to notice me."

"So if they ask you out, you can turn them down?"

"Exactly."

"Your breasts are fine, Stacy. And you're young. They have several more years to fill out."

A male voice intruded. "Um, Deputy Marshal?"

Alexa turned and saw a portly, middle-aged officer from the Tucson Police Department standing there. With all the sirens and teenaged whining, Alexa hadn't heard him approach.

She hoped he hadn't overheard the conversation about teenaged breasts. Judging from the awkward look on his jowly face, he had.

"Hold on, Stacy," Alexa said. "What is it, officer?"

"An Agent Barrett of the FBI just arrived. He says he has some news for you."

"I'll be right there."

Alexa waited for the officer to leave and then got back on the phone.

"Sorry, Stacy, I've got to go. I'm actually working at the moment. Is there anything else you wanted to talk about?"

"No. That's it. Oh, I got Wesson to jump over the three-footer!"

"Awesome! You wearing your helmet?"

"I always wear my helmet when I jump."

"Good girl. I need to go."

"Love you!" the girl chirped.

"Love you."

Alexa hung up, feeling much better. A dose of the normal, sane world was better than any professional therapy.

Squaring her shoulders, she headed back inside, ready once again to face the sad scene and whatever news that FBI agent had brought her.

She saw Agent Barrett standing by the squad car as an officer put the perp in the back seat. He turned to Alexa as she approached.

"Looks like you were right," he said. He did not look like he was conceding that easily.

"He's one of the men who broke Drake out of the prison bus," Alexa said, glaring at the prisoner.

"You sure?"

She gave a curt nod. "Same build. Same voice."

Agent Barrett looked to the suspect and then back at her. He was obviously thinking the same thing the perp had, that with a mask on, and Alexa injured, it would be all but impossible to convince a judge and jury about that identification.

They'd need more. Alexa would make damn sure she'd get it.

It was time to get this animal in human form back to the station and grill him.

CHAPTER FIFTEEN

The prisoner was handcuffed to a steel chair in the interrogation room when Alexa and Agent Barrett walked in. They had let him stew alone for a couple of hours as they checked his prints, his vehicle, and the phone he had been using.

In that short time, they had already learned a lot. The car had been stolen in Phoenix a week before, with fake plates added. His prints had given up a match because he had a criminal and prison record. Several counts of assault, theft, and one of sexual assault. He really must have been under Drake's spell not to repeat that particular crime when he had the chance.

The phone had been stolen just like his vehicle—from the victim herself.

The records on the phone showed that the video the perp had taken had been shared on thirty different websites specializing in violent content in eight different countries. No doubt it had since been downloaded and shared countless times.

That woman's suffering and humiliation had become the cheap entertainment of a world of deviants, and would remain on the Internet forever.

Alexa had forced herself to watch the entire five-minute video. It only showed the final part of the attack, before switching to the woman being tied to the tree and having those insulting words written all over her.

All through the torture, the perp had repeated, "This will make you stronger. This will make you stronger."

When they finished watching it in the police station, Alexa turned away in disgust. Agent Barrett looked pale.

"Cruelty is always worse than violence," he muttered.

Alexa gave him a sharp look. "Let's grill this son of a bitch."

They went to the interrogation room. A couple of the police officers sat in the observation room. None came in with her or Agent Barrett.

Fine by her. The Tucson police department had a reputation for shoddy work, corruption, and poor public relations. Once, a few years ago, a local man had reported his van stolen. The police couldn't find it until three weeks later, when one of the men's friends happened to pass the police station and saw the stolen van parked just down the street. The affair made all the local news outlets and the police chief, instead of responding with an apology, accused the van owner of playing a trick on the police department.

Alexa didn't need those jokers in the interrogation room with her.

"Ricardo Montañez," Agent Barrett said as he swaggered into the interrogation room, looking through a printout. "You've got quite a sheet on you."

"Montañez," Ricardo said, correcting his pronunciation.

"Whatever." Agent Barrett sat down. Alexa remained standing. She edged around the table so as to stand behind the prisoner, close enough to get into his space.

Ricardo leaned back and took a deep breath. "Mmmm. You smell nice. That chick was fine but I bet you'd be finer. Too bad we didn't have a chance for some fun at the old race track."

"Where is he?" Alexa demanded. She couldn't count the number of times a suspect had sexually harassed her. It didn't affect her at all anymore.

"Where is who?"

"Don't play games with us," she snapped. "Drake Logan."

"Don't know him," Ricardo turned back to Agent Barrett. "You're not a cop. Where's your uniform?"

"I'm Special Agent Stuart Barrett of the FBI. I'm down here helping with the Logan manhunt. If you help us, we might be able to do something for you."

Ricardo chuckled. "Oh, so you're playing good cop and she's supposed to be bad cop? I guess she'd have to, after losing her partner."

Alexa felt rage rising up in her. This was the man who killed Robert Powers. This was the man who cut his head off right in front of her eyes.

"You know that there's still a death penalty in Arizona," she said through gritted teeth. "Killing a cop gets you death."

"Unless you cooperate," Agent Barrett said in a level voice.

Ricardo ignored him and looked over his shoulder at Alexa, his eyes taking in her body.

"I didn't kill anybody."

"Like hell you didn't! I recognize your voice!" Alexa leaned in close, fists clenched, resisting the urge to beat this guy.

"Calm down," Agent Barrett said, and that level voice and reassuring hand were just as annoying to her as the smug killer shackled to the chair. The FBI man turned back to Ricardo. "Tell me about the crime."

"What crime?"

Alexa almost smacked him then, but with all those other officers watching, she didn't want to lose her cool any more than she had already.

She knew what they'd think. A hysterical woman who shouldn't be in uniform. Well, they hadn't seen their partner beheaded.

"I'm talking about that woman you assaulted," Agent Barrett said. "Why her? And why Marana? And why did you do it the way you did it?"

Ricardo put on an innocent face. "You mean why did I tie her to a tree? I'm an environmentalist."

Alexa took a deep breath and stepped away from him. It was the only way she could ensure she wouldn't rip this guy's head off.

Agent Barrett went on. "I'm referring to you tying her up and writing those words on her, and then calling in the crime so you could make sure she was discovered."

Ricardo shrugged. "I was making her strong."

"You said that in the video. Why?"

That got only a grin in return.

"Answer my question," Agent Barrett said.

Ricardo inclined his head toward Alexa. "Ask her."

"Why should I ask my partner?"

You are not my partner, Alexa thought, leaning against the far wall with her arms crossed. *Robert Powers is my partner, and this guy killed him.*

"She knows. She understands," Ricardo said.

"The only thing I understand about lowlifes like you," Alexa growled, "is that you should be locked away for the rest of your lives."

Ricardo gave her a saucy smile. "You didn't kill me when you had the chance. That was disappointing. I'm thinking you're one of the weak. That chick in Marana is going to end up stronger than you."

"Why, because you attacked her and then humiliated her to the whole world?" Alexa said, her anger rising even more.

"She fought like a champ," Ricardo said. "Half the bruises you see on me I didn't get from you, I got them from her. She's taken lots of self-defense classes. I could tell. Thought she was strong, at least until I got the upper hand."

And suddenly Alexa understood. Ricardo had picked someone fit, someone who looked like she could take care of herself. By beating her down, humiliating her, and then posting it all to the Internet, he was proving to her that she was wrong.

Thus leaving her with a choice—be the victim and spend the rest of her life afraid, or turn into something stronger than she was before.

It fit perfectly with Drake's philosophy. And every step—the hunt, tying her up, writing those words on her, and posting it online, all of that had been meticulously planned by Drake.

He was sending out his followers to create victims they hoped would become a new generation of people adhering to Drake's ideas. Ricardo wasn't just a sidekick, he was a missionary.

There would be more missionaries. Alexa felt sure of that.

More attacks. More humiliations. He won't kill. He's changed his plans. Now he wants to spread misery, thinking it will unlock people's potential.

And that's where Drake Logan was wrong. She had spent a lot of time talking with victims of crime, and they did not prosper from their experiences. Most were broken, or if they did manage to put their lives back in a semblance of order after getting robbed or raped or mutilated, they always carried with them a shadow that dimmed even their brightest days.

Some took to the bottle, or to the sleepwalking death of opioid painkillers. Some lashed out, hurting others like they had been hurt.

Drake wasn't going to help the human race. He was going to drag it down into the mud.

The next thing Ricardo said snapped her out of her thoughts.

"She'll be a star one day. She has potential. I could see it. She'll move from being weak to being strong. Strong in a good way. Some strong people just get in the way. Those kind need to be put down so the great work can continue."

Ricardo looked Alexa in the eye when he made this last statement. A smug smile tugged at the sides of his mouth.

A red haze settled over Alexa's vision. She watched herself, as if from a distance, push off from the wall on which she had been leaning and striding over to the prisoner. As she did, he burst into laughter. Her hands reached out, ready to strangle him, ready to choke the air out of that laughing throat, to erase that laugh, that smugness forever …

"Whoa! Hold up."

Agent Barrett intercepted her. She snarled and tried to duck around him, forcing him to grab her by the shoulders and push her back.

"Don't do it, Deputy Marshal Chase," the FBI man said as Ricardo cackled in the background. "It's what he wants. You lay a finger on him and his lawyer will get him off, and it will cost you your job."

"That's right, Alexa," Ricardo called over. "Don't lose your head!"

"Why you—"

"Out," Agent Barrett ordered, backing up his command with a firm push.

Alexa struggled, but the Army veteran was stronger. The door to the interrogation chamber opened, a cop standing there, looking concerned, judging this female officer who couldn't keep her head. Alexa felt ashamed and enraged at the same time. Who were these guys to judge her? They hadn't lost a partner to that slime shackled to the chair.

Agent Barrett got her into the hallway, and the local cop slammed the door to the interrogation chamber, cutting off Ricardo's mocking laughter.

"Calm down," the FBI man repeated. "He wants to get a reaction from you. Look, the local P.D. can take over the interrogation from here. Other than that babble about creating strong people I don't think this guy is going to reveal anything more. Why don't we go to the motel and catch some sleep, eh? We've had a long day and we're going to have a longer day tomorrow."

Alexa stood there for a moment, grinding her teeth and trying to catch her breath. She couldn't get the vision of her partner's decapitation out of her mind. Ricardo did it, she was sure of that. He had all but confessed. And he sat in there, safe and sound, reveling in the fact that he had violated a woman a few hours before and shared the act all over the Internet. He deserved to die.

But not tonight, Alexa told herself, trying to calm down. Both men in the hallway watched her, waiting to see what she would do. She needed to get a grip. The last thing she needed was other people on the manhunt to start thinking she had cracked. She had barely gotten back on the case. She didn't want to jeopardize that now.

She had a killer to catch.

"Let's go to the motel," Agent Barrett repeated.

Alexa nodded, not trusting herself to speak. Agent Barrett patted her on the shoulder, an overly familiar and condescending gesture she immediately resented. She drew away, frowning, then felt bad. She'd been acting horrible to everyone, and this guy was only trying to be supportive. Sure, she had plenty of reason to feel bad, but she shouldn't take it out on someone who was trying to nab Drake. They were a team, after all, at least for a moment.

"You're right," Alexa forced herself to say. "Let's go get some rest. We did some good work today … the both of us."

They headed down the hall, leaving Ricardo Montañez sitting happily in custody, savoring the memory of his many acts of evil.

CHAPTER SIXTEEN

That night at the motel, Alexa tossed and turned. The events of the previous few days swirled around in her mind, especially the horrible scenes in the video Ricardo had taken of his victim.

She could feel it happening again. She could feel herself slipping into the awful mindset of the animals she hunted. It was what made her career in the FBI, and it was what broke her as a person.

Her time at the FBI had been short, only two and a half years, and yet in that time she had run down several serial killers. Alexa had shown a talent for anticipating their next moves.

The only way she had been able to do that was to think like them. She had to put herself in their mindset, like what they liked, hate what they hated. It was like a dirty form of method acting.

It yielded results, but at what cost. Every day at work had led to a darkening of her soul, to the point where she could barely recognize herself anymore. The line between her thoughts and the thoughts of the animals she hunted became blurred. While that helped her catch them, it made her feel like a stranger inside her own head.

It got to be too much. The dark dreams, the evil waking fantasies. The reluctant familiarity with those who had killed so many and in such creative ways. She had to quit, leaving the East Coast to return to the familiar desert that she loved so much.

After a short lull of doing not much of anything at the family ranch, their old family friend Robert Powers had saved her by inspiring her to join the U.S. Marshal Service. He had known her since she was a kid, and knew she wasn't a quitter. He told her that she could stay in her beloved Southwest, fighting the crime that threatened the way of life she treasured. It would be a more straightforward, cleaner form of law enforcement. She wouldn't have to sully herself by having to think like the insane, only outwit common criminals. She had donned the new uniform with pride and a renewed self-confidence.

Only to get faced with the worst serial killer of her career.

That almost sent her fleeing back to the ranch, but Robert Powers's strong assurance, his constant quiet mentorship, had bolstered her. It hadn't been so bad facing down a serial killer when she had a man like him by her side.

But now, with Powers gone, she felt herself slipping again.

Turning over in bed, Alexa tried to relax, tried to clear her mind. If she didn't get any rest, she'd never be able to work tomorrow, and this torture would continue.

Her spirit wouldn't get any real peace until Drake Logan was behind bars again.

She pulled out her phone, wincing at the light it shone in the darkened room. 2:30. Ugh. She really needed to sleep.

Turning the phone's brightness down, she opened the picture Stacy Carpenter had sent of herself standing and smiling between Smith and Wesson.

Alexa's mood soothed a little. At least there was some good in the world.

She stared at it for another minute and, feeling a bit better, turned off her phone and rolled over.

After a few minutes, sleep came at last.

But it proved anything but restful.

The dreams came in bits and snatches as they always do when one drifts into sleep.

Faces, sounds, and scenes flashed behind Alexa's eyes, all in chaotic confusion until one resolved itself into lifelike clarity.

Olivia Powers, Robert's wife. Friendly companion at many a backyard barbeque. She looked right at Alexa, anger stamped on her tear-stained face.

Why him? She demanded with words Alexa felt but did not hear. *Why did he have to die and not you?*

I'm sorry. Please forgive me, Alexa begged. *I am so sorry.*

Drake let you live because he loves you. You're just like him. You've never been one of us. You fooled Robert. Betrayed him. He should have arrested YOU.

Alexa's eyes snapped open and she let out a cry.

Groaning, she turned over, told herself it was a dream, and tried to go back to sleep.

Faster than she expected, the fragments of images and words returned.

Faces, mostly. Faces of the dead. Pictures and crime scenes from her past. A prostitute with her throat slashed in a filthy alley. An elderly man shot in the head while out for his early morning jog. A child packed inside a shipping crate and tossed into a river. So many dead. So many scenes of horror.

And the worst—the scenes in the Pine Barrens.

A thick woodland of pines in New Jersey, and the dead it contained.

Staked out on the ground and gutted. Burned alive in heaps of pine needles. Tied to trees to starve to death.

A flash of a goat-like face, slitted eyes, and curved horns.

Alexa woke with a start. This time she sat up, rubbed her face. She felt tempted to look at Stacy's photo again, but no. Alexa did not want to sully that girl's happy image with the foul memories of the past.

With a sigh, Alexa lay back on her bed, staring up at the dark ceiling, knowing that sleep would not come for some time. It never did when New Jersey came back to her in the small hours.

A killer as bad as Drake. But that wasn't what really haunted her.

What haunted her was what she had to do to catch him.

* * *

Early the next morning, haggard and worn out, she met Agent Barrett at a diner next to the motel. He looked like he had slept just fine. Another annoying thing about this guy. He'd gotten a solid eight hours while she had snatched a few brief respites of unconsciousness here and there between the horrors of the dark.

"Have you looked at the morning report?" Agent Barrett asked as he tucked into a Denver omelet.

"Not yet," Alexa admitted. It was only in the hour past dawn that she had been able to drift off and get a halfway decent stretch of sleep.

"There isn't much there, unfortunately. Every law enforcement agency in the region is working on this. I've never seen anything like it. Border Patrol talked through an intermediary to some of its connections among the coyotes and warned them not to let Drake or his people across the border. Apparently the coyotes agreed without any fuss."

"Not surprising," Alexa grunted. "The coyotes are people smugglers, not serial killers. They don't have much heart, but they do have heads. A sicko like that out on the loose is bad for everyone."

"Like *M*."

Alexa looked at him over her second mug of coffee.

"*M*?"

"Old German film," Agent Barrett explained. "Peter Lorre's first big role. He plays this child killer terrorizing a German city. The cops are after him and so is the underworld. The underworld doesn't like the increased police presence on the streets and they also don't like child killers."

"Never seen that film."

Agent Barrett smiled. "My dad is a big fan of old movies. I saw a lot of them growing up, and every time I go visit him in Boston he shows me more. I swear that guy has never watched anything in color. Half the time the films don't even have sound."

"So who catches him?"

"Who? Oh, Peter Lorre? The criminals do. They put him through a kangaroo court and execute him."

"Maybe we'll get lucky and Arizona's underworld will do the same thing," Alexa said. "We could use a bit of luck on this case."

"We got Ricardo, at least. As we thought, Tucson P.D. didn't get any more out of him. Not much else to report, I'm afraid. They've questioned a ton of people who either knew Drake before he went to prison or who corresponded with him. Hell, they even have foreign police questioning his correspondents. Canada, Germany, Japan, you name it. They're really going after every thread in this thing. Not sure what we should do. What do you think?"

Alexa studied him for a moment. Yes, he really did want to know her opinion. That, at least, had changed since last night. She had been right about the old race track, or at least half right. Agent Barrett might be annoying, but he wasn't so arrogant not to know results when he saw them.

And if he had gotten to where he was today, he must be a halfway decent law enforcement officer.

Alexa had been in the FBI too, so she knew.

"Before we try to figure out his next move," Alexa told him, "we have to figure out his motivations."

"Survival," Agent Barrett grunted.

"Yes, but not in the way most people mean. He's too smart not to know he'll get caught sooner or later. So what does he want to do until then? His time on the outside is precious to him and he'll want to spend it in the best way he knows how. He wants to survive in a different way. He wants to create a new generation of Drake Logans. Turning the weak into strong, creating people who will carry on what he thinks of as his life's work."

"Like that poor woman last night? I don't see her becoming a serial killer."

"Neither do I. Drake has his own sense of logic, though. The important thing is that *he* thinks he can make converts this way."

Agent Barrett nodded. "Good point. But that doesn't get us any closer to finding him."

Alexa thought for a moment. No, it didn't.

What would Drake be doing right now? While sending out his minions to make converts was part of his plan to spread his sick philosophy, he wouldn't be content just to sit back and give orders. He liked to get his hands dirty.

So what would he do, knowing his time might be short? Something special. Maybe some unfinished business?

Then she snapped her fingers. "Amy Doherty!"

"Who?"

"Amy Doherty was one of Drake's earliest victims, and the only one to survive. He stabbed her multiple times in her home but her boyfriend came back from the supermarket before he could finish her off."

"The boyfriend is lucky he didn't get killed too."

"He was carrying a pistol."

Agent Barrett snorted. "Oh yeah, this is an open carry state."

"Concealed carry too."

"That must make you feel so much safer as an officer of the law."

Alexa shrugged off the sarcasm. "It's a problem for us, and it leads to a lot of shootings. It can stop crime in some cases, though."

"So the guy shot Drake?"

"Tried to. Drake was stabbing Doherty in an upstairs room. The boyfriend ran up and opened up on him. Drake only survived by leaping out the window. He landed right on a barrel cactus."

"Ouch."

Agent Barrett snickered. Even though the story she was telling was deadly serious, she couldn't help but see the funny side and smiled in return.

"Got covered in spines," she said. "Landed butt first."

"Good! We'll have to remind him of that when we catch the bastard. So you're thinking Drake might go after the victim he never finished off?"

"I think he might. Because get this. I did a follow up with her after we captured Drake. He was on the loose for three years after the attack on her before we finally ran him to ground. In that time she became a New Age guru and a pacifist. The boyfriend became a vigilante and got arrested for attacking someone he thought was a burglar. Turned out to be a sixteen-year-old Hispanic kid sneaking into his girlfriend's house while the parents were asleep."

"Whoa. Did the kid die?"

"No. Shot him in the leg. Bad enough to put the guy in jail for second degree attempted murder. He's still there. The kid recovered."

"Good." Agent Barrett cocked his head, thinking. "So Amy Doherty failed the test and the boyfriend passed."

"Exactly," Alexa said.

Finally, somebody gets it. Maybe this guy will be some help after all.

"So you're thinking Drake is going to go after the girl, try to kill her since she failed the test?" Agent Barrett asked.

"Yes. He'll want to make an example so the others he puts through the test will steer in the right direction. And he might try to reach out to the boyfriend too. He's in prison so he wouldn't be much help to Drake, and not much of a danger to anyone except fellow prisoners."

"Still in jail for second degree attempted murder after all this time?"

"No, he got out, then got busted for violating his parole by carrying an unregistered firearm."

"Sounds like a real charmer. You got a lot of good old boys down here. We need to talk to him."

Alexa waved the suggestion away. "We'll have someone else handle that. We'll focus on Amy Doherty. Let's call into the operations center and see if anyone's gotten in touch with her."

Just as she said this, Agent Barrett's phone buzzed. He held up a finger to tell her to hold on and answered it.

"Hello, Agent Barrett speaking. Yes, sir. No, sir. We're getting right on it, sir. We think we have a new lead. Yes, we think he might go after one of his early victims, the one who survived. We're following that up now. Yes, we'll be in touch, sir."

Agent Barrett hung up and bit his lip. "That was Deputy Director Sandford breathing down my neck. Wanted a progress report. As if catching one of Drake's henchmen isn't enough."

Alexa caught his eye. "It isn't."

Agent Barrett popped the last bit of omelet into his mouth. "Then we better get to work."

They hopped in the car and headed to the Tucson operations center. Alexa checked her messages and calls. No one had contacted her. Her eyes narrowed as she looked at the blank screen of her phone. So they asked Agent Barrett for an update and not her? Did they think he was the senior partner, even though she was the expert on Drake Logan and had helped catch him in the first place?

Yeah, you helped catch him, and then you let him slip through your fingers. That's what they're thinking. They don't think you're up to handling this case on your own. They think that not only do you need help, you need direction.

Alexa dialed the number for the operations center. When one of the officers answered, she said, "I need you to pull all the information you have on Amy Doherty."

"We will, Deputy Marshal. In fact, we already tried to get in contact with her. One of the guys figured she should be informed of Drake's disappearance just in case she didn't hear it on the news."

"That's not likely," Alexa said. "The story has been everywhere."

Briefly that made her wonder what her family and Stacy must be thinking. She shoved that aside and focused. No time to worry about that now.

"Yeah, turns out she did hear about it," the officer said. "She's gone missing."

Alexa tensed. "Missing?"

"That's right. She's not at her home, and neither is her vehicle. And she's not answering her phone."

"We'll be right in," Alexa said, hanging up.

"What's up?" Agent Barrett asked, glancing over from the driver's seat.

"She's gone missing!"

"Fled?" he asked. "Or abducted?"

"I don't know," Alexa whispered, "but if she's been abducted, we'll have another murder on our hands. We need to find her and we need to find her right now."

CHAPTER SEVENTEEN

As important as his great work was, Drake Logan didn't dare go to any built-up areas. He couldn't even go to some rural gas station or convenience store. His face was everywhere. He had things to do, and needed time to do it. So only his followers could go into town.

At least until the time was right, and now was not yet the time.

Luckily, he didn't have to go into town to see Amy Doherty.

She was camping.

Amy had picked a little cluster of Native American style teepees on a bluff just to the east of Sedona, a town in northern Arizona famous for two things—its beautiful red rocks and its large collection of New Age inhabitants.

The view was certainly breathtaking. Drake watched the campsite through a pair of powerful binoculars from the edge of a pine forest, his lungs filling with clean mountain air. The teepees were arranged in a circle on a grassy field, and beyond them rose a series of smooth hills of red rock.

At sunset they must look incredible, Drake thought.

He'd missed nature while in prison. The world's natural beauty was humanity's rightful inheritance for those with the eyes to see it.

And yet so many didn't see. They caged themselves up in cities and ugly apartment buildings, watching TV and playing video games and never seeing what the world had to offer. No wonder they were so weak. They willingly allowed themselves to be hypnotized by the media and society.

And even though Amy Doherty was out here enjoying nature, she was still blind to it. She didn't see the natural beauty of its colors or the organic justice of stronger creatures eating weaker ones. Instead she saw invisible ley lines of spiritual energy converging at this spot that allowed people to align their chakras and speak with spirits from other realms.

Yes, he thought sadly, Amy Doherty had become a New Ager.

Just look at that campsite! All these teepees painted with stars and rainbows; trees adorned with dream catchers, crystals, and little bells; a medicine wheel made of colored stones in the middle of the camp, and a bunch of middle aged, middle class people wearing white robes.

He didn't see a single Native American in the bunch.

Aw hell, and now they were all gathering around the medicine wheel and chanting. A mountain breeze caught their words and they lilted over to him at his vantage point half a mile away.

"Oh Earth Mother, bring us peace,

Oh Sky Father, bring us breath

Oh Sun God, bring us light

Oh Moon Goddess, bring us wisdom."

Drake shook his head in disgust, feeling like he was going to puke. Some people were born victims. Too bad he didn't get to kill the bitch the first time he tried. It would have been a service to the human race.

Well, if at first you don't succeed …

Mike Harwell, on the other hand, that guy had been a champ. Drake remembered with a smile how Amy's boyfriend had burst unexpectedly into the house, gun blazing. Good thing there had been a window right next to Drake, or his great work would have ended right then and there.

Pity they caught him for that firearms violation. Mike had a good run while it lasted, though. If he ever got out of prison, Drake would like to shake his hand and invite him to join his army.

His ex-girlfriend, however, would have a different sort of meeting …

Drake could see her now. She'd gained weight, and had a placid, blank look to her face. Pity he was too far away to see the scars. The idiot had a lot of them.

Amy Doherty stood in a circle with the other white robed self-style visionaries, chanting to the sky while hoping the world would change from a struggle for survival to some sort of global love-in.

Why? Drake shook his head. *Why would they want that? Don't they understand that the struggle is what makes us what we are, that fighting against others to claw your way to the top was what unlocks your full potential? If these idiots got their dream—which they never would because they're too damn weak—it would mean the end of the human race.*

He should kill every one of them. It would help the gene pool.

But he didn't have the time. He'd just have to settle for killing one of them.

* * *

"Still no sign of her?" Alexa asked the police officer on the other end of the phone as Agent Barrett sped them north on Interstate 10.

The Phoenix police officer on her phone said, "Sorry, Deputy Marshal. We checked her house and place of business and she isn't there. Her employee says she hasn't been in since the news hit that Drake Logan escaped. Looks like she's gone into hiding."

"Or grabbed by one of his henchmen," Alexa said. *They got me and Powers, after all.*

"We haven't found her vehicle or gotten any ransom note."

"You won't get a ransom note. Keep on the lookout for the vehicle, though," Alexa said. "We're just about to get off the highway. We'll talk to you soon."

Alexa gave Agent Barrett the address to Doherty's place of business.

"But the local P.D. said she wasn't there," he objected.

"No, and I'm sure they asked where she was and didn't get an answer," Alexa said crossing her arms across her chest. "I'm going to get an answer. I'll make damn sure of that."

Agent Barrett took the next exit, taking the off ramp and driving into the ugly concrete sprawl that was Phoenix. Alexa crinkled her nose in disgust. It was like a chunk of L.A. landed in the Arizona desert. What a waste of natural beauty.

As they drove past strip malls and housing developments, gas stations and billboards, signs of so-called civilization that reflected nothing of the natural environment and could, indeed, be anywhere, Alexa thought through what the Phoenix P.D. had discovered.

It was precious little. Amy Doherty, now known as Willow Skylark, ran a New Age bookshop in Scottsdale, one of the several cities that made up the sprawl that was collectively called Phoenix. There was little or no boundary between Phoenix proper, Scottsdale, Glendale, Peoria, Tempe, Chandler, or Gilbert. That history buff friend of hers had told her all about how they each had started out as separate settlements and had distinct histories.

Not anymore. Now they were just names in an unbroken mass of concrete.

Scottsdale was the most affluent of these cities. Alexa wasn't surprised "Willow Skylark" had opened her shop there. There were a lot of rich people in the area who wanted to feel spiritual and one with the land.

If you want to feel spiritual and one with the land, Alexa thought, *just walk into the desert and stand watching the sunset for half an hour.*

Alexa looked around at the high rises and liquor stores, the strip malls and 7-11s, and realized that living in a place like this sapped the soul. It was no wonder people turned to violence or clung to silly beliefs. To be a real person, one had to be surrounded by the beauties and dangers of nature.

Agent Barrett parked the car along a leafy street shaded by lush trees that, while providing welcome shade, sucked up far too much water from the valley's already scarce supplies. The trees were an import from the north, along with many of Scottsdale's residents. Along both sides of the avenue stood cafes and boutiques. Well-dressed men and women in whites or pastels strolled along and looked through the windows, seemingly without a care in the world.

"GPS says it's just down that way," Agent Barrett said, pointing.

After half a block they saw an ornate green sign saying "Mystic Life Books." Crystals hung from the sign, sparking in the sunlight. The smell of incense wafted over to them, as did harp music.

While the local police had already checked Amy's place of work, Alexa wanted to see for herself. If anyone knew where she had run to, it would be the employee.

As Alexa and Agent Barrett passed through the open door, they saw a small shop with crystals, wind chimes, and Native American dream catchers hanging from the ceiling. Two aisles were devoted to books on meditation, yoga, crystal healing, UFOs, and various spiritual practices Alexa had never heard of. Another aisle offered various paraphernalia such as candles, incense, and crystals balls.

Alexa and the FBI man exchanged an amused glance. They walked to the back of the store, where a young woman in her twenties who did not match Amy Doherty's description stood behind a glass counter displaying jewelry and tarot decks.

This may be a New Age shop, but the small, valuable, and easy to steal items are all behind glass. I guess some of their customers figure shoplifting is a valid part of their spiritual path.

The young woman eyed Alexa's uniform, then Agent Barrett's suit. Alexa figured not many guys in suits came in here.

Agent Barrett pulled out his FBI ID.

"We're looking for Amy Doherty," he said.

"Her name is Willow Skylark," the woman said in an overly relaxed voice. Her eyes were glassy but clear. Stoned but covering up with Visine? "She changed it when she rose to a higher vibration."

"She's in a great deal of danger," Alexa said. "Ms. Doherty, um, Skylark, was—"

"A victim of a blackened soul. Yes, I know. She often talks about it. Everyone asks her because of the scars. She's not here. I told the police the same thing yesterday, and this morning."

"Do you know where she is?" Alexa asked.

Those glassy eyes shifted away. "No."

Alexa looked around the shop for a moment, letting the silence draw out. A good way to make people nervous. She noticed a wire stand by the counter with leaflets in it.

Going over and looking through the leaflets while the woman fidgeted behind the counter and Agent Barrett gave her The Look, Alexa found several leaflets for classes that would teach you how to read tarot cards or have out of body experiences, plus announcements for upcoming lectures at something called the Third Age Institute.

One leaflet caught her eye. It showed a circle of teepees with the famous red rocks of Sedona as a backdrop. The title read "Rise to a higher level at the Path of Light Campground."

She pulled it out and held it up for the shop worker to see.

"Did she go here?"

Those glassy eyes got shifty again.

"We're trying to protect her," Alexa said.

"The people she's with will protect her."

"No they won't. Not against a monster like that," Alexa said.

The woman looked at her feet and mumbled, "I don't know where she is."

Agent Barrett leaned over the counter, "Ma'am, I detect the presence of marijuana. I'm going to have to ask you to step out from behind the counter and empty your pockets. Also that purse I see on that back shelf over there."

The young woman's eyes bugged. "Yes, she's at the Path of Light Campground. She went there when she heard Drake Logan broke out. She didn't want me to tell you. She thought she'd be safer if no one knew."

"Thank you, ma'am," Agent Barrett said, a sly smile tugging at the corners of his mouth. "A search won't be necessary."

The young woman visibly relaxed.

"Who else knows about this?" Alexa asked.

"I don't know. I'm her only employee and I don't hang out with her friends. I'm just working at this place to get through college. I don't believe in any of this crap."

"Good for you. Do you think she told any of her friends?"

She shrugged. "I suppose. Willow talks a lot. She's always sharing with everyone who will listen. Everything from her attack to talks she has with her spirit animal."

"What's her spirit animal?" Agent Barrett asked.

"A unicorn."

"That's not an animal," the FBI man snorted.

"Look, I just work here."

"Thanks for your help," Alexa said, handing her a business card. "If you think of anything else, call us."

They walked out of the shop.

"So you spotted that she was high too, eh?" Alexa said.

Agent Barrett gave he a sheepish grin. "I was in the army in Iraq. Lots of guys smoked. Even a lot of the terrorists smoked. They're not supposed to drink, so they get high."

"I hope you don't still get high." After what her big brother Malcolm had been through, she had a low tolerance for people who took drugs.

"You kidding? The FBI makes you take piss tests all the time. And yeah, they know I used to. Everything comes out in those entrance interviews. They use professional interrogators. Scary. They don't care as long as it's behind you. Besides, I was a dumb kid back then."

You're not so bright as an adult.

Agent Barrett pulled out his phone. "I'll give a call to the police and have them pick up Amy Doherty and put her in protective custody. Glad we found her. At least she's safe."

"Yeah," Alexa grumbled, "and we're at another dead end."

CHAPTER EIGHTEEN

Amy Doherty, who only referred to herself now as Willow Skylark, looked out over the red rock hills of Sedona, then turned to take in the beautiful desert.

It was so peaceful here. Just what she needed.

From the campground of teepees nearby, she could hear the low chanting of some of her brothers and sisters, and smell the sage they burned to purify themselves before the afternoon ritual.

It was a ritual of healing, one that would be conducted just for her. As usual, the community she had found here was gathering to help. They knew of her past, and knew that even the thought that Drake Logan was out of prison was tainting her aura. The ritual would help her heal.

As did this gorgeous view.

Climbing onto a flat rock, she sat, getting into the lotus position, took a deep breath of desert air, and closed her eyes.

A deep breath. Another. She could feel the tension slipping away. So easy in the desert, not like in the middle of the city, where the filthy economic system forced her to stay just to make a living.

She should give thanks to the spirits, though. Her shop allowed her to meet so many kind and wise people.

Willow took another deep breath, allowing the ley lines running through Sedona to fill her with energy.

At the edge of her hearing, she heard someone running.

The running came closer.

Willow tensed. Was it …

Yes! Someone was running right at her.

"No!" she screamed, her eyes snapping open as she leapt to her feet and spun around.

* * *

Willow, feeling miserable, tried to meditate in the back of the police car. She closed her eyes so as not to see the toxic auras given off by the two police officers up front, and tried to bring her mind to a happy place. Once she got herself centered, she'd try a purification ritual. So much negative energy had passed through this vehicle. She could feel it.

And not just from all the poor lost souls who had been arrested and trapped in here. These police officers, one male and one female, gave off bad energy. They thought their laws and their guns gave them superiority over other creatures, when in fact they didn't know they were simply energy beings passing through an earthly existence. They needed to be realigned.

But before she could go through with the purification ceremony, she needed to realign herself. The wail of the police siren, the lights, the uniforms, the crackle of the radio, the guns … they had all brought back that horrible night. And now she was sitting in the back of a police car being driven to a safe house. She'd be a virtual prisoner until they found Drake Logan, if they ever found Drake Logan.

She doubted they would. That man wasn't human. He was a demon spirit in a human body.

Many in the movement didn't think evil existed. They thought that all energy beings were essentially good but had strayed into evil deeds because of poor alignment. They thought that everyone had some good in them.

Willow Skylark knew better.

And that knowledge kept her from concentrating.

She couldn't get into a meditative state, not in this sort of environment, and not with that creature of darkness pursuing her.

"Can I light some incense?" she asked the officers up front.

"I'm afraid not, ma'am," the male officer said.

"It would help purify the air in here."

"Against regulations to light anything in the squad car, ma'am. Is it stuffy back there? Would you like me to open a window?"

"That won't release the negative energy."

The female officer glanced over her shoulder. "The what?"

"The negative energy. You'll never reincarnate into a higher form while channeling energy from the dark side."

The female officer didn't reply. Instead she whispered something to her partner. Both of them snickered. Willow thought she caught them saying something about Star Wars.

Willow Skylark crossed her arms and looked out the window. People always laughed. She wished she was back at camp. People understood there, and she would be safe in their healing embrace.

She winced, her lower lip trembling, because deep in her heart she knew it wasn't true. After the attack she hadn't felt safe at all. So many stitches, and plastic surgery to take away the worst damage to her face. And they had to surgically reattach her right forefinger. She still couldn't bend it.

Mike Harwell had raged, and raged. He seemed more upset about not killing Drake than how badly she had been injured. That had insulted his masculinity, and that masculinity had turned ever more toxic. When he had bought three more guns and joined a vigilante group, Amy had to let him go from her life for the sake of her own mental health.

That had been the first step in a long spiritual journey. Therapy had helped a little. Her friends helped too, although their concern always made her feel conspicuous. They always agreed with everything she said, tiptoed around her as if afraid of saying or doing anything to upset her, like she was some delicate porcelain figurine that would shatter if handled too roughly.

She knew they were only trying to help, but they tried too hard, and that made her feel like a perpetual victim.

So she sought out a new community. First she did yoga, which led to meditation, and that led to her finding a whole network of spiritual seekers who followed many paths to seek enlightenment. The term "New Age" was a corny joke for most people, but she embraced it. Didn't the world need a new age? The current one only led to wars, pollution, and spiritual isolation.

And monsters like Drake Logan.

Those fellow seekers had taught her about how we are all only energy beings passing through a physical manifestation, and that to move on to a higher plane of existence we must all try to align our energies with that of the greater universe.

Amy had joined in eagerly, learning meditation techniques, the resonance of crystals, Native American spirituality, earth mysteries, the lore of angels and other beings of legend that were in fact real. It soothed her. Gave her a new purpose.

And then, on the third anniversary of the attack, she and some fellow spirit travelers had gathered at the Path of Light Campground for her final cleansing ceremony. A shaman had given her a new name. Willow Skylark. A new name for a new life.

She had felt rejuvenated. With her savings and a small business loan, she had opened Mystic Life Books in Scottsdale, which soon became a meeting ground for the community she loved so well.

Willow had worked hard to build a new life. It had been a long path, but it had ended in acceptance and peace.

She stared out the window, trying to regain some of that peace. The red rocks of Sedona dwindled in the distance but remained as breathtaking as ever, and all around stretched beautiful upland desert. Arizona was truly a blessed place. Someone like Drake Logan could never appreciate it.

Her gaze idly moved from one side of the car to the other, and in the brief moment she looked down the road ahead of them she thought nothing of the bright yellow Hummer speeding toward them on the otherwise empty road.

More toxic masculinity. The guy had even added an extra big bumper on the front. It looked like those cattle guards they put on the old steam locomotives.

She gazed out the other window, smiling as a rabbit darted between two clusters of cacti. Such a beautiful creature, so gentle and so free.

The male officer let out a cry. There was a flash of yellow in Willow Skylark's peripheral vision.

She turned just in time to see the Hummer slam into the patrol car.

The world seemed to explode. The crash of metal on metal jabbed her ears, and her vision spun. The patrol car somersaulted several times before landing hard on its roof.

Willow Skylark blacked out.

She couldn't have been out long, for when she cautiously opened her eyes she could hear the wheels of the car, now up in the air, still spinning.

The next thing she noticed was that, other than a pain in her midriff from the seatbelt, she appeared unhurt.

"What happened?" she asked. Her voice came out groggy, as if she had just awoken from a deep sleep.

The officers in front didn't reply. The male officer groaned, holding his bleeding head, while the female officer cursed and struggled to free herself from her seatbelt.

A tromp of approaching boots on gravel. To both sides of the upended car appeared a group of men and women. Willow Skylark could only see them from their legs down.

"Help us!" she called.

The only answer she received was a hail of gunfire.

Willow Skylark screamed and covered her face as the bullets pockmarked the front side windows. After a few moments, the bulletproof glass could no longer resist the fusillade and the bullets punched through, tearing into the flesh of the two officers in front. Willow Skylark screamed again as she felt their blood spatter on her arms.

The gunfire stopped. Willow peeked through her dripping fingers.

Just in time to see a booted foot kick out the damaged window.

An arm reached around and unlocked the back door.

"No! No! This can't happen again!" she screamed.

For now Willow understood. Drake Logan had come for her, like she always feared he would.

She clutched the medallion around her neck—a crystal bought on a trip to Mexico, and a little gold unicorn, her spirit animal.

Rough hands grabbed her, unbuckling her seatbelt and making her fall on her head. She kept clutching her medallion, whispering to herself.

"The spirits of light will protect me. The spirits of light will protect me."

They dragged her out, and Willow found herself lying on her back in the middle of a circle of masked men and a woman.

And one man who did not wear a mask. Drake Logan.

He looked down at her and smiled. "Amy Doherty. How nice to see you again."

"Get away from me, dark spirit!" Amy shouted. She no longer felt like Willow Skylark, her reborn name. No, she was back to the old days, the days of suffering. "I call upon the spirits of light and all aligned energy beings to cast you out of my presence!"

Drake Logan raised an eyebrow.

"Seriously?"

CHAPTER NINETEEN

Alexa fidgeted in the passenger's seat as the red rocks of Sedona came into view ahead of them. She wished Agent Barrett would drive faster, although to be fair he had been driving like a maniac ever since getting the news that the patrol car picking up Amy Doherty had gone missing. The three and a half hour drive from Tucson had taken only two.

As they sped on, the updates kept coming in. No radio contact from the patrol car. A call to the Path of Light Campground confirmed that they had picked up Amy Doherty and left. The officers who picked her up had not made the precaution to radio in their route back to Phoenix, and there were four different paths they could take. The understaffed Sedona police department, already occupied with policing a county fair, could only spare two patrol cars to check the routes.

The first two routes picked up nothing. Repeated attempts by dispatch could not get the missing car on the air.

Then the patrol cars went along the other two routes, and found the missing vehicle.

Its three occupants were all dead.

"Don't touch anything until we get there," Alexa had told them. She had no idea if her command would be followed, so she called the ops center and had them relay it too.

At last they drove down a gravel road between Sedona and the camp. This was the least used of the four roads the officers could have taken. Alexa guessed that the officers had picked this lonely road as the least conspicuous, figuring they'd be safe.

They had been terribly wrong.

And, as usual, she had been right, but too slow to stop Drake from striking again.

Agent Barrett slowed the vehicle as the flashing lights appeared up ahead. Two police cars blocked the road on either side of an upturned patrol car. An ambulance was parked nearby, although by now Alexa knew the ambulance was unnecessary, a sad attempt to help those who were beyond all help.

They slowed to a stop. Alexa leapt out before Agent Barrett put it in park. She sprinted to the scene, passing several officers and EMTs. Someone said something to her but she ignored it, still running for the patrol car.

And stopped short.

The two officers were still in their seats, trapped upside down by their seatbelts. They had been riddled with bullets.

Alexa's stomach churned. It was just like that pair of poor prison guards on the bus.

The back seat was empty, one door hanging open.

An officer and a police photographer standing a little way off the road told her where to look.

This being Arizona upland, tall grass and bushes grew alongside the road. It was trampled down in one spot. Flecks of blood clung here and there to the plants. The trampled area delineated a path leading away from the road toward the two officers standing about a hundred yards off.

They dragged her. Dragged her into the desert.

Trembling, Alexa followed the path, keeping to one side so as not to disturb this meager bit of evidence. The CSI folks would comb the path of Amy Doherty's last journey for any trace the killers might have left.

The ground sloped down slightly. Two Sedona police officers stood over the body, partially blocking Alexa's view. From what she could see, Amy Doherty lay on her back, arms stretched wide, one leg flat and the other slightly flexed.

It was only after she got a bit closer that Alexa saw that Amy Doherty had been decapitated.

Nausea rose up in Alexa, threatening to overwhelm her. Her knees grew weak and her head swam. A vision of her partner getting his head cut off right before her eyes superimposed itself on the sorry scene in front of her.

She took several deep breaths, gulping for air, trying to get it together.

Alexa closed her eyes for a moment. Once she open them again, her stomach and the world around her had stopped spinning, and Robert Powers's last moments alive had faded into the background.

Not that what she saw looked any prettier.

The body lay in a circle of darkened ground where the thirsty Arizona soil had drank up Amy's blood. Her head sat upright about a foot away, eyes hooded and half closed, the mouth slack. A pendant with a crystal and a gold unicorn was set on top of her head.

Now Alexa started shaking again, this time with anger.

Drake hadn't fled. He hadn't gone to ground in some isolated compound or tried to sneak across the border.

No, he was close. He was still in the game.

* * *

Agent Stuart Barrett looked at the scene by the road and gritted his teeth. He could feel the sweat trickling down the inside of his suit. The upturned car … the shattered bulletproof glass … the blood and bodies by the road …

Not much different than an IED.

The Iraqi insurgents could never beat coalition forces in a toe-to-toe fight, and so they had gotten tricky, sniping at patrols from the tops of minarets or tossing grenades from alleys before running off. And their favorite method of all was the IED, the Improvised Explosive Device. A bomb hidden in a house or buried by the side of the road.

In a country awash with weapons, high explosives were easier to find than medication. Often the insurgents used artillery shells. The actual artillery pieces were useless to them—they'd get spotted and blown to pieces before they even finished setting up—but the shells could be rigged with wires or a cell phone attached to a detonator to be set off from a distance. Buried just under the ground by the side of the road, it could take out coalition vehicles and cause grievous damage. Stuart had seen Hummers flipped over just like this police car. Trucks aflame after their gas tank got hit. Stryker armored vehicles with their front ends crumpled like paper. Sometimes even tanks got their tracks shattered or their armor punctured.

Stuart had seen a lot of roadside death. Far more than he could ever wipe from his mind.

Nevertheless, he tried to shake off the memory. He had more pressing problems in the here and now.

He watched his partner from a distance, feeling a mixture of pity, concern, and alarm. For someone who had witnessed her partner getting killed just days before, she was holding up remarkably well.

She'd kept her head clear enough to provide some insights into Drake's motives and movements.

But the strain was showing. Even though he didn't really know her, the signs were clear—the lack of sleep, the impatience, snapping at everyone around her, the shaking.

She would crack before long.

They had to catch Drake before she did, because as bull-headed as Deputy Marshal Alexa Chase could be, she was their best hope of catching him.

Yes, Alexa knew Drake well. The question remained, though, how well did Drake know *her*?

Because it seemed Drake was leading them on a merry chase. Many serial killers liked to toy with the police. It gave them a sense of power. And many formed a strange bond with one of their pursuers, a competition based on a mixture of hatred and respect, fear and anger. At times, it could even border on love.

Drake Logan had formed such a bond with Alexa Chase.

The idea had been in the back of Stuart's mind for a while now, but like with all half-formed theories, he had allowed it to simmer, waiting for fresh evidence for it to become a full certainty.

And he was certain now.

First, Drake hadn't killed her during the breakout. Instead, he had taunted her, made her watch Marshal Powers get killed in a most gruesome way. Then he had struck in Marana, near Tucson, where he knew she would go as it was the closest major city to the breakout. And he had told Ricardo Montañez to hide out in a place where he figured Alexa, with her deep knowledge of Drake's interests, would be sure to look.

Who got set up there, Alexa or Ricardo? Drake seemed to be playing a double game. Ricardo might have killed her, which would have helped Drake in his escape, or things could have turned out the way they did, with Alexa capturing Ricardo.

Why would Drake want that? Just so Ricardo could taunt her, push her buttons and getting her more wound up than she already was? What purpose did that serve?

Stuart wasn't sure, but it seemed to be what Drake wanted. Because now he had shifted to the northern part of the state in order to take out this poor woman, a previous victim, and to cut her head off in imitation of what had happened to Powers.

Two birds with one stone. Finish the job on Amy Doherty, and goad on the deputy marshal even more.

Deputy Marshal Chase came back up the slope, her legs wobbly. Briefly she looked at him, and then turned her eyes toward the ground.

"He's always one step ahead," she muttered.

"He's messing with you," Stuart said.

She looked at him sharply. "Messing with me?"

"If there's one thing Drake Logan is good at besides killing, it's psychology. He's developed a bond with you. He's obsessed. He's probably spent years in the pen analyzing your character, and now he's playing with you, goading you on."

Deputy Marshal Chase waved off his suggestion. "Ridiculous. He's smart, leaving a trail of bodies for us to follow, but it's all a dead end. He's doing that on purpose to get us off the scent. He wasn't even present for the attack in Marana."

"He was present for this one. He wouldn't have let an underling kill Doherty," Stuart said.

The deputy marshal didn't have a response to that other than to curse under her breath and scan the landscape, as if hoping Drake was somewhere in sight.

Maybe he is, Stuart thought. *Maybe he's watching us through a pair of binoculars from one of those distant rocks, gloating.*

That got Stuart looking around too, before realizing he was wasting time when he should be talking to his temporary partner. If Drake was out there, there was no chance of them finding him, not in this vast, rough terrain. Of course a dragnet had been put out, but of course it would lead to nothing.

"This is personal for him," Stuart said. "It's not uncommon for serial killers to develop a bond with one of the people hunting them. Look at the Zodiac Killer writing coded letters to the local newspaper. Or the Florida Highwayman writing the Tallahassee chief of police. Son of Sam did it too. Hell, even Jack the Ripper did it."

"Scholars proved the Ripper letters were faked by journalists. Learn your history," Deputy Marshal Chase grumbled.

Stuart swallowed his irritation and went on. "You're missing the point. Lots of serial killers do this, and he's done it with you."

"No," she said flatly, "You're wrong. He's just cold blooded and very clever, that's all."

"Then why did he let you live?" he asked gently.

The deputy marshal rounded on him. "How the hell am I supposed to know why he let me live?" The shout made everyone turn and stare. "I've been thinking about practically nothing else! It's been going around and around in my mind ever since it happened! You know what I think? I think he just wants to show his power. He's always talking about the will of the strong. He thinks he's God, able to kill or save whoever he wants. He just did that to inflate his own ego and add to his myth."

"No," Stuart continued patiently. "He did it because he wants to turn you."

Deputy Marshal Chase blinked and took a step back. "Turn me?"

"You yourself said he wants to create converts, that he's sending out people like Ricardo Montañez to create a new generation of Drake Logans. I think that's what he wants to do with you. He—"

"Nonsense!"

"He keeps pushing you and pushing you, hoping you'll snap. He probably wanted you to win that fight with Montañez. He was hoping you'd be so enraged by the video that you'd kill the guy."

"Well, if he thinks that then he's got me all wrong. I've never injured a suspect once they were in custody. The only person I want to kill is Drake. Person? What am I saying? He's a wild animal and he needs to be put down. I'd like to—"

The deputy marshal stopped midsentence, realizing what she had just said. She looked at Stuart, frowned, and waved her hand as if to wave away what she had revealed about her innermost feelings.

"You know what I mean," she grumbled. "Let's get back to Phoenix. I still have to follow up on Fiona, that meth dealer. Drake has got me running around half of Arizona and is keeping me from doing any proper police work."

"We," Stuart said softly.

Another frown. "What?"

"*We* have to follow up on Fiona," Stuart said in as gentle a voice as his anger could manage. "Drake has *us* running around Arizona. I'm on this case too, Deputy Marshal."

"Like you've even read through all the files. I've been dealing with this case from the very beginning. And once we finally ran that wild dog to ground and I thought I could put it all behind me, his goons break him out and I have to do it all over again. I'm the one who has to do everything."

OK, that's too much.

"Maybe you shouldn't," he growled.

While it was a lot less than what he wanted to say, Stuart knew he had said too much.

"What the hell is that supposed to mean?" Alexa demanded.

"Maybe you should step back. You haven't recovered from your injuries and … " Stuart almost added 'trauma' but stopped himself at the last moment " … it might be better if you pulled back a little. Take a few days off. Or at least get out of the field and work in the ops center. I think you're too close to this, and I think he's too close to you."

Stuart held his breath. He knew he had gone too far, but this frustrating, overly driven woman was teetering on the edge and needed to be pulled back.

He needed her. He hadn't been lying when he had said she was their best chance at catching Drake, but he needed her mentally whole. If she cracked, she wouldn't be any help at all.

And a lot more people would die.

He expected her to shout, to rail at his lack of knowledge of the case, to call him some big-city snob come to the countryside to lord it over local law enforcement. Or he expected her to dismiss everything he said, maybe even walk back to the car and drive off without him.

What he did not expect was Deputy Marshal Chase to take a step forward, eyes glittering with rage, and for her hand to twitch.

Her gun hand.

Just a little, so little that an untrained eye wouldn't have noticed.

But Stuart had seen it. The start of a motion, cut off almost immediately, a perhaps entirely unconscious move toward her holster.

Stuart's heart froze.

She's not seriously going to …

His hand moved an inch closer to his own weapon.

The deputy marshal paused, and Stuart could see something click in her mind. The rage vanished, replaced by a flushed embarrassment.

She turned on her heel, hung her head, and walked away.

Stuart let out a long, slow breath as she walked stiff-legged back to the car.

A snickering behind him made him turn. One of the Sedona police officers sauntered up to him, a middle-aged good old boy with a deep tan, a poorly groomed moustache, and mirror shades.

“Must be that time of the month,” the cop said with a chuckle.

“Shut the hell up,” Stuart snapped, then followed Deputy Marshal Chase.

CHAPTER TWENTY

This was getting downright fun.

Drake Logan sat on a deck chair amid a cluster of a half-dozen trailers off a county road. There were no electrical or water hookups this far out of town, but solar panels on the trailers and large water tanks took care of that. And he didn't care about modern conveniences anyway. He had his freedom, lungsful of fresh air, and the chance to continue his great work.

Plus a little hands-on fun like he had with that crystal-clutching idiot. There was a born victim if there ever was one.

Good times. Good times.

Taking a drag of his menthol cigarette, he studied the thug sitting opposite him.

Antony Keene was a heap of a man, nearly three hundred pounds of muscle and fat. He had worked as a bouncer, a repo man, an enforcer for various low-rent drug gangs, and a bodyguard for a pimp. He was stupid, very stupid, but he was tough.

And more importantly, he had no criminal record. That was a rarity in the crowd Drake hung with.

That made him valuable.

He wasn't on any of the police lists. He wasn't even a suspect. His license plate had never come up on any police lists. It was like Keene lived a charmed life.

Drake hoped some of that charm would rub off on his mission.

"You've studied the photo?" Drake asked.

"Yeah."

"You know the address of the Phoenix ops center?"

"Yeah."

Drake took another drag of his cigarette. "You know what you need to do?"

"Yeah."

"Quite the conversationalist, I see. Tell me what you need to do."

"Hang out in the Burger King. When I get the call that she's close I hunt her down. Use a knife and not a gun."

"Or you can beat her to death with those twin boulders you call your fists. Your choice. But take her out. Make sure it's in broad daylight with plenty of witnesses."

"OK."

"And then what do you need to do?"

"Run around the corner to 14th Street and a car will be waiting to take me away."

"What kind of car?"

"Nissan Sentra. Blue. Tinted windows."

Drake nodded, surprised Keene was able to remember all this.

"Then it's all set," Drake said, stubbing out the end of his menthol on the heel of his boot.

"Isn't it risky?" Keene asked.

"Not at all. You just run around the corner and we pick you up. The car is stolen but we have legit plates on it. No one will stop us. It will all happen so fast you won't have to worry."

Keene's face took on an eager, worried look, like a child about to do a dangerous stunt and who wants to make sure his parents are there to watch and protect him.

"And you'll be there, Drake?" he asked.

Drake Logan cracked a grin. "Of course I'll be there. I want to see everything."

* * *

Alexa was nearing the end of yet another frustrating day. After coming back from the crime scene in Sedona, and checking in with the dragnet in the region, which of course had come up with nothing, Alexa had spent the rest of the afternoon in Phoenix, looking for Fiona, her brother's old meth dealer who had links to the Glory of the Sun cult.

And that brought up a ton of old feelings, all of them bad.

Not only did it bother her that her own brother had an indirect link to Drake, but seeing all these trashy neighborhoods recalled the many times, years ago, when she would go hunting for Malcolm to try and bring him home.

This duty always fell to her. Dad always said, "that lump of uselessness will come home when he damn well wants to." Wayne wouldn't hunt for him either. Dad had forbidden him to and Wayne always did what Dad said.

“Wayne needs to stay on the ranch,” Dad always said. “He’s needed here, not gallivanting around some concrete eyesore talking to druggies and hookers.”

So a younger, more foolish Alexa Chase had gone alone to find her lost brother in the middle of the night to the worst neighborhoods of Phoenix. People had tried to sell her drugs. People had tried to mug her. Twice they had tried to rape her. Every one of them had backed off when they got a pistol shoved in their face. One potential rapist took a bullet in the kneecap before he curbed his lust. Word got out on the street that Malcolm’s little sister shouldn’t be messed with.

After a few such trips, the street people started bringing Malcolm to her rather than have to deal with Alexa causing trouble and screwing up their business.

That was a blessing. She hated going into the cheap bars and abandoned buildings, climbing creaking steps past unconscious addicts and pools of stale urine to find her brother lying half out of his mind on some flea-ridden blanket.

“Shooting galleries” they called them. Places where heroin addicts shot up. He’d tried junk for a while, then managed to kick it in one of his many attempts at recovery, only to fall hard for meth when that came into fashion.

After he got into meth, she wouldn’t find her older brother lying on a dirty blanket. She’d find him running around the street half naked and screaming his head off. Or losing fights to random people. Or screaming at telephone poles.

And today she had to revisit a lot of those old places. Some of the shooting galleries had been torn down or gentrified. One of his favorites was still in business. Alexa didn’t bother making any arrests as she scanned the crowd of addicts staring wide-eyed at her uniform and gun. All she cared about was finding Fiona. No one seemed to know where she was anymore. Several knew of her, but said she hadn’t been on the scene for at least three months.

Long enough to help plan the breakout? Had it really been Fiona who had shot the prison guards?

Next Alexa had visited the old fountain where she had once found Malcolm beaten up and shaking in withdrawal. Someone had mugged him and he hadn’t gotten his fix. She had visited the street corners, the cheap bars, the laundromat where deals went down between the dryers. No Fiona. It was like she had vanished.

Throughout all this searching, Agent Barrett had trailed her. Despite their argument, he refused to let her go alone. White knighting for her once again. How annoying.

Exhausted and dispirited, they had returned to the decent part of town, parked, and walked to the operations center.

Since the police station didn't have enough room for such a big operation as the interagency hunt for Drake Logan, the state had lent them an old registry office that hadn't been used in years. The only problem was that the parking lot had been sold to a developer who had built a car dealership on it. So while there were plenty of parking places still on the spot, they were reserved for cars nobody actually used. The officers at the ops center for the Logan hunt had to use a parking lot three blocks away. Typical state government oversight.

Alexa and Agent Barrett got out of the car and began to walk. It was already past five, the sun slanting low to the west, soon to set off one of Arizona's unforgettable sunsets, but Alexa had no thought of quitting for at least another five or six hours. Drake was out there somewhere, planning his next move.

"I'm going to get a coffee," the FBI man said. "You want one?"

"Huh?" Alexa said, coming out of her own thoughts.

"I'm going to get a coffee," he repeated, pointing to a Starbucks down the street. "Do you want one?"

"Sure."

Anything to get away from you.

He walked off. Alexa continued to the ops center.

So where the hell did Fiona go off to? No one seemed to know anything. The state troopers had launched a nighttime raid on the Glory of the Sun cult's desert compound but found no evidence that Drake had been there or had been in touch. They found no evidence of Fiona either. The state troopers had hauled in all the members anyway, on the excuse of a small amount of drugs found on the scene, and had been grilling them ever since. So far, that had yielded no useful information.

This case is nothing but loose ends.

Alexa passed a Burger King across the street and the smell of cooking meat and fries made her stomach grumble. When was the last time she ate? Breakfast? She'd need to order something. Not from Burger King, though. After being raised on Dad's home-cooked ranch steaks, she was picky about her meat.

A huge man came out of the fast food restaurant and lumbered along the sidewalk in the same direction she was walking, wearing jeans and a loose army jacket.

Damn. He'd make a good riot control cop.

Alexa took her phone out and checked it. Nothing. Shouldn't they have gotten an update by now?

Oh, my shadow from the FBI probably got the update. I think everyone in the ops center has decided he ranks me.

That'll be the day. He probably hadn't even studied this case until he was flying over here.

Drake Logan has an obsession with me? Get real! He just wants to hurt me, figuring he can break me psychologically and keep me from finding him. Not going to happen.

Something made Alexa get out of her own head and look across the street again.

The man mountain had disappeared.

She glanced over her shoulder. He was walking right behind her.

Normally, that wouldn't have bothered her. They were downtown and it was broad daylight, with several other pedestrians in view, but when the guy looked immediately away when she looked at him, alarm bells began ringing in her head.

He hadn't looked away the way guys will when you catch them looking at you. He was far more nervous than that.

And that got Alexa nervous.

She turned to him, moving her hand closer to her gun.

"Can I help you?" she said in a demanding tone.

Most people would stop and offer and apology. Or freeze when they saw her hand stray near her gun.

This guy didn't do either of those things.

Instead, he attacked.

He rushed Alexa, closing the few yards between them with remarkable speed. He swung a meaty fist at her while the other went to the inside of his jacket.

Alexa backpedaled, the fist whooshing by her face, missing by millimeters.

She kept moving back. Someone screamed. As she pulled her gun, he pulled out a Bowie knife from inside his jacket.

Just as she was flicking off the safety, he struck.

The knife slashed down at her gun hand, aiming for her wrist. Alexa managed to pull back enough to keep her hand from getting lopped off, but the heavy steel blade hit the body of her Glock so hard it jolted from her grasp.

It fell to the pavement with a clatter, leaving Alexa helpless.

Not quite helpless. Her attacker was confident or dumb enough to pause and give her a triumphant grin, so she snapped out with a kick to the shin. Oddly, it reminded her of the many fights she'd had with her big brothers as a kid.

And it had a similar effect. Almost.

Wayne and Malcolm would howl and clutch their shin, stopping whatever annoying thing they had been doing. Of course, they'd plan some revenge later.

This guy wasn't a teenaged kid, though, and only let out a grunt and staggered enough to stop his next swing with the knife.

And he sought his revenge right away, and not in a brotherly way.

"Bitch!" he bellowed.

He charged her again, slightly slower this time. Alexa retreated, going for the pepper spray stuck in a little holster on her belt. She fumbled, had to duck to the side as that deadly blade sliced down, hitting nothing but air, and circled.

She leaped back from another swing, not having time to get the little bottle out of its holster, and then had to leap back again, hissing with pain as the tip of the Bowie knife sliced across her breast.

"Hey!" the man stopped and shouted, eyes bugging as he stared at a blue Nissan Sentra with tinted windows pass by.

The distraction gave her the chance she needed. She pulled out the pepper spray and gave him a full blast square in the face.

He let out a bellow like a bull being put down.

He didn't stop, though. Scrunching up his face and nearly blinded, he made a swing with his knife Alexa easily dodged.

She sprayed him again.

The guy charged. Alexa ducked out of the way and he ran right into the metal pole of a streetlight with a loud *clong*.

Grinning, Alexa pulled out her telescopic metal baton, flicked it open, and swung for the back of his knees.

No one, no matter how big, can stay standing when hit like that. He fell to his hands and knees.

The guy still had the knife in his hand. Turning and seeking her out with teary, blood-red eyes, he stabbed at her, making her back off.

He kept stabbing and swinging, crawling forward. Alexa ducked and wove, taking care not to get too close until the right moment when he had just made a big swing and was pulling his arm back for another.

When the right moment came, she brought her baton down. The knobbed tip hit him square on the wrist.

The sound of cracking bone, followed immediately by the clang of the Bowie knife falling on concrete.

"You bitch!" he cried out, clutching his ruined wrist. "I'm going to cut your head off like Ricardo cut off your partner's!"

Alexa snarled and brought down the baton again. The huge man had just enough time to bring up his good arm to keep her from hitting his head.

Instead he took it on the forearm. He cried out and toppled over. Alexa, seeing red, brought the baton high and smashed it down on him again, hitting him on the broad chest. She thought she heard a bone crack.

Good. Let's crack some more bones.

Let's crack them all.

She raised her baton again …

CHAPTER TWENTY ONE

"Alexa! No!"

Agent Barrett's voice cut through her red fog.

"Don't interfere," Alexa growled. Her voice didn't sound like hers. It came out low and savage. It didn't even feel like it was arising from her own throat.

She swung the baton down again,

A strong hand gripped her wrist. She struggled for a moment, turning to Agent Barrett.

"Get off!"

"Stand down! He's subdued. You got him."

"I said get off!" Alexa screamed, trying to wrench her arm from his grasp.

"Look!" Agent Barrett said, pointing across the street.

A pedestrian was filming with her phone.

Alexa stopped, the heat of her rage suddenly chilled out of her.

Visions of going viral passed through her mind. The snap judgements of the press and millions of YouTube viewers. The investigation. The second guessing by everyone on the force.

She knew what they'd see. They'd see a monster.

And they'd be right. Damn.

What's happening with me?

The same thing that happened in the FBI. That's what.

She turned to face the camera. She wanted this civilian and the viewers on her YouTube channel and Facebook page to get a good look at the red line across her chest. Even as she did it she realized it was a lame excuse. An officer of the law, no matter how badly hurt they might get, doesn't abuse a prisoner.

Agent Barrett cuffed the attacker, who did not resist, the fight having gone out of him. Then he called in for backup. The woman across the street kept filming.

"He has accomplices in a Nissan Sentra," Alexa said to Agent Barrett as he was talking on the phone. "Blue with tinted windows. Went northbound just a minute ago."

Agent Barrett relayed that to dispatch.

"He got out of it?" he asked her.

"He called out to them."

The FBI man relayed that to dispatch too.

"We have to go after it," Alexa said, picking up her gun.

"Wait. You can't leave the scene. How will it look on camera?"

"The hell with the camera. They're getting away. Come on!"

"We can't leave the suspect here alone."

"You stay here and give me the keys."

Alexa held out her hand. The FBI agent shook his head.

"No. Calm down. Dispatch is already alerting every patrol car in the area. That's all we can do. If you flee the scene of a police beating, your career will be over five minutes after the seven o'clock news."

Alexa looked around. Several people were filming now.

Jesus Christ.

"You all right?" he asked indicating her cut.

"Just a scratch. Stings like hell, though."

She winced. Now that she was cooling off, the pain began to kick in.

"Let's take him to the ops center," Agent Barrett said. "We need to get you fixed up."

Alexa retrieved the knife, which was red with her own blood, and put it in an evidence bag.

They headed out, stepping over the coffees that Agent Barrett had fetched, now just a puddle on the sidewalk.

At least I'm not lying in a puddle on the sidewalk.

Several civilians followed them. Alexa and Agent Barrett got met halfway to the ops center by several officers who took charge of the perp.

* * *

Back at the ops center, a female agent gave Alexa first aid in the bathroom.

She felt miserable. She had really lost control with that guy. That had been several steps too far, knife or no knife. She could feel herself slipping.

At least her injury wasn't too bad. As Alexa had suspected, the tip of the Bowie knife had barely grazed her. While she was bleeding, she didn't need stitches and she did not need the aid of the EMTs who came to help her attacker.

The female officer put some surgical tape across the gash as well as cotton gauze and a big bandage, and even sewed up the tear in her uniform shirt.

"That will keep the guys from ogling you," she told Alexa with a smile. "But you're going to want to get changed as soon as possible."

"I will when I have the time. Thanks."

Alexa headed back out to the ops center to find the perp. She came up to him just as they were preparing to put him on a stretcher and take him to the hospital with a police escort. She shouldered her way through the EMTs. A couple of officers from the Phoenix Police Department stood nearby, giving her uncertain looks.

"He sent you, didn't he? Where is he?" she demanded.

The perp looked up at her through bloodshot eyes and grinned.

"Answer me!" she snapped.

"Take it easy," a police sergeant said.

"Quiet," she said, eliciting an angry glare from the sergeant. She ignored that and turned back to the perp. "Who was in that car that drove past? Drake?"

The guy's eyes shifted. "What car?"

"The blue Nissan that passed by. That was supposed to be your getaway car, wasn't it? But they ditched you. Drake doesn't care about you. He doesn't care about anybody. Tell me where he is."

The man grunted. "I'm one of the strong."

"No you're not. You're an idiot who got duped into trying to killed a U.S. Deputy Marshal, and now you're going to jail for life. Minimum twenty-five. If you tell me where he is, the judge might go easy on you. You might get out in ten or fifteen."

"I don't know nothing."

"He tricked you. That car wasn't for your getaway; it was so he could watch."

"You're wrong," the big man blurted. "He wasn't even in it!"

He pressed his lips together, realizing he had said too much.

"So where is he, then?"

"I don't know nothing."

"He betrayed you. What do you owe him now?"

"He made me one of the strong."

Alexa gave him a smirk. "Is that why I beat you?"

The man looked at the floor.

"All right," the Phoenix police sergeant said. "That's enough. We need to get this guy to the hospital before some public attorney gets on our asses. We'll book him there. Let's go."

The EMTs moved the stretcher out of the room and down the hall. Alexa stood watching him go, fuming.

From down the hall, after he was already out of sight, the voice of her attacker came back to her.

"He's coming for you! I heard him swear that he'll get you sooner or later!"

Alexa sat down heavily on the nearest chair, feeling exhausted and a bit ill.

Agent Barrett came up to her. "I just talked to dispatch. No sign of the blue Nissan."

"Of course not," Alexa grumbled. "These guys would never catch them. I could have, though."

"*We* couldn't go after it ourselves. Even if *we* had, by the time we got back to our car, it would have been long gone."

Alexa didn't reply. He was probably right. That didn't matter. She had wanted to go after them anyway. She couldn't just let someone else take care of Drake and his followers. Then they always got away.

She was the only one who had caught any.

Twice now, and both times she had nearly gotten killed.

She heard the ping of the elevator down the hall as the EMTs and their police escort took the perp away. Alexa turned to the FBI man and held out her hand.

"Give me the keys," she demanded.

"Why?"

"I need to follow them to the hospital."

"You're not going to get to question him. Not until after he's been treated. And by then he'll have lawyered up and you won't get a word out of him."

"I know, but I need to follow them in case there's another ambush."

"*We* need to follow them."

Agent Barrett pulled the keys out of his pocket and walked out the door, still holding them. Grumbling, Alexa followed.

They passed through the ops center in silence, Alexa feeling all eyes on her. On the street out front as the EMTs were putting the perp in the back of the ambulance, she went up to the police officer in charge.

"Wait for me to get my car," she said. "I'm coming with you."

The guy didn't even look at her. "We got to get him to the hospital pronto."

"I'm the arresting officer."

"We can take it from here," he said with a dismissive tone that said, *don't you think you've done enough?*

Agent Barrett stepped forward.

"Wait for us," he snapped.

The police officer straightened a little. "Yes, sir."

Jesus.

Shaking her head, she said to Agent Barrett, "Come on, let's not keep them waiting."

She walked at a furious pace for the parking lot. Agent Barrett kept up beside her.

This guy is nothing if not persistent, she thought with grudging admiration. I've not exactly been the best company, but he's still here, doing the job. Not a bad cop.

"You think Drake will make a move this soon after the attack?" Agent Barrett asked.

"I don't know."

I hope Drake does makes a move. I'd love a chance to shoot him right between the eyes. This is probably another false lead, though. Damn, he's got us running around in circles.

Once they got to the car, they circled around to join the ambulance and patrol car as they headed to the nearest hospital.

Agent Barrett remained unusually silent. Alexa gave him a sidelong look. He must have seen it, because he gripped the steering wheel, sat up a little straighter, took a deep breath and said,

"This attack proves it. He's got a thing for you."

"Oh, come on, he—"

"He could have sent any number of experienced killers after you. He knew your movements. He could have done a drive-by with a couple of guys firing AR-15s. Instead he sent that lumbering idiot knowing you'd beat him. He also … " Agent Barrett looked uncomfortable and continued in a quieter voice " … hoped you'd kill your attacker."

"I'd never do that!"

The FBI man didn't reply.

"I'd never do that," Alexa repeated.

"I never said you would," the FBI man said. *But you think that.* "He was hoping you would, though. He's trying to turn you, make you one of his followers."

Alexa snarled and rounded on him. "Look, I'm sick of you saying that. He's not trying to make me a follower, he's trying to make me suffer!"

"Exactly, just like Yvette Ramirez. Hurting her to make her stronger."

"Oh, he's hurting me all right. He's trying to kill me."

Agent Barrett gestured at the ambulance in the road in front of them. "With that loser? No. If he wanted to kill you, he would have done it in the prison breakout. Or if for some sick reason he wanted to extend your suffering and kill you later, he would have come for you himself, or sent someone a lot more capable. This guy was more of a patsy than Lee Harvey Oswald."

"And so am I!" Alexa shouted, the last emotional resistance snapping. "He knows I'm tortured about Powers, and he knows I won't investigate properly. The only way I can catch Drake is if I get into his head, and he knows I won't do that. He *knows*. How the hell can he know that? It's like he's read my FBI file!"

Alexa paused. She knew she had said too much, but the turmoil roiling around in her heart wouldn't let her stop. When Agent Barrett glanced at her, confused by the FBI reference, she explained.

"My last case at the Behavioral Affair Unit. It burned me out."

She did not mention that she had to go see an FBI therapist to deal with it.

"The Jersey Devil?" Agent Barrett asked. "But you cracked that case."

Alexa cringed at the mere mention of the name.

After a long pause, she went on quietly. "Yeah, I cracked it. And it cracked me. Someone was killing people in the Pine Barrens of New Jersey. There was no pattern to it. Men, women, children. Stabbed or shot or strangled. One case of a kid being buried alive. No witnesses. No really good material evidence. The only link I could think of was the one the media had already picked up."

"The folklore monster. The Jersey Devil," Agent Barrett said.

"Yeah. A devil-like creature that's supposedly haunted the Pine Barrens since the old settler days. I figured the killer was taking advantage of a local myth to make a name for himself. I figured he was obsessed with all that. So I delved into the myth, and, damn, it took me down a hell of a rabbit hole. Folklore, cryptozoology, demonology, astrology, radical religion, Satanism … "

Her voice trailed off and she shuddered.

"But you caught him," Agent Barrett said. "You figured out the pattern of killings when no one else could, and you were at the location where he would kill his next victim. You saved that little boy."

Alexa nodded, remembering. She had ambushed the killer, who had hauled an eleven year old boy deep into the Pine Barrens to carve him up with a butcher's knife. As soon as Alexa leapt from her hiding place, the Jersey Devil—who she later learned was an out of work plumber named Bruce Thornton—dropped his knife, laughed, and stepped back from his intended victim. He had made a name for himself, implanted himself forever into local folklore, and that's all he really wanted. The killing was just a means to an end.

Years later, Alexa still regretted not killing him. She had him deep in the woods, the only witness a child so scared out of his wits he couldn't speak straight. She could have shot him. Rid the world of a monster.

But she hadn't. Every day since then, she had regretted not pulling the trigger.

Even worse, she regretted the three victims who the Jersey Devil killed before she managed to get into his head. If she had acted sooner, been a little braver, those victims—Helen Jo (46), Lenny Garth (31) and Rita Ashford (10)—would still be alive.

"You solved a case no one else could," Agent Barrett said, turning a corner and still following the ambulance and patrol car. "You're like a legend at the FBI. I joined a couple of years after you left, and everyone was still talking about you. People studied your cases. I did too."

Alexa blinked. He had studied her? Admired her? She didn't think there was much in her time at the FBI to admire.

But I guess it looks that way from the outside. I did solve a lot of cases, after all.

After a moment's hesitation, in which she felt strangely shy, she asked, "I never got a chance to read much of your file. You start in the BAU?"

"Yeah, right out of the academy. I did some counterintelligence ops in the Army, trying to anticipate what the various factions in Iraq would do next. Managed to stop a couple of car bombings." The pride in his voice was obvious, but it did not last. "That wasn't exactly transferable to homegrown American psychos."

"You must have done good if you've been put on this case." Alexa's estimation of the man had slowly risen during the past few days. He was still annoying, and still not the expert on Drake Logan, but he was a good enough assistant.

And she was beginning to realize he was right about Drake's opinion of her.

"I got good. I didn't start good," he said.

And that regret she heard in his voice was certainly something she could relate to.

"What happened?" she asked.

His knuckles went white on the steering wheel.

"Screwed up on my very first case," he said, his voice heavy with guilt.

CHAPTER TWENTY TWO

Alexa's mood softened. She knew a lot about guilt.

After a pregnant pause, Agent Barrett went on.

"It was a new case. A series of prostitutes had been suffocated with plastic bags tied around their heads and dumped in the warehouse district of Baltimore. CSI didn't pick up much. Part of the guy's M.O. was to kill them on rainy nights and leave them in puddles under drainpipes so they got water pouring all over them. Washed away a lot of evidence. The only real leads we had were some vague sightings by witnesses and the type of bags the guy used."

"What kind were they?"

"Chemical waste disposal bags, like they use in hospitals and industry. So we did a lot of legwork at those kinds of institutions, questioning everybody. We already had a long list of suspects, but nobody had any clear connection to the chemical industry, waste disposal, or medical care. We came up against a dead end."

"There's a lot of that in this job," Alexa said, feeling sympathy. As annoying as this FBI agent could be, he was, after all, one of the good guys.

"Tell me about it," Stuart grunted, then made a face like he had tasted something bitter. "But it wasn't a dead end. We just weren't seeing right. Well, to be honest, *I* wasn't seeing right, because I was lead investigator. It was all my responsibility."

"You were lead investigator? But it was your first case."

"The lead caught the flu and there was no one available to take his place. So I was lead for a week. And that's the week I screwed up."

"Nobody's perfect. You can't beat yourself up over every case that didn't go right."

Looks who's talking.

Agent Barrett went on like he hadn't heard her. "Most of the guys on our long list were johns from that area, or locals who had a history of violence against women. There was this one guy I didn't think about much. He had gotten a bad case of the clap from one of the local hookers—"

Something sparked in Alexa's mind. "Chemical waste. He saw the women as polluted and he wanted to cleanse himself by killing them off."

Stuart groaned and slapped his palm against his forehead. "Yeah. Exactly. And I should have seen that. Instead he got away with another murder and then got caught by pure luck when someone stumbled on him as he was finishing off the victim. He got away, but the witness's description was enough to nail the guy. I didn't actually solve that serial murder at all."

"I'm sorry that happened to you," Alexa said, meaning every word. "This is a hard job, and it's hard to bear failure when it can mean people's lives. We all have to accept that we're human and even in working the most important jobs we all make mistakes. I'm sure your military service taught you that."

"Oh yeah," Agent Barrett said in a heavy voice. "It did."

The FBI man did not elaborate and Alexa decided not to ask.

The ambulance and patrol car they had been following arrived at the emergency room entrance to the hospital. Agent Barrett idled the car as the EMTs, under close watch from the Phoenix police, took Alexa's attacker out of the back and into the admissions hall.

"You want to go in after them?" Agent Barrett asked.

From his tone it sounded like he didn't think she did.

"No," she replied. "Drake's not making a move now. He would have made it on the way over. I think he's got something else he wants to do."

"And what's that?"

"I'm not sure ... " Alexa said, thinking it over. "The attack on Amy Doherty doesn't fit into the pattern. It wasn't a trap for me and he wasn't trying to make a convert."

"So what was it for?"

"It's like ... " then it hit her. "It's like he wants to clean up unfinished business. She was the only victim to get away."

"So what other unfinished business could he have?" Agent Barrett asked. "Revenge on your partner was one."

Alexa winced. "Yeah."

"Converting you."

Alexa didn't reply.

"If there's something else, we need to figure it out," he said. "Revenge on fellow prisoners? No, he already took care of them. Other arresting officers?"

"There was just the two of us."

Powers had been so proud, Alexa thought, feeling a pang of misery.

The FBI man looked at her, and she could see something clicking in his head. It hit her the same instant.

Agent Barrett spoke first, and said exactly what was on her mind. "Drake Logan's mother! She's the one who turned him in. But wait, didn't she already get picked up by the police?"

"She should have been, let me call the ops center."

Agent Barrett was already pulling out of the emergency entrance, even though he didn't know where to go yet. Alexa got on the police radio fitted onto the dashboard.

An officer answered at the ops center. "Deputy Marshal? Marshal Juan Hernandez called asking after you. We reported the attack, of course."

"Tell him I'm fine. Look up the current location of Fuchsia Logan."

Alexa heard a keyboard tapping in the background. After a moment, the officer said, "She's at her home in Lordsburg. She refused to leave, so the police have a female officer staying with her."

"Just one?" Alexa asked, incredulous. *That'll never stop him.*

"Yes."

"Text me the number for that officer."

A moment later he texted her the number. She put it on speed dial on her phone and called. A female voice answered.

"Officer Gerrold speaking."

"Hello, this is Deputy U.S. Marshal Alexa Chase with the Drake Logan investigation. Give me a status report."

"Staying here with Mrs. Logan. We're doing split shifts. I get twelve hours and then another officer gets another twelve."

"How is she? Has she said anything?"

"Mrs. Logan is pretty frail." Alexa nodded. The strain of the trial had led to her having a stroke. "She usually has a nurse who comes in to check on her once a day, but the nurse so scared of Drake Logan that she won't come anywhere close to the house. So I'm doing a lot of nursing duties too."

The officer didn't sound too happy about that.

"The house? So she's at her own house?"

"She refused to leave. And legally we can't force her."

Alexa rubbed her temples. *Why are people so damn uncooperative*?

"All right. We have reason to believe Drake might come after her. He just killed an early victim who got away at the beginning of his killing spree several years ago. Try to get backup. We'll come to you."

"All right."

Agent Barrett glanced over at her as he drove down a street busy with evening traffic. "We're going to see the old lady?"

Alexa gave a grim nod. "She lives in Lordsburg."

"Where the hell is that that?"

"Little town in New Mexico, not far across the state line. We can get there in two hours on the Interstate. The way you drive we'll be there in half that."

"One of the best things about being in law enforcement is you can drive the way you feel like," he said with a smile. "We have to stop off at the hotel first, though."

"Why?"

Agent Barrett gave her a grin. "You need your spare uniform. You can't go running around like that."

"Doesn't matter. Get on the highway."

"All right," Agent Barrett said with a shrug. He took a turn that would lead to the access road. After a moment he asked, "Is Lordsburg a big place?"

"No. And from what I hear she lives in a small ranch house outside of town. The town is famous, though. Billy the Kid washed dishes in a hotel there when he was a kid."

"That's it's only claim to fame?"

"Well, Pat Garrett was from there."

"Who's Pat Garrett?"

"The guy who killed Billy the Kid."

Agent Barrett shrugged. "I'm not too into history."

"You should know law enforcement history. It's always bothered me that people know more about outlaws than the people who catch them."

"Well, I can sure agree with that."

They got on the Interstate and Agent Barrett developed a lead foot. Alexa's phone rang. Marshal Hernandez. Her boss.

First time he's called in a while. Do people only call me when things go wrong?

"Hello, sir," Alexa said in as neutral a voice as she could muster.

"You all right?" he asked.

"Just a scratch. One of the officers gave me first aid. We're on our way to Lordsburg right now."

"I heard. I put in a call to the local police department and told them to put some backup on the Logan home. They were dismissive until I told them what happened in Sedona. I suppose you didn't see the five o'clock news?"

Alexa looked at the clock on the dashboard. It said 5:30 pm.

"No, sir. We were just leaving."

"Well, Sedona was all over the news, and so was your little fight with one of Drake Logan's hitmen."

Alexa flushed. She had really gone overboard subduing that guy.

Subduing? Almost killing.

When Alexa didn't reply, her boss went on, sounding irritated.

"It was the first story. Apparently the news folks thought it was more important than the fallen officers in the Sedona incident."

Alexa flushed even further. "How did it look?"

"Like hell. Oh, I'm not blaming you. You got attacked. But the way you beat down that guy? Looks terrible. The public is going to be all over this."

"But Logan sent him. And he slashed my chest with a knife."

"I know that. The press knows that. But the public sure doesn't know that. They didn't show the part where you're getting attacked, and they didn't show your wound."

"I faced the camera so they'd see!"

"Good idea, but they cut to the announcer before it came to that part. Oh, they mentioned it so they can pretend to be fair and balanced, but that's not going to stick in the public's mind. What's going to stick is the image of you using a metal baton to beat down a man already on the ground and giving up."

"He wasn't giving up!"

"The TV stations were saying that you 'beat a man after he had apparently surrendered.'"

Alexa slumped back in her seat. "Jesus."

"We're working on a press conference. Damage control. We'll reveal he was sent by Logan to put a hit out on you and we'll stress your injury. We'll also put the screws on them to show the full video. But in the meantime, lay low. Avoid any dealings with the press."

"There's nothing I'd love better," Alexa grumbled.

"Good luck." The way Hernandez said it, she could practically hear the unsaid addition, *you'll need it.*

And she would need it, because they hadn't made it more than five miles down the highway before she got another call. Melanie, her sister-in-law and Wayne's wife. A reporter for Action News in Phoenix. Alexa had never liked her, and sure wasn't in the mood to speak with her right now.

She felt tempted not to answer.

Yes, the press is a pain, Powers once told her. *But they can be cooperative if handled right. And always remember, it's worse not to talk to a reporter than to talk to one. If you don't feed them something, they'll just fill in the blanks. And when they do that, they almost always get it wrong.*

Steeling herself, Alexa answered.

"Alexa! Are you all right?" Melanie actually sounded concerned. Well, actually more excited than concerned.

"I'll recover. That attacker slashed me with a knife. It was pretty bad but I got some first aid pretty quick."

"Yes, I saw the raw footage. It was bleeding pretty badly."

"It would have been nice if you had left that part in the newscast," Alexa grumbled.

"Time constraints. You know how tight our program schedules are. We made sure to mention it."

Alexa suppressed an angry response, took a deep breath, and said. "My boss will be having a press conference soon and—"

"We got the announcement. We'll be there."

"He'll give a full account. Marshal H—"

"I'm more interested in your account."

Alexa took a deep breath and tried to be patient. One of Melanie's more annoying traits was that she constantly interrupted people. She did it on the air too. "All I can tell you at the moment was that my attacker was sent by Drake Logan to kill me. He attacked me with a knife and I pepper sprayed him—"

"So he was already subdued when you pulled your baton."

"Obviously not, or I wouldn't have pulled my baton. You saw the size of that guy. He—"

"Alexa, Alexa, don't get defensive. I'm on your side. Where are you now?"

"Following up more leads."

"You're not in the hospital?"

"No."

"So the injury wasn't too bad."

"He cut me with a knife. I—"

"I'm so glad he didn't hurt you badly. The video showed a lot of blood, but appearances can be deceiving. I'll be sure to reassure our listeners that you weren't badly hurt."

Alexa gripped the phone so hard she worried it would break. Saying that would only make it look like the beating she had given that guy hadn't been warranted. It's always so easy for someone sitting in an easy chair at home to make snap judgements about situations they weren't involved in.

"Look, I've got to go," Alexa said.

"Would you like to come on the air and do a face to face interview?"

"I'm busy," Alexa grumbled.

"Of course. I mean after they catch Drake Logan."

After they *catch him?*

"I've got to go," Alexa said, and hung up before she could get interrupted again.

Agent Barrett stared at her.

"Look at the road," she grumbled. "You're going ninety."

He looked back at the road. "Who was that?"

"My sister-in-law. She's a reporter on TV."

"Oh," he said in a quiet voice.

"Yeah," Alexa said, crossing her arms and glaring at the road ahead of them. "Oh."

Her phone rang again. Reluctantly, she looked at the screen, and saw it was someone she wanted to speak to even less.

CHAPTER TWENTY THREE

Her father was calling.

Like Melanie, Dad would keep calling until she picked up, so Alexa picked up.

"You all right?" he demanded.

"I take it you saw the news."

"Everyone saw the news! They say he came at you with a knife."

"Yeah. Just a scratch."

"Wait, he cut you?"

"Yeah, didn't the news report mention that?"

"Not the one we saw up here!"

"Ugh. Well, yes, he cut me. Just a flesh wound. I didn't even need stitches."

Still burns like hell, though.

"Well, then I'm glad you beat that son of a bitch. You really laid into him. Good girl!"

Alexa smiled. While Dad had always been sparing with his praise, to say the least, he was a real law and order type.

"Look, Dad. Drake sent him. I'm afraid he might come after people close to me."

"I figured that. Each of us is carrying a sidearm on our belts and keeping a rifle or shotgun within reach. And we got the dogs all out in the yard."

"You gave Malcolm a gun?"

"Oh, don't worry. He can handle a gun as good as any man. It's one of the few things he can do."

"Yeah, but when he was fifteen he—"

"That was just for attention. Don't worry about that wimp. Worry about yourself."

Alexa didn't have the energy for an argument. Instead she said, "Just be careful, all right? And have Wayne keep Melanie off my back. She just called me."

"Aw, hell! He told her not to bother you when this whole thing started. She said she wouldn't call."

"Well, she did."

"It's that damn video. The commies are going to drag you through the mud."

"There aren't any commies in Arizona, Dad."

"All those college liberals? Commies, every one of them. Public defenders are commies too. Heck, half of America has gone commie. Vegetarians, druggies, nudists, surfers, skateboarders, environmentalists, hikers, swingers—"

"OK, OK, Dad. Whatever you say. Just be careful, all right? Thanks for calling." Suddenly a terrible thought came to her. "I need to go. I just remembered I have to call someone else."

Stacy. If Drake finds out my home address, he might check it out and find her there.

She glanced sidelong at Agent Barrett, who kept his eyes on the road. He might have fought terrorists in Iraq, but he didn't have the courage to get involved to someone else's family squabbles. Smart man.

Alexa called Stacy. She hadn't checked in for a while and needed to make sure the girl was all right.

Finally, something to get my mind off the case for a moment.

The kid was good at that.

Not this time. Before Alexa even got to say hello, the girl blurted,

"Oh my God, I just heard! Why did you tell me you were in a car wreck?"

Alexa slumped. So Stacy had finally heard about Drake Logan getting busted out. The press had mentioned Alexa's name the previous day in connection with that. Even a kid who never watched the news was bound to hear eventually.

"I didn't want to worry you," Alexa said.

"Well, now I'm worried! You could have been killed. And I'm *so sorry* about your partner. That must have been horrible. Why aren't you taking time off?"

"Because I'm the only person who knows how to catch the people who did it."

That got an annoyed look from Agent Barrett. Alexa turned away from him.

"But are you OK?" the girl asked, anxiety cutting her voice.

"I'm fine."

Alexa realized she had just reversed roles with her. It was usually Alexa asking Stacy if she was OK, and the teenager dismissing the question with the meaningless term "fine".

"You are *so* not fine. Come home."

"I can't."

"Even my parents are worried about you. Is it safe to be here?"

That was the very question Alexa had asked herself. Drake knew so much about her; did he know her address too?

Even if he did, he knew she was busy chasing him around the state. Home was the last place to look for her. Alexa really, really wanted to believe that.

And hopefully he didn't know Alexa had taken in a neighbor girl.

Still …

"Put some extra feed in for Smith and Wesson and stay away from the house for a couple of days."

"But Mom and Dad—"

"It's safer to be away from my house until we get this guy."

"But they're … you know … "

"I know, and I'm sorry. You're a strong girl and you're just going to have to bear with it for a while, OK?"

Silence on the other end of the line. Stacy didn't like it when Alexa came even close to mentioning her parents' drinking. This situation was too important to dance around the subject, though.

"It's better to steer clear of the house, all right?" Alexa said. When she didn't get an answer, she added, "Promise?"

"I promise," Stacy grumbled.

"And don't watch the news or look at the Internet about this case, all right?" She didn't want the girl to see that video of her beating down a suspect while bleeding from a knife wound. She got enough trauma at home.

"Why not?"

"Just don't, all right?"

"OK."

"Pinky promise?"

"We can't do pinky promise. We're on the phone."

"Just hook your pinky and touch the phone," Alexa told her.

Stacy giggled. "All right, I'm doing it."

Alexa hooked her pinky around the phone. "There, so have I. Now go home. I'll call you as soon as I can."

"All right. But be careful, all right? And call lots."

"I will. Love you."

She hung up.

"I didn't know you had a kid," Agent Barrett said.

"Oh, she's not my kid."

"You talk to her like she's your kid."

"A neighbor's kid. Bad parents. Its's a long story."

Agent Barrett shrugged. "Family is what you make of it. My big brother is ten years older than me. He dated this older girl for a while who had a kid. Gunther. He was twelve when I was seventeen. My big brother would always bribe me with beer to babysit Gunther while he was going out with his mom. Well, more like staying in with his mom. So my job was to keep Gunther out of the way. We really hit it off. Taught him how to throw a curveball, work a barbeque, all that stuff a dad's supposed to teach. Except he didn't have a dad. It was fun teaching him that stuff and he ended up being my little brother. I'm the youngest and I always wanted a little brother and so I got one." He laughed. "I got a lot of free beer too. My brother and Gunther's mom broke up after a few months but Gunther and I still hung out. He just graduated from NYU. We still call each other brothers."

"That's really sweet."

"Like I said, Deputy Marshal Chase, family is what you make of it."

"Why don't you call me Alexa? We're partners," Alexa said, then quickly added, "for the time being."

"All right. Call me Stuart, but no *Beavis and Butthead* jokes, all right?"

"*Beavis and Butthead*?"

He looked at her. "You seriously never heard of *Beavis and Butthead*?"

"Of course I have. Never watched it, though. My brother Malcolm loved it."

Explains a lot.

"Well, there's a guy named Stuart in it. The dorky kid. Beavis and Butthead are fans of Metallica and AC/DC. Stuart is a Winger fan."

"Oh God, I remember Winger."

"Yeah. And he wets his bed and has no social skills. Gunther always made fun of me for being called Stuart. Always asking me if I've wet my bed or finally gotten a girlfriend."

"Sounds like a typical little brother."

"He is," Stuart said with a chuckle.

They continued driving, the tension between them relaxed a little.

"You think we can get Drake's mother to talk?" Stuart asked after a while.

"Sure. I'm not optimistic she'll know anything, though. After she put two and two together and realized her own son was responsible for a string of murders, she called the police and helped them arrange to trap him. He's never spoken to her since."

"That's hardly surprising. She might have some insights into his behavior, though."

Alexa nodded. "That's what I'm hoping. She was pretty insightful during the investigation and trial. And even if she doesn't give us anything new, I think that's where he's going to show up next. The Fiona connection is a good lead, but I think this one is stronger."

"So do I. He must know he can't hide from us forever. He needs to get what he wants done finished before we run him down. You know, I didn't get a chance to delve too much into Drake's early life. What was it like?" Stuart asked.

"Troubled. Abusive father who beat his mother in front of him. He used to flee to his grandparents' house where he felt safer. But he resented his grandparents. They were his mother's parents and they were alcoholics, incapable or unwilling to help their daughter get out of an abusive relationship."

"So he got into crime early?"

"Actually not. He was a quiet kid, small for his age. He's still small, but didn't have the violent streak he has now. Got bullied a lot. What people didn't realize was he was getting back at his tormentors secretly. One bully discovered his dog had been killed. Another got food poisoning. It was only later, when this got traced back to Drake. He got away with it for a while but that sort of passive aggressive behavior didn't really satisfy him. He began to steal, and used the money for self-defense classes."

"I've heard he's pretty dangerous. In prison he's killed people twice his size."

"Several times, although usually with a shiv. Drake doesn't take risks unless he thinks they're important to spreading his message. But yeah, he got good at hand to hand fighting. Got kicked out of two different self-defense classes for being so aggressive with sparring."

"And then he took out his aggressions on the bullies?"

"He did more than that. He recruited every wimp in the neighborhood and started his own self-defense class. A lot of them didn't make the grade, but soon he had built up a little army of scrawny, geeky kids who had a lot of pent-up anger inside. They would hunt down bullies as a pack and beat the hell out of them."

"He must have seemed like General Patton to these kids."

"Oh, yeah. And that's what started it all off. Of course as he grew older he started getting in trouble with the law, and his crimes began to spiral. He became the terror of Lordsburg before moving on to bigger cities like Phoenix where he could find more opportunities. And through it all he kept his charisma and his ideology of making supermen out of the weak."

"That's sure made him dangerous."

"Yeah," Alexa said. "He's got a pack of people willing to do anything for him. We're not just dealing with a serial killer; we're dealing with a small army."

And that small army might already be in New Mexico. Waiting for us.

CHAPTER TWENTY FOUR

A porch light shining up ahead told them of their destination. Through the desert night Stuart could make out a low ranch house with faded green paint and a sagging porch. A waist-high chain link fence enclosed about an acre of bare dirt. In the dirt lot out front they could see two parked police cars with their lights off, and a battered old station wagon.

"Real charming place," Alexa said.

Stuart slowed the car, a tingling going up his spine. On impulse he switched off the lights and gunned the engine, driving half blind down the dark county road.

"What did you see?" Alexa said, scooting down low in her seat, hand on her gun.

"Nothing. It didn't feel right."

"What do you mean it didn't feel right?"

Stuart thought for a moment. The feeling always came before the thought, and that feeling had saved his life several times.

"Nobody came out to greet us, or even look through the window. I know, I know, I'm probably being paranoid. But you've been attacked twice now."

"You just talked with them on the radio not fifteen minutes ago," Alexa said.

Stuart nodded, driving slowly down the dark road. He had talked with the female officer, who told him that Fuscia Logan was safe and "sleeping like a rock." She had revealed no valuable information.

"I'll give them a call," Alexa said, digging into her pocket.

"Call them on the radio," Stuart said, indicating the police radio fitted into the dashboard.

"Why?"

"I want to hear them."

Alexa shrugged, picked up the radio, and called, "Unit 12, unit 12, this is Deputy Marshal Chase. You at the Logan residence?"

The answer came back, crackling slightly. "Roger, Deputy Marshal. Waiting for your arrival."

"Hear the quality of that signal?" Stuart said. "They're calling from further away than the house."

"Could be atmospheric disruption. I've heard that before. Let me check."

Alexa switched channels to the Lordsburg police station. "Lordsburg P.D., Deputy Marshal Chase checking in. Is Unit 12 still at the Logan residence?"

"Roger, deputy marshal. Both units 12 and 5 are at the residence."

Stuart and Alexa exchanged looks. That transmission had come in loud and clear, even though it was several miles further away.

"Pull off by the side of the road and we'll come at the house over land," Alexa said.

"Good idea."

Stuart's heart beat fast as he pulled off onto the shoulder and switched off the engine. When he got out of the vehicle, he stooped low, a habit borne of countless patrols in the Al-Anbar governate. He took the car's shotgun with him and went around to open the trunk.

"Come on, let's go," Alexa said, her voice impatient. He couldn't see her well in the late dusk, but could tell she was looking at him with irritation.

"Kevlar," he said, handing her a bulletproof vest and pulling one out for himself.

He saw Alexa's dark form hesitate, unconsciously moving a step toward the lights of the house half a mile down the road, then stopping. She was pulled between the chance of getting after Drake Logan as quickly as possible, and the good sense of armoring up before doing so.

Good sense won and she donned the Kevlar. Stuart wondered how often her impulsiveness won out over good sense.

"Let's walk along the road part of the way and then cut through the yard," Stuart said. He found himself whispering. "Quicker and quieter approach, but we don't want to be on the exposed road once we get into the sight of anyone in that house.

"All right," Alexa whispered back.

They headed out. Stuart gripped the shotgun and glanced along either side of the road. He was still uncertain whether he was being paranoid or simply cautious, but the quality of that radio transmission made him nervous. He did not want to walk into an ambush. He had had enough of those for one lifetime.

If he was wrong, the local P.D. could have a good laugh at his expense. He could shrug that off no problem.

But if he was right …

The desert evening was quiet, with only a gentle wind blowing on a few bits of scrub. His shoes crunched on the gravel. Too loud. He moved closer to the center of the road where traffic had ground down the gravel to a tight surface that made no noise as he walked on it. Too exposed. He hunched down a little and wished Alexa would do the same.

Too much combat on this case. When he had joined the FBI he knew he'd be seeing some pretty grim things, especially in the Behavioral Affairs Unit, but he didn't think he'd see much gunplay. Your average soldier in Iraq gets into more firefights in a week than your average law enforcement officer does in their entire career. That made him look at his new job as a lifelong vacation.

Some vacation.

They approached the house. No movement at any of the windows. No crackle from the radios of either of the police cars. That would carry clearly through the still desert air.

They stopped and stared at the house for a moment.

When nothing moved over there, Alexa whispered, "Let's go around the back."

"We'll have to hop that fence." It was only waist high, but he worried about the noise.

Alexa didn't reply. She probably figured the same as he did—that hopping the fence would be better than coming at the house from the front, from where they were expected to come. Whoever was there should be wondering why they hadn't shown up yet.

They picked their way carefully through the rocks and scrub. Stuart kept out a sharp eye for snakes. After a few steps he stopped, seeing a black, curved form on the lighter desert floor, then realized he was looking at a stick. They moved on. A few steps later he winced as he brushed by a cactus and a few spines jabbed through his pants.

I hate working in the boondocks.

They cut around to the back of the house without making too much noise. Two windows faced them, both with drawn curtains backlit by the lights inside.

Creeping toward the house, eyes and ears alert, they still saw no sign of life from within. Now Stuart felt sure something had gone wrong.

They got to the fence. Stuart edged to a spot where one of the upright poles held up the fence so it would make less noise as he gripped it. Then he took a big step and hauled himself over. The fence let out a little squeak.

Stuart hurried over to the house and hunched under one of the windows.

Now it was Alexa's turn. Being shorter, she made considerably more noise getting over.

That still didn't bring any response from the house.

Alexa came over at a crouch and they worked their way around to the side. There they saw a window with the blinds partially open.

Stuart dared a peek.

He could see a bedroom with a lumpy old bed covered by a handmade quilt. Through an open door he could see into the hall and part of the front living room.

And the bottom half of a pair of legs of what looked like an old woman lying on the floor.

She was not moving.

Alexa took a peek, cursed, and hurried around to the front of the house.

"Wait," Stuart hissed.

The impulsive deputy marshal did not listen, too obsessed with catching her nemesis to pay attention to police procedure or even her personal safety.

He hurried after her.

At least she had enough sense that, when she hopped on the porch, she kept clear of the front door and windows. Stuart did a quick scan of the front lot, illuminated by the porch light, and saw no one in or around the three cars.

Alexa had made enough noise getting on the porch to alert anyone alive inside. The time for sneaking was over. Now for the direct approach.

"FBI! Drop your weapons and put your hands up!"

Stuart, shotgun leveled, gave the door a hard kick.

The cheap old wooden frame splintered and the door popped open, hitting the wall with a bang.

Stuart got behind the doorframe, sighting down the barrel of his weapon. He saw no one in the front room or the hallway beyond.

No one, that is, except the old woman lying with a tight cord wrapped around her neck. Her face was purple, eyes bugged, swollen tongue sticking out of her mouth.

He killed his own mother.

Stuart suppressed a shudder and his combat reflexes kicked in. Taking point, and trusting that Alexa would follow his lead, he burst into the room, then systematically went through the kitchen, bathroom, and two bedrooms, looking for the enemy. The best approach when clearing a house was to go through as quickly as possible, not giving the surprised occupants time to plan or to hide.

Although back in Iraq, he had gone in with an entire squad at his back, not a lone deputy marshal.

He didn't find the enemy, although in the laundry room in back he found the two police officers.

They lay in a heap, stuck between the washer and dryer. A note was pinned on the female officer's chest.

"Check the backyard," Stuart told Alexa. "I'll look for signs of life on these two."

He moved forward. Alexa, instead of going to the nearest window, grabbed him and pulled him back.

"Look!" she shouted once they had made it to the other side of the small room.

Stuart followed her pointing finger. A thin wire crossed between the washing machine and a laundry hamper heaped with dirty clothes.

He crouched down. Between the various blouses and dresses he could just make out the side of a large coffee can near where the wire passed through the plastic mesh of the laundry hamper. He had no doubt that if he had tripped that wire, the explosives inside that can would have gone off. He bet the can was packed with nails and BBs, and maybe a bit of rat poison to make the wounds fester.

He had seen the same thing in Iraq. Too many times. But he had never expected to see it here.

An IED, right here in the laundry room in a cheap house in New Mexico. Stuart trembled, then walked slowly back to the far end of the room, eyes scanning for more wires.

Stuart stood at the far end of the room, his mind numb as Alexa carefully stepped over the wire and checked on the bodies. She turned to him, shook her head sadly, and stepped back over the tripwire.

"What did that note say?" Stuart asked, pointing at the piece of paper pinned to one of the dead officer's chests.

Alexa grimaced. "If you're reading this, you've been blown to bits."

They searched the rest of the house and yard, Stuart running on automatic. Whoever had set the booby trap was long gone. Alexa called in the crime scene while Stuart leaned on the front porch railing, utterly spent.

Private Barrett.

Private Barrett had been in Stuart's platoon. One day they had been clearing a village, looking for insurgents. After a long, hot morning of finding nothing, Private Barrett had gone to check a toolshed in a garden behind one of the houses. Stuart had been standing nearby. Private Barrett had told Stuart he was going to check it out and Stuart, hot and tired and stressed, had only nodded. It was only a toolshed, after all.

The explosion had thrown Stuart ten feet across a lane and into a concrete wall, knocking him out. They didn't find much of Private Barrett.

After that, Stuart had sworn never to let a partner down, never to let someone go off alone into danger, and for years he had managed to do that.

Until tonight. Until through his own oversight he had nearly blown up them both.

He had wanted to protect his partner, and instead she had saved him.

But could they save themselves? Stuart wasn't sure.

Stuart wasn't sure if they were hunting Drake Logan, or if he was hunting them.

CHAPTER TWENTY FIVE

The desert around the Logan home was lit up with police cars, the flashing lights painful to Alexa's tired eyes. A bomb squad was going through the house with a fine-toothed comb, looking for other devices. They had already neutralized the one bomb they had found.

Stuart stood nearby, drinking coffee from a thermos and looking preoccupied. Every now and then the radios in the patrol cars crackled with the news that the search through the desert and the dragnet the local police and highway patrol had set up had found nothing.

Of course they hadn't. Drake was like a vengeful ghost, striking and then disappearing.

He had been here, though. He wouldn't have left the murder of his mother to an underling. She bet he had been watching too, waiting to see if his childhood home blew up. She wondered if he felt disappointed, or pleased, that Alexa had escaped another of his traps.

Alexa knew she needed to change tactics. Everything she had been doing had failed. Drake Logan was leading her around, playing on her impulses and emotions to get her exactly where he wanted. Put her in positions where she could compromise herself, hoping she'd break and come over to his own dark way of thinking.

Stuart was right about that. She knew that now.

The FBI man came up to her. "Look, it's really late. Let's go get a hotel and head back to Phoenix in the morning. It's all over here."

Alexa nodded, preoccupied, then the look on her partner's face took her out of her own thoughts.

He looked ragged, pale. His hands trembled slightly.

Poor guy. He probably saw a lot of bombs in Iraq.

"All right," Alexa said. "Let's get some sleep. I'll drive."

"I'll do it."

"It's OK, I can—"

"I'll do it," he said, heading for the car.

Whatever gets your mind off things a bit, Alexa thought, following him.

They drove in silence into Lordsburg to get a motel for the night. It was now close to midnight and they had no energy to drive all the way back to Tucson. So they'd stay in New Mexico and resume the search in the morning, or run off to a new location if Drake summoned her once again.

Yes, Drake wanted to make her into some sort of disciple, but he didn't mind if she failed the test either. Ricardo could have killed her at the racetrack. The second attacker might have gotten her too. And spotting that tripwire was as much luck as anything else.

He was playing with her life as much as with her soul.

Just like he had played with the lives of the two men who had been after her. They could have succeeded, made the grade, but when they got captured, Drake probably hadn't cared all that much. He had given them the chance to be strong and they had failed.

But with Alexa? She seemed to be getting a whole string of chances. Again and again Drake tried to get her to come around to his way of thinking. Her soul was worth more to him than the souls of the others. He had become as obsessed about turning her as she had about capturing him.

She needed to use that against them.

But how? She thought about this as Stuart drove through town, looking for a decent place to stay. Then something he said gave her the answer.

"He's cracked the police communications."

"Why do you say that?"

"Remember how that phony transmission back at the Logan house sounded distant? That's because they were transmitting from miles away, luring us into that booby-trapped home."

"They could have used one of the radios in the patrol cars."

Stuart shook his head. "They wouldn't have had time to get out of sight before we showed up, and neither of the radios were missing. No, they have their own radio. You can get illegal descramblers to monitor and transmit on police frequencies. That's how he keeps staying one step ahead of us."

Alexa stared at him. "That would explain a lot."

"We could track his position if he stayed on the air long enough. Use two sensitive receivers in two different vehicles to triangulate his position."

"He's too smart to do that," Alexa said.

Stuart nodded grimly, turning into the parking lot of a Motel 6.

"We need to keep any essential communications off the radio," he said. "Cell phones only."

"All right. But that gives me an idea."

She got on the radio and called the Lordsburg P.D. dispatch. "This is Deputy Marshal Chase and Special Agent Barrett. We think Drake will head back to Phoenix. We're heading there right now."

"Roger, deputy marshal. Safe travels."

"You think he'll head to Phoenix?" Stuart asked once she returned the handset to the dashboard.

"I know it," Alexa said with a smile. "He's obsessed with me, like you said. He'll go to Phoenix and monitor police communications until he hears from us. That's when he'll make his next move. Phoenix has a lot more law enforcement than this little town. That will help. Also we have the main ops center right there. If we're going to catch him, Phoenix is the best place to try. In the meantime, we can catch some sleep in safety. He won't be looking for us in Lordsburg."

They parked and got out of the car. Luckily, both of them had been smart enough to pack their things and leave them in the trunk.

"Getting him to Phoenix isn't enough," Alexa said. "We need to bait him instead of having him bait us."

Stuart closed the trunk. "How do you mean?"

"He wants me so we'll give him me. I'll be the bait."

"What?!"

"We're already luring him back to Phoenix where we can count on more backup. Once he's there, we need to figure out a plan where he thinks I'm alone and we can ambush him."

Stuart shook his head vigorously. "No way. Too dangerous. This last attack proves you can't be left alone for a second. We need to stick together. We'll use regular police procedures to—"

"Regular police procedures aren't working! All that gets us is more dead bodies."

The FBI man looked her in the eye. "And I don't want you to be one of them."

Alexa paused, studying his face. She saw determination there, and worry, and she knew she would not be able to convince him.

So she'd have to go her own way.

* * *

They returned to the Phoenix ops center by ten the next morning. For the rest of the work day Alexa was stuck in the office dealing with a huge amount of paperwork dealing with their investigation, expenses, and the killings in Lordsburg. They also had to attend several meetings to get up to speed on what the various agencies were doing to hunt down Drake Logan and his followers. Several of his partners in crime from the old days had been arrested, but none had revealed anything of value. The members of the Glory of the Sun cult were still in custody, and still being tight-lipped.

Alexa figured Drake had kept them all in the dark. Otherwise surely one of the detainees would have broken by now.

Marshal Hernandez and Deputy Director Sandford both called, wanting updates and wanting results. Alexa and Stuart had none to give, and that put even more pressure on them.

Despite a frustrating day of getting nowhere, Alexa felt strangely calm. It would be better for her to launch her trick at night. It was Drake's preferred time, and what she needed to do would seem more convincing in the evening on the drive back to the hotel.

She only hoped that Drake would be listening.

And just as the sun set, Alexa got a break from an unexpected source.

Malcolm called.

As she picked up, her heart clenched with fear that something had happened at the ranch.

"Are you all right?" Alexa blurted before her brother got to say a word. Stuart looked up from his desk at her.

Her brother's tremulous voice came over the line. "Yeah, everything's fine here. Dad's got us all patrolling the ranch like we're under siege."

"For once I agree with Dad. Stay careful."

When Stuart heard she was speaking with her family, he put his head down and got back to work.

"Alexa?"

"I'm here, Malcolm. I'm all right. Look, I'm really busy right now."

"I got news of Fiona."

Suddenly Alexa was all ears.

"Really? Where is she?"

"I'm not sure. I heard from a guy I used to hang with that she was living in an apartment in Tempe."

"Where in Tempe? You have an address?"

"Yeah." He gave it to her. She hurriedly wrote it down on a pad and stuffed it in her pocket.

"Thanks a million Malcolm. I love you."

"Love you too. You sure you're all right?"

"I'll be fine. How about you?"

"Taking it one day at a time. I wish Dad wouldn't drink whiskey around me, though. The smell drives me crazy. Makes my mouth water."

Their father's voice could be heard in the background. "I'll drink when I want to in my own home. Just work on your damn self-discipline!"

Alexa rolled her eyes. "I really have to go, Malcolm."

"All right. Love you."

"Love you too. Bye."

She sat staring at her desk for a long time, thinking.

There was a good chance Drake would be at Fiona's address, or if he wasn't, Fiona would be there and they might be able to pump her for information.

But what if it was another dead end? They might not be there at all.

But there was a way to ensure they would be. Drake, or one of his underlings, would be monitoring police communications at all times. If they announced over the air that they were heading to Fiona's place, Drake would set a trap.

But a trap wasn't good enough. They needed to get Drake, not an ambush from his underlings, and certainly not another bomb.

So how to get Drake to stay at Fiona's place?

Being the bait, like I said.

If I announce over the radio that I'm going over there alone, he'll be there to greet me.

Alexa felt a tremor of fear, her entire body going chill.

That chill did not last long. It got warmed by the growing heat of rage.

This man killed my partner. He almost killed my new partner. And it's me he wants.

Well, then it's me he's going to get.

If we go over as a group, we'll never find him. We'll chase him all over the Southwest, him always a step ahead and leaving a trail of victims behind him.

If I go alone, I can take care of him myself.

And this time, I won't be merciful like I was with the Jersey Devil.

The light outside had dimmed into another night. Drake's favorite time. It was time to act.

She got up, made a show of stretching and rubbing her eyes, and turned to Stuart, who sat at the desk opposite, looking through some police reports from various towns scattered across the region. Since Drake Logan had hit the news, the number of sightings had been staggering. Most of the false, of course. All leads had to be checked, though. This case was too important not to follow every trail.

"You hungry?" she asked, putting an annoyed edge into her voice that she didn't feel.

"Yeah, now that you mention it," he said, still reading.

"I'll go get some takeaway."

Stuart looked up from his work. "It's better if we go together."

"I don't need you watching over me every second of the day," she said with false irritation. "For Christ's sake, Stuart, I'm just going down the street."

A couple of the officers working nearby glanced over.

The FBI agent looked confused. "But yesterday you got attacked just down the street."

Alexa didn't reply. There was no rational rebuttal to that, after all. So she simply turned and left.

Stuart followed her all the way outside.

Damn it. How to get rid of him?

She walked over to her car, which was parked three places down from his.

"Wait, Alexa, we should—"

"Enough! I'm sick of you hovering over me like I'm some damsel in distress!"

"Damsel in distress? I'm your partner."

She got into her car and turned on the engine. Looking through the mirror, she could see Stuart hurrying to his car, obviously not wanting to get left behind. She hadn't even told him what restaurant she was going to.

Alexa peeled out of the parking lot and got around a corner before he had a chance to get his engine started.

Her phone rang. She ignored it.

Alexa took the first corner, then the next nearest corner, not caring where she was going, just needing to get away from him.

Then she got on the police radio.

"Agent Barrett, you reading me?"

"Yeah. Where did you go off to? You didn't even tell me where this restaurant is."

"Doesn't matter. I'm off the case, thanks to you."

Stuart's confusion came in over the air. "Off the case? What are you talking about?"

"You got me taken off the case, you son of a bitch."

"Huh?"

"That call I got from the higher ups? That was to relieve me of duty. Oh, administrative leave is what they called it. They want to do damage control for that video of me beating down that guy Drake sent."

"Wait, I never heard—"

"And you asked them to do it, didn't you? All the way to Lordsburg and back you kept lecturing me about how I was too close to this case, and how I couldn't think straight."

"Alexa, no—"

"Well, you got what you wanted. Now I'm off the case. But I'm not off the case, Agent Barrett. Not by a long shot. I just found out where that meth dealer's apartment is and I'm going to hunt her down. And when I find her, damn it, I'm going to *make* her tell me where Drake is."

"You found Fiona's address? What is it?"

"Not so fast. You'd like to take all the credit, wouldn't you? Get in good with the FBI after your past mistakes."

"Hey, that's not fair!"

Now he sounded hurt, and that hurt Alexa. He was a decent guy who didn't deserve to be treated this way, but it had to be done.

"You've been cutting me off this entire investigation, and that's getting in the way of capturing Drake. Nobody knows him like I do. Who captured him in the first place? Who's grabbed two of his men? I'm in his head, and that's because I know this case inside and out. You just stepped in a few days ago and you think that just because you're coming from the FBI you know how to do everything? I'll handle this myself. It's the only way I know it will get done right."

She returned the handset to the dashboard and turned off the radio before he could sputter out a reply. It felt terrible embarrassing him like that on the air. Dozens of local cops must have heard. Hopefully, Drake's crew had heard too.

Still, it was a horrible thing to do even if it was necessary. She'd apologize to him later.

The important thing was he was out of it. Drake wanted her, and her alone. Those poor officers in Lordsburg had been killed because of her. She wouldn't let Stuart get killed too. Now he was safe. She could explain it all to him later.

If she survived.

CHAPTER TWENTY SIX

Drake Logan lit a menthol and settled into the armchair in Fiona's living room. The police scanner Harry had set up on the coffee table had just broadcast some wonderful news. Those idiots in the U.S. Marshals Service had taken Alexa off the case, even though she was the only one who had even a tiny chance to catch him. And now she was going to do what the strong always did—whatever the hell she wanted.

She was coming for him herself.

How had they found Fiona's address? It didn't matter so much. Here was as good of a place for the final lesson as anywhere else.

Taking another drag from his cigarette, he turned to Harry and Fiona and the rest of his core group of followers.

"Get ready. You all know what to do."

"What if the police come?" Fiona said, obviously concerned. It was her apartment that had just become forever useless, after all.

"Didn't you hear? Alexa found your address but didn't share it. She wants to face me alone. Deep inside, she wants to face the final test."

"But the police might—"

"You take care of the police. Leave Alexa to me."

A slow grin went across all their faces. They knew what was in store for Alexa, once Drake got her where he wanted her.

Drake grinned back. He wondered if Alexa would be ready.

He sure hoped so.

* * *

What the hell just happened?

Stuart was confused. That argument had come out of nowhere. While Alexa had been prickly all through this investigation, he thought they'd finally begun to hit it off in Lordsburg, or at least work together on a more professional level.

And now she was picking a fight for no reason.

Because he was sure she hadn't really been kicked off the investigation. He had been talking to his boss just a couple of hours ago and the director hadn't mentioned anything. And when Alexa had spoken with her own boss, there hadn't been any tension in the conversation, just a routine update, from what he could hear.

Wait. There was a reason for her sudden blowup. She hadn't started it in the office, and she hadn't called him on the phone. She had used the police radio.

The police radio she knew Drake was most likely listening in on.

She was going ahead with her plan to set him up.

And doing it alone.

She said she was going to that meth dealer's place. But we never found out where she lives.

Wait ...

A memory tugged at the back of Stuart's mind. Didn't she talk about some address with someone on the phone?

She was talking to Malcolm! Her family found out the address somehow. Yeah, it was an address in Tempe. Where the hell's Tempe?

He pulled into a strip mall parking lot and checked his phone. Tempe was one of the cities that made up Phoenix. Perfect. But *where* in Tempe?

Her family knows.

He called back to the ops center and identified himself.

"What's going on with your partner?" the local cop who answered the phone asked.

Stuart's heart sunk. His "partner" had just humiliated him in front of the whole office.

"You had the police radio on?"

"Of course. We always have it on. So what's going on with—"

"Never mind. Deputy Marshal Chase's family lives on some ranch somewhere. Do you have their home number?"

"Sir, we're not allowed to divulge—"

"Never mind what you're not allowed to do," Stuart snapped. "Give me that damn number or you'll be issuing parking tickets in Alaska for the rest of your career!"

"Hold on," the officer grumbled. Stuart could hear him tapping on a keyboard. "OK, I'll text it to you."

As soon as the number came in, Stuart dialed it.

It rang. And rang.

Stuart let it ring ten times before hanging up.

Cursing, he tried to think of what to do next.

His phone rang with an unknown number.

Oh God, have they captured her family?

He picked up, his skin prickling, fully expecting to hear Drake's mocking voice punctuated by the screams of Alexa's relatives.

Instead he heard the gruff tones of an older man's voice.

"Who's speaking?" the man demanded.

"This is Special Agent Stuart Barrett of the Federal Bureau of Investigation."

"Oh God, a fed! What's he done now?"

Stuart stared at the phone, baffled. "What's who done now?"

"My useless son. He trafficking in that junk or something?"

"Sir, could you please identify yourself?"

"Identify myself? You called me!"

In Stuart's head, something clicked. "Wait, is this Alexa Chase's father?"

"Who do you think it is, Santa Claus?"

No, sir. I would never mistake you for Santa Claus.

"Mr. Chase, I'm working with your daughter on the Drake Logan case. She's … busy right now and I really need to know the address of a woman named Fiona who lives in Tempe. Did you provide her that information?"

"No, that was my useless son. You sure he isn't in trouble?"

"He's not in trouble, sir. But I really need that information right away."

"Hold on." Stuart heard the phone being put down, footsteps receded, then a distant shout. "Malcolm, stop with that hippie shit and get over here! The feds want to talk to you, and you can thank your chakras that they're not here putting the cuffs on you."

The sound of approaching footsteps and a low grumble, "Come on, Malcolm. Get the lead out."

The phone got picked up.

"Hello?" a high-pitched but male voice warbled.

"Hello, Malcolm Chase? This is Special Agent Barrett of the FBI. I'm working with your sister and I need the address of the meth dealer named Fiona."

"Why didn't Alexa call me? Is everything OK?"

Suppressing his impatience, Stuart struggled to keep his voice calm.

"She's fine." *I hope.* "She's just busy and working with another unit at the moment and can't be disturbed. I really need that address."

"Oh. It's 450 East Rio Antiguo Street."

"Thank you so much, Mr. Chase."

"Is Alexa—"

Stuart hung up, punched the address into the GPS, and sped out of the parking lot, nearly sideswiping a pickup truck. The driver blared his horn and gave Stuart a one-fingered salute.

Stuart ignored him, weaving through traffic and running three red lights as he shot through evening traffic to get to Tempe. He was amazed he didn't get stopped by the police. They were either as incompetent as Alexa had said the Tucson police were, or they were all out hunting for Drake Logan.

Briefly he thought he should alert the police and get backup, but the way he was driving he didn't have the chance to pull out his phone without serious risk of a head-on collision. He could use the handset to the radio, but that would tell Drake exactly what he was planning.

So he hunched over the wheel and concentrated on driving. Alexa only had a few minutes' lead on him and was driving at a normal speed. If he drove fast enough, he could head her off.

His police radio crackled. "Agent Barrett, this is ops center dispatch. Please give your location."

Stuart groaned. They must have been confused by the argument and his demanding phone call and were now trying to figure out where he was and what he was doing.

He ignored it. No way he was touching that radio.

They called several more times, and called Alexa too. She kept radio silence as well.

He arrived in a quiet residential neighborhood in Tempe without running anyone over and reduced his speed to something approaching normal. The GPS said Fiona's apartment was just two blocks away. Stuart slowed further and found a parking space by the side of the road.

As he got out, he checked his gun was ready inside his jacket, and took a look around.

The street was fairly quiet, with a series of ranch houses and the occasional small apartment complex. A car passed him. A van went by slowly on the nearby intersection. An older woman was out walking her dog. A jogger huffed by him, leaving a trail of sweaty air.

A normal neighborhood. Peaceful and dull.

Except a meth dealer lived two blocks away, and her serial killer pal was coming there intent on killing a U.S. Deputy Marshal.

Stuart began to walk, keeping alert. Another car passed by, and for a moment Stuart did a doubletake, thinking it was Alexa. But no, it was just a similar make and model.

He got to an intersection and looked to the right, to where he knew Fiona's apartment complex would be. This street was equally quiet, with just a couple of people getting into a car half a block away. Stuart headed for the apartment, passing by several houses and their cars parked in the driveways.

Just as he passed one house and was approaching the driveway of another, he paused.

A van was parked in the driveway with the engine idling, a plain white model with tinted windows up front and no windows in the back. And he swore it was the same van that had passed him a couple of minutes before.

But that van had been going another direction.

Was that movement he saw behind the tinted windows? Was someone sitting in the passenger seat?

Just then, the back of the van opened up and two men and a woman leapt out, all wearing ski masks. The move was so sudden, and the van so close, they were on him almost before he managed to draw his gun.

Almost, but not quite.

Just as the first man grabbed him by the collar, the knife in his other hand glittering in the streetlight, Stuart yanked out his gun and shot him in the gut. The man let out a gasp and doubled over.

Stuart raised his gun to take out the other two, but the woman swung a tire iron and knocked his gun away. The gun went off, sending a bullet into the night air.

Stuart backed off, narrowly avoiding another swing by the tire iron. The third attacker, a lean man, rushed him, a nightstick in his grip.

No guns. They had obviously wanted to subdue him quietly and throw him in the van without anybody noticing. Too late. He could hear screams from the couple who had been getting into the car on the same street, and a shout from somewhere else.

That was all he had time to notice before the man with the nightstick came at him.

The guy was quick, but untrained. Stuart grabbed his wrist, locked his elbow, and flipped him so he landed hard on the pavement.

Then Stuart spun around, lashing out with a kick at the woman wielding the tire iron.

She was too quick for him and ducked to the side at the last moment.

Then that tire iron was coming down. Stuart dodged, then dodged again as the woman's backswing nearly caught him on the jaw.

A kick to his ankles. The guy on the sidewalk had recovered enough to lash out at him. The kick was weak, just making Stuart stumble instead of fall, but that was enough.

The tire iron caught him hard on the side of the head.

Stuart blacked out.

CHAPTER TWENTY SEVEN

Alexa parked three blocks away from Fiona's apartment. She needed to approach quietly and on foot. Drake would be coming for this location, might already be here, so she had to take care.

In fact, he had probably beat her here. When she had sped away from Stuart, she had only made it about a mile before a patrol car started shadowing her. She got off the main road, taking a right down a quiet residential street, and the patrol car followed. She cursed, thinking she was being tailed. That impression grew stronger when she took another turn and the police continued to follow, maintaining a discreet distance.

Then another patrol car appeared in front of her.

She hit the gas, peeling around the corner into another street and zigzagging through the neighborhood before cutting across a main road and losing herself in another residential area. She left the police far behind.

All this took time, and by the time she made it to Tempe she had figured that those two patrol cars hadn't been shadowing her, that Stuart hadn't put out an A.P.B. on her vehicle. It had only been her guilty conscience working on her rationality.

So now Drake, after hopefully hearing her announcement to go to Fiona's, would have had time to get there. He would be waiting.

The only advantage she had was that Drake assumed she was unaware of his presence, that she'd simply walk up to the apartment and try to do a routine arrest.

Plus, because this wasn't one of his planned tricks; he wouldn't have had time to arrange any of his nasty little surprises.

She'd surprise him instead.

Alexa loosened the gun in her holster, pulled out the pepper spray with her off hand, and approached the address.

It was a cheap apartment complex like so many others in Arizona, a two-story concrete building faced with stucco with a common walkway open to the parking lot out front and a series of back porches for the apartments behind, each separated by enough space from the others so that no one could climb onto the porch of their neighbor. The building was in the shape of a U, enclosing a small swimming pool.

The pool was empty at this hour, but a couple of porches had people on them. Two college students drank cans of beer while listening to the radio. A middle-aged woman read by the light coming from the open sliding glass door to her apartment.

Fiona's apartment was number 25, on the upper floor. Alexa passed the back at a distance and saw dim light shining behind drawn curtains. No one was on the porch. Her designated parking spot at the side of the building had a battered old white van parked in it.

When Alexa went around front to peer at the entrance from behind the shelter of a pickup truck, her heart froze.

The door stood open.

Has he killed her and fled? Or am I being invited in?

Alexa pulled out her gun and, gripping the pepper spray in her other hand, went around the corner to the far end of the building out of sight of the apartment. Quietly she climbed the stairs.

She moved along the walkway toward the corner of the building, from where she could get another look at Fiona's open front door just twenty yards away. Light shone from the interior to cast a rectangular patch of yellow on the pavement. For a moment she stood there in silence, listening. Other than the regular street sounds, she heard nothing.

Until she heard her name being called.

"Alexa! We're not playing hide and seek anymore. Come on in."

Drake Logan.

She paused, hands gripping the Glock and pepper spray.

"Come on, Alexa. I won't shoot you. I want to talk with you. You're not going to be able to do what you want to do from all the way out there."

How the hell did he figure out I'm here already? He must have people watching.

Fine. I'll subdue and arrest as many goons as he feels like throwing at me.

Squaring her shoulders and taking a deep breath, she moved to the doorway and peeked inside, leading with her gun.

At the other end of a small living room, Drake sat in an armchair. He had an unlit cigarette in one hand and a lighter in the other. He raised them as if to show he was unarmed, then lit the cigarette. The rasp of the lighter sounded loud in the silence.

Alexa ducked low through the doorway, ready to shoot anyone lurking unseen beside it. There was no one. They were alone.

Drake chuckled, then took a long drag of his menthol.

"Aaah. The last cigarette. You'll have to excuse me as I savor this."

He took another long drag, studying her as she kept the gun and pepper spray trained on him from a few feet away.

"Which one of those do you plan to use?" he asked. "You going to spray me in the face and then beat me down? I saw the video of what you did to Keene. Ouch! He's going to feel that for a long time. You're almost there, Alexa. Almost there."

Alexa's gazed roved around the room. No hiding places here. An open doorway led to a small kitchen. The lights were off, but she could see enough to tell no one was in there. A hallway led to three doors, all closed. No lights shone from beneath them. Were they really alone?

Drake Logan gave a sharp whistle and Alexa turned back to him.

"You came up with a nice little plan to catch me with my pants down. You were correct that I was staying here, listening to your operations." He nodded toward a police scanner on the coffee table, now turned off. "And you were correct that I'd have no time to set up a bomb or arrange an ambush. At least so you thought. What you didn't take into account was how well I know you."

"Put your hands in the air."

The distant wail of a police siren interrupted whatever Drake was going to say next. He nodded toward the open door.

"We had a bit of a dust up a few minutes before you showed. The police will be here shortly. If you're planning any more police brutality, you'd better get started."

"Raise your hands," Alexa ordered.

Drake shook his head and continued. "I got connections everywhere, and I do mean everywhere. I even have a pal in the FBI. He got me access to your old files."

Alexa took a step toward him, aiming between his eyes. "I said put your hands in the air."

Drake looked her in the eye. "No. What will you do if I don't? Shoot? Well then, shoot." When she paused, feeling the anger simmer inside her at his callous, dismissive attitude, he went on. "I got to see your psych file. Took me ages to get it, I tell you."

"Bull. You'd never get access to an FBI file."

The serial killer took another drag, let out a long exhalation of smoke, and smiled. "Nightmares. Violent fantasies. Guilt over beating a farm hand at age sixteen and—"

"You bastard!" The red haze was beginning to settle on Alexa's vision. It had taken all her strength to admit her worst fears, her worst faults, to that therapist, and to have Drake, of all people, looking through all her darkest confessions. She gripped the gun tighter.

The police siren drew closer.

"Yes, I really did get that file. Fascinating reading. You showed strength at an early age. Most girls in your position would have become a victim, and would have carried that burden the rest of their lives. Never speaking about it, always letting it color their emotions. Not you. You smacked that guy's jaw with a horseshoe and left his teeth on the floor of the stable. Well done. Where you did wrong was feeling guilty about it."

"How dare you look at my personal life!" Alexa heard her voice break, and hated herself for it.

Drake shrugged. "How else could I get to know you? Oh, I knew there was something to find. Just looking at you I could tell you had a past, that you had a violent side yearning to get out. That's why you chose law enforcement. You wanted to swing that horseshoe at a bad man's face. Again and again and again."

"If you don't put your hands in the air right now, I'm going to unload this pepper spray on you."

"Hold on a minute. There's something I'd like you to see." He gave a little whistle as if summoning a dog.

One of the doors in the hallway opened. A man and woman came out, holding Stuart between them. They had to support him as he stumbled along, a huge welt on the side of his head. Each had a gun in their free hand they held to Stuart's body.

Alexa's rage got overwhelmed by fear and guilt.

She had underestimated Stuart. He had seen her writing something down when Malcolm called, and put two and two together. He had also heard her call her brother by name. So he had found the number to the ranch and called them. Then, while she had been evading an imaginary pursuit, his famous lead foot got him here before her.

She had tried to keep him out of it, tried to keep him safe, and had instead endangered his life.

Focus. You'll never get the two of you out of here alive if you don't focus.

She studied Stuart's two captors.

The woman matched Fiona's description. Seeing her, now Alexa felt doubly sure she had been the woman who helped break Drake out. The man she didn't recognize, but Alexa had no doubt he was a killer too.

"Your partner figured you out just like I did," Drake said. "He got here before you but Harry and Fiona ended up getting him. Shot one of my guys, though. That's what the cops are responding to. Someone called 911 reporting they heard a shot and they just dispatched a patrol car to check. We've been listening in on the police scanner. Harry's our communications expert. Figured out a way to descramble police radio. Smart guy. Close the door, Alexa. We don't want to be disturbed."

Alexa hesitated and looked at Stuart. "You all right?"

Stuart nodded weakly.

"No, he's not all right," Fiona snapped. "And he'll be dead in a second or two if you don't close that damn door."

Alexa stepped over to the door and, without moving her gun from Drake, closed the door with her foot.

"That's better," Drake said, smiling and taking a puff from his cigarette. "Now we can have a chat. We don't have much time, though, so you better hurry up and kill me."

"I will kill you if your goons don't drop their weapons."

Drake shook his finger, making the smoke from his cigarette do a little dance. "Correction. They won't drop their weapons and you will kill me. If you don't kill me, they'll shoot him."

Confused, Alexa looked into his eyes. It was a hard thing to do. They radiated power. And this time they did not show his usual brash confidence cut with a hint of mockery for the world. Right now they practically glowed with intent, a superhuman will like an acrophobic skydiver about to leap from an airplane.

What had he said when I came in? "The last cigarette."

"Wait. You really do want me to kill you," Alexa said, baffled.

Drake gave her a kindly smile. "It's what you really want to do. It's in your nature. I want to help you, Alexa. You're like me. And in a different situation ..." Drake looked away for a moment. Was she seeing right? Was he actually blushing?

He gathered his cool quickly enough and looked back at her. "That siren's getting louder. They're almost here. It won't take long for them to search the area and they'll probably bust in here sooner or later. There were witnesses. You don't have much time. Release your inner strength. Kill me."

"I'm going to arrest you and let the state execute you," Alexa said. "Don't worry, I'll be in the execution chamber when they fry you."

Drake shook his head. "That won't satisfy you. It would be like watching porn instead of having sex. A cheap substitute for the real thing. I never liked how they let the family of the victim watch executions. The family should either pull the switch themselves or get lost. And if I die in the electric chair it will be meaningless. If I get shot down by some other cop it will be meaningless. If the prison gangs finally take me out it will be doubly meaningless. I want my death to signify something, because I know it's close. No one can run forever, not even me. I want my death to liberate someone else. You."

Alexa's hand trembled. She looked down the sights of her Glock, straight into Drake Logan's eyes.

"Do it, Alexa. Do it. You know you want to. Do it to save your partner."

God, it would be so easy. Nail him right between the eyes. Powers would be avenged. Given the situation, I'm not sure I'd even get in trouble.

"If you don't kill me, Alexa, think how many more bodies I'll produce before I'm run down. Cops. Criminals. Innocent bystanders. Him." Drake nodded toward Stuart.

Alexa didn't look at Stuart. She couldn't bring herself to. She didn't want to know what expression he wore.

He and the two criminals Fiona and Harry remained silent.

Drake is right. Killing him would save lives.

Her gun shook a little.

And it would feel so, so good.

"Come on, Alexa," he whispered. "Make me proud. You didn't kill the Jersey Devil when you had a chance, and you've been carrying that weight ever since. Don't carry this too."

"Damn you," Alexa growled.

Drake leaned forward, careful to keep his head in the line of fire.

"You're like me. And you know it."

Alexa shuddered.

No I'm not.

She bent down and set the gun and pepper spray on the floor. She could not bring herself to look at Stuart.

She couldn't bring herself to look Drake in the eye either.

"That's disappointing," Drake said quietly. He took a final drag of his cigarette, extinguished against the heel of his boot, and reached behind him, pulling out a Bowie knife.

"I'll kill you quick," Drake said, leaping up and rushing at her.

Alexa slapped the lights out, plunging them into darkness.

CHAPTER TWENTY EIGHT

Alexa had to dodge to the side as she heard and felt Drake close in on her. The knife whistled through the air and she felt the breeze as the blade cut close.

With no time to grab the gun or pepper spray lying on the floor, Alexa cut to the left, hoping to get to the kitchen where she might be able to grab a knife. The sound of a struggle on the other side of the room told her Stuart was back in the fight.

Her shin banged into something and she found herself falling. She landed hard on the floor, with what felt like a coffee table falling with her. Another loud thud was probably the scanner.

As Alexa got to her hands and knees, she felt something metallic and heavy about the size of a toaster but much heavier. The scanner.

She grabbed it and felt its reassuring weight.

Someone let out a cry. The room flashed as a gun went off, leaving garish afterimages in her eyes.

Alexa stood, stumbled over the table again, and took two steps to steady herself.

The lights flicked on again, and she found herself facing Harry. His hand was on the light switch, his other hand gripping a gun. He raised it.

Alexa smacked him upside the head with the scanner.

Harry grunted and slammed against the door, legs buckling. His gun went off, a bullet burying itself in the ceiling.

Alexa hit him hard twice more. He crumpled to the floor. Alexa kicked the gun away, scooped up her Glock lying nearby, and spun on the others.

Only to find Stuart holding a gun on Fiona. Fiona sat on the floor holding her shoulder as blood seeped through her fingers.

"Where's Drake?" Alexa said.

"I heard someone move toward the back of the apartment," Stuart replied.

Alexa rushed past him, flicking on the hallway light. The furthest door was open.

She advanced, keeping her gun level, trying to maintain caution while a rising edge of panic told her Drake would get away.

Bursting into the last room, she found it was a bedroom. A sliding glass door led to the balcony. It was open.

"Damn it!"

She got to the balcony just in time see Drake running across the parking lot. The police siren had stopped. Flashing lights told her the patrol car was parked on the opposite side of the building. Drake angled away from it, heading for a corner.

Alexa aimed for his legs and fired. The bullet sparked off the concrete inches away. Drake didn't even slow down as he rounded the corner.

Cursing to herself, Alexa clambered over the railing and jumped down onto hard dirt below, ankle twinging with pain, her legs narrowly missing a cactus.

Alexa sprinted across the parking lot, ignoring the ache in her ankle.

She rounded the corner, leaving some space between her and it so Drake couldn't leap out at her, and checked the side of the building.

He was gone.

There was nothing but a pair of dumpsters side by side, a chain link fence, a couple of parked cars, and the balconies of the apartments.

Had he hopped the fence? It looked too high for him to have made it in time, and it wasn't shaking. Through the fence she could see the side of another apartment building. No sign of him there.

Had he gone into one of the apartments? All the doors to the balconies were closed and, knowing this neighborhood's crime rate, locked. She would have heard him break in.

That left him hiding behind the dumpsters or behind one of the parked cars.

A police officer ran around the far corner.

"Hands up!" he shouted.

"Deputy Marshal Alexa Chase," she shouted back just as the cop took in her uniform. Good thing he wasn't too trigger happy. "Did you see anyone go your way?"

"No."

So he's still here, within a few yards of me.

"Where's your partner?"

"It's just me."

Alexa grimaced. Budget cuts meant many patrol cars only had one officer in them. She heard another siren in the distance, approaching. Not soon enough.

"Drake Logan is either hiding behind those dumpsters or behind or under one of those cars. Keep an eye on them. Drake! You're surrounded. Come out with your hands up."

Silence.

She looked at the cop. "I'm going to check the car nearest to me. Cover me."

The cop nodded and moved to the chain link fence to get a better angle of fire.

Alexa got on her hands and knees and looked under both cars. She saw nothing. So he wasn't lying underneath either vehicle. He could be crouching behind one of the wheels, though.

Getting up, she moved around the first car, keeping enough distance that Drake couldn't jump out before she got a shot off. Alexa couldn't gun him down when he was helpless, but if he attacked her, she would not hesitate.

She found herself hoping he'd try.

Whipping around the first car, she found nothing.

Now for the next one. She could hear that police siren getting closer, and another in the distance. No chance they'd get here in time for anything more than cleaning up. It was just her and this patrolman.

She approached the second car.

"Drake. Come out with your hands up."

Just as she rounded the car, a noise above her made her look up.

Someone had opened a window, saw the gun, yelped, and slammed it shut.

A half second of distraction. Enough to make the difference between life and death.

She brought her aim back down to bear on the space behind the second car …

… and saw nothing.

"Damn," she muttered, and turned to the two dumpsters.

They were big metal things with bright yellow plastic lids. He could easily hide behind them, in the narrow space between the dumpster and the chain link fence. Or he could squeeze between them.

"OK, Drake. We know you're hiding behind the dumpsters. Get out of there."

Silence.

Of course he's going to make me go get him.

Alexa motioned to the cop and they approached the dumpsters. She peeked behind them from a distance, but it was all shadows there, and heaps of trash bags some resident had been too lazy to throw in the dumpster.

Briefly she thought of sending the cop around to the other lot to look from a better angle, but she didn't want to be alone with Drake. Despite putting down her gun in the apartment, she still didn't quite trust herself.

Motioning for the cop to cover her, she moved in closer. He helped by shining a flashlight in. Nothing.

"He's in between them," the cop said, and then did something terribly stupid.

He sauntered around the dumpsters to get to a point where he could see between them.

He kept back, but not enough.

For just then the lid of one of the dumpsters flew open and Drake sprang out, hitting the police officer square in the body, both of them going down. The officer lost his hold on both his gun and his flashlight

The cop managed to tuck in his head as he fell so he didn't strike it on the pavement and get knocked out. Drake raised his Bowie knife. The officer desperately grabbed his arm and they struggled.

Alexa couldn't get a shot in without endangering the officer. She moved closer. The cop and Drake struggled, rolling along the pavement.

Drake would win. She knew that.

As Drake rolled on top, Alexa landed a kick to his ribs. The serial killer grunted. For a moment it looked like the cop would be able to get on top, but with a supreme effort, Drake wrenched his knife hand free, slashed the cop across the chest, and then leapt at Alexa.

She couldn't fire with the officer right behind Drake. So she lashed out with another kick, hitting Drake in the knee and making him stumble.

That didn't stop him, though. Nothing ever did.

He ploughed right into her, tackling her like a football player. Her back slammed hard against the dumpster, hitting at an angle and making her almost fall down.

Somehow she kept on her feet. She struck him a glancing blow with the butt of her Glock, making him loosen his grip. He backed off, slapping her arm up and away before she could shoot him.

And then she couldn't, because the cop had risen to his feet. His uniform was sliced open across the chest, revealing Kevlar beneath. Apparently this was a bad enough neighborhood for the police to routinely wear it.

The officer raised his baton high, swinging it down on Drake's head.

Drake spun around, grabbed the officer's arm, twisted, and flung him against Alexa.

Again she almost went down. By the time she regained her balance, Drake had the baton in his grasp and swung it across the cop's jaw, knocking him out cold.

Alexa raised her gun, only to have it smacked from her hand by the baton. She gave Drake a hard hook with her other hand, then tried to flip him.

Drake was ready for the move and when she tried to throw him to the ground, he tripped her, and they ended up on the ground together.

"Well ain't this cozy," he laughed, cutting off as she punched him again. "What will it take to get you to shoot me, girl? Grab your titties?"

"Shut up!" She slammed his head into the pavement.

"That's the way!" he cackled. "Knock my teeth out with a horseshoe!"

"Shut up! Shut up! Shut up!" She slammed his again into the pavement again and again until he went limp. Then she scrambled to her feet, grabbed her gun, and trained it on him.

Kneeling down, she checked the cop and found him alive, just knocked out.

Drake moved, groaning. His hand went to his head.

Before he could turn over, she put a knee on the small of his back and leaned her whole weight onto it. His head turned, neck craning so he could look up at her. She put her gun in his face. He blinked, focused, and grinned, showing teeth stained with blood.

"Good girl."

Alexa held her aim steady. The sirens had stopped.

"They're here," he said. "You only got a moment."

Alexa didn't reply, reaching for the handcuffs on her belt.

“Go on,” Drake said gently. “One pull of the trigger and you’ll become what you truly are.”

“I am Deputy Marshal Alexa Chase of the U.S. Marshals Service, and I’m placing you under arrest.”

CHAPTER TWENTY NINE

Alexa put Drake's hands behind his back, and cuffed him.

She put the cuffs on too tight. She allowed herself that little bit of satisfaction.

A pair of officers with guns out, ran around the corner.

"I got him," Alexa said.

"Got who?" the officer said.

She blinked. Well, how would he know?

"A nobody. A ten-cent philosopher who no one will remember a year from now."

Drake chuckled. "Even someone as weak as you knows that ain't true."

"Weak?" Alexa snorted. "I beat you."

"The only thing you beat is your own spirit."

"You keep telling yourself that as you sit on death row, waiting for your meaningless death."

Drake Logan slumped, and Alexa knew she had scored a hit. He had revealed himself too much in that conversation in Fiona's apartment. Showed that he, in fact, was one of the weak. He couldn't stand thinking that he was normal, and would do anything, even get killed by Alexa, to prove that he was not.

And now he would be just another prisoner, until one day his time would be up and he'd take that slow walk to the execution chamber.

Alexa turned to the two policemen. "You, help this officer. You, come with me to apartment 25. An FBI agent is injured there and holding down two prisoners."

As they walked, the patrolman who came with her radioed in the news. Alexa smiled. Too bad Harry wasn't around to hear that. She had broken that scanner over his head.

They climbed the stairs to Fiona's apartment, telling several curious neighbors peeking out doors and windows to get back inside.

They found Stuart sitting in the armchair Drake had once sat in, still looking a bit dazed but managing to keep a gun on Fiona and Harry. Harry was cuffed and lying face down on the floor. Stuart hadn't been able to cuff Fiona with her injured shoulder so he had cuffed one ankle to the wrist of her good arm. He had also patched her up to keep her from bleeding out.

A good man, Alexa thought. *Helping someone who tried to kill him. That's what real law enforcement does.*

I could learn a thing or two from him.

Stuart looked up, eyes going wide when he saw her leading Drake.

Is he surprised I didn't kill him? Alexa thought, embarrassed that he would think that.

"You did the right thing," he said.

"Thanks for the vote of confidence," she said, standing. She looked him in the eye. "I mean that."

Stuart hesitated, then said, "You shouldn't have tried to go it alone. I know you were trying to keep me out of harm's way, and I know you were trying to test yourself, but you can't do that to a partner."

"You're right. I'm sorry. I'm especially sorry about chewing you out on the air. I'll tell everyone what really happened. And I'm sorry I didn't rely on you more …," she paused for half a second, " … partner."

He gave a tired smile. "I guess this is job done."

CHAPTER THIRTY

Alexa pulled into her little ranch outside of Phoenix. For the past two days, she and Stuart had been buried in paperwork and debriefings. Fiona copped a plea bargain and told the police the location of every one of Drake's followers that she knew of. Various agencies rounded them up, and several of the suspects confessed to the locations of several more in Drake Logan's gang. Searches brought up stashes of drugs and illegal guns, leading to more charges. A wave of arrests rippled through the Southwest's criminal community.

Now that the investigation could be left to local law enforcement, Alexa had been given a well-earned rest. Two weeks paid leave. More if she requested it.

She needed time to heal, both physically and emotionally.

And the best place to do that was as far away from the city as possible.

As she pulled up in front of her quiet little home outside Phoenix, she saw Stacy's bike leaning up against the front wall.

Alexa smiled, turned off the engine, and went into the house.

And nearly burst into tears.

Balloons covered the living room floor, and a bright hand-drawn banner saying "Welcome Home, Heroin!" was hung over the doorway. She recognized Stacy's handwriting. And spelling.

"It's good to be home," Alexa murmured, wiping her eyes.

She passed through the living room, her feet bumping balloons out of the way, and passed through the kitchen. Judging from the dirty dishes, Stacy had stayed here last night.

As usual, the girl was out with the horses. She had an arm around Wesson as she took selfies of them together. For a moment Alexa watched from the back door, enjoying the simple happiness this girl had when she had a place where she could be a kid.

Stacy looked up from her phone and spotted her.

"Alexa! You're back!"

She clambered over the fence and ran to her, giving her a huge hug. Alexa's ribs still hurt, but she didn't tell the girl to stop. The hug felt too good.

"Don't worry," Stacy said, pulling away. "I didn't come to the house until I heard you got that psycho. It's safe now, right?"

"Yes. The house is safe. It's all right now."

Except for Powers being dead. So no, Stacy, things won't be all right with me for a long, long time.

At least you make things a bit better.

"Awesome! Sorry about the balloons. I put them up right after you arrested him but that was a couple of days ago and they're not floaty anymore."

"That's OK. We can put up some more. I got two weeks off."

The girl's eyes lit up. "Cool! We can spend it riding. We'll go out first thing tomorrow morning."

"Don't you have school tomorrow?"

"Helloooo?" Stacy said, tapping her finger on the side of Alexa's head. "It's Friday. That means the weekend. No school tomorrow."

"Ugh. I'd completely forgotten what day it is."

"You work too much."

"So I've been told."

"So we can ride for two days straight!"

"We'll have to put that off until next weekend. I'm just passing through, I'm afraid. I told my father and brothers I'd head on up to Bumble Bee and spend a few days with them."

Alexa would rather just stay here and sleep for two weeks, but Malcolm was so fragile after all this. He needed her.

Stacy's disappointment seemed to ooze out of every pore. "Oh. Family only."

Family is what you make of it. Isn't that what Stuart said?

Alexa suddenly had an idea. She pinched Stacy's cheek and smiled. "You're family too. Why don't you ask your mom and dad if you can come up for the weekend?"

Stacy's face lit up. "To your dad's ranch? With all that land and horses you told me about?"

"Sure thing. We'll ride all weekend."

"I'll go ask them right now," she said, already bolting out the door.

“And don’t forget to pack your homework!” Alexa called after her. She wasn’t sure the girl heard over the sound of the screen door slamming.

Alexa smiled, although the smile wasn’t an entirely happy one. She felt sure Stacy’s parents would agree. That would be the perfect opportunity for them to go on the mother of all benders without their daughter’s disapproving glare to ruin the party.

While Alexa waited for the girl to come back, she called her father.

“Hey Dad, I’ll be up in a couple of hours. And I’m bringing Stacy.”

She decided to tell him, not ask him. You don’t have to ask to bring family home.

“That girl with the loser parents you take care of?”

“You could put it that way.”

“All right. I’ll have Malcolm make up the spare bedroom. Why haven’t you brought her up before?”

Alexa blinked. “Um, just too busy I guess.”

“Well, look forward to meeting her. See you in a bit.”

* * *

A couple of hours later, Alexa and Stacy pulled into the ranch outside Bumble Bee. The dogs came to the gate to bark their heads off as usual, and they could see her father sitting on the porch. He gave a lazy wave.

“I’ll get the gate!” Stacy said, leaping out of the truck like she had been to the ranch a thousand times. The dogs ran up to her, but she didn’t show any fear and soon they stopped their barking and started wagging their tails and leaping up on her playfully. She unhitched the gate, petted them all, and Alexa drove slowly in.

Dad stepped down from the porch as Alexa parked.

“Where’s Wayne and Malcolm?” she asked.

“Wayne is out back preparing the barbeque. Malcolm is at his meeting.” Alexa’s father turned to Stacy, who was just walking up after closing the gate. “You must be my daughter’s stable girl. She’s told me a lot about you.”

Stacy stood up a little straighter. “That’s right, Mr. Chase. I take care of Smith and Wesson while she’s out hunting bad guys.”

“No need for that Mr. Chase stuff. Call me Uncle Fred. Now I bet you’d like to see our stables, wouldn’t you?”

"Sure! Alexa says you got seven horses."

"We do, and we got a mare about to foal. Let's go take a look."

Alexa pulled out their bags. "I'll put the things away and say hi to Wayne while you two get acquainted."

Dad looked at her. "Staying long?"

Alexa shrugged. "I'll need to get her back to school for Monday."

"Then you're coming back here to rest, right?"

Alexa looked away. "Well, I haven't really given it much thought."

Dad walked over and put a hand on her shoulder. "You should. I want you to. And if this half pint kid is as good a stable girl as you say she is, she can come back up next weekend too. In the meantime, I think you and I have a few things to work out."

He looked her in the eyes as he said this, something he rarely did, and squeezed her shoulder.

"All right, Dad. I'd like that."

They hugged. After a moment, her father pulled away, embarrassed. Then he turned to Stacy. "Well don't just stand there gawking, fill up that bucket over there at the hose and let's bring the horses some water. You want to hang out at this ranch, it's going to cost you some work."

"OK, Uncle Fred."

Stacy ran to fetch the bucket and Dad ambled off, following her.

Alexa chuckled and carried the bags to the porch. After she mounted the steps, she looked out over the familiar front yard, the dogs lolling in the dirt, the line of her family's pickups, and the broad open desert stretching as far as the eye could see.

Yeah. This is where I should be for the next couple of weeks, with my screwed up but loving family and adopted family. This is where I belong.

Her phone rang. She put down her bags and checked the number. Marshal Hernandez.

Uh-oh.

"Hello, sir."

"Deputy Marshal, I just wanted to congratulate you once again on your excellent work on the Drake Logan case."

"Thank you, sir," she replied, immensely relieved he hadn't called with bad news.

"Have you started your vacation?"

"Yes, sir."

"Good. Now I want you to take off those two weeks, and I mean the full two weeks. You've more than earned it. While you're relaxing, I do have something I'd like you to think about."

"What's that, sir?"

"I was speaking with Deputy Director Sandford of the FBI this morning. He was equally impressed with your performance. He spoke with the people upstairs and they think the collaboration was a success. They want to take it into the midterm and they think you and Agent Barrett would make the perfect team."

Alexa blinked. "You want us to be partners?"

"For a little while at least. There are a number of open cases that we feel an interagency collaboration might help solve. Many of them are here in the Southwest so it wouldn't involve a move, at least not for you."

"And what does Agent Barrett think?" Alexa asked.

"He's already agreed to come over in the short term, although he said he wanted to discuss some things with you first."

"Oh."

What things? Probably a list of demands like "be a real partner," "don't run off without telling me," "don't get me on the five o'clock news." Those sorts of things.

Sane things, in other words.

"So give it some thought," Marshal Hernandez said. "We have some big cases that could use your touch. There are serious ones, though, with some of the worst criminals the region has ever coughed up. It's going to be tough."

"I'd like to do it if he's willing," she said, her assured tone matching her feelings.

"Oh, you don't need to answer now. You can have a few days to mull it over."

Alexa thought of Stuart and how brave he had been in the field, how concerned he had been about the victims, and how his keen mind had solved several of the problems they had faced.

He wasn't Robert Powers, but then again neither was she.

Neither was anyone.

"I don't need to mull it over, sir. I'd like Agent Barrett as my new partner."

Alexa hung up, picked up the bags, and carried them inside. She dropped her own bag in her old bedroom, the one she'd known her entire childhood, and looked around.

Home.

She was home.

NOW AVAILABLE!

<u>THE KILLING TIDE</u>
(An Alexa Chase Suspense Thriller—Book 2)

THE KILLING TIDE (An Alexa Chase Suspense Thriller—Book 2) is book #2 in a new series by mystery and suspense author Kate Bold, which begins with THE KILLING GAME (Book #1).

Alexa Chase, 34, a brilliant profiler in the FBI's Behavioral Analysis Unit, was too good at her job. Haunted by all the serial killers she caught, she left a stunning career behind to join the U.S. Marshals. As a Deputy Marshal, Alexa—fit, and as tough as she is brilliant—could immerse herself in a simple career of hunting down fugitives and bringing them to justice.

But with her last case a big success, the FBI and the Marshals have decided to make their joint-task force permanent. Alexa, reeling from her own traumatic past and her PTSD of hunting serial killers, has no choice: she will now have to work with an FBI partner she dislikes and hunt down serial killers whose jurisdiction intertwines with that of the U.S. Marshals. Alexa finds herself forced to confront the thing she dreads the most—entering a killer's mind.

Two federal judges are murdered, and startling evidence points to the work of a serial killer with a vendetta. But the judges have tried and convicted hundreds of people over their long careers, and with the suspect list a mile long, Alexa is in the race of her life to find the killer before he kills another judge on his list.

And when the next victim offers a shocking twist, it throws everything Alexa thought she knew into doubt.

Is this truly a vendetta? Or is this killer far more diabolical then he seems?

To find this diabolical killer, Alexa will have to do what she fears most—enter his twisted mind, before he can strike again. It's a life-and-death game of cat and mouse, and it's winner takes all. But will the darkness swallow her whole?

A page-turning and harrowing crime thriller featuring a brilliant and tortured Deputy Marshal, the ALEXA CHASE series is a riveting mystery, packed with non-stop action, suspense, twists and turns, revelations, and driven by a breakneck pace that will keep you flipping pages late into the night.

Book #3 in the series—THE KILLING HOUR—is also available.

Kate Bold

Debut author Kate Bold is author of the ALEXA CHASE SUSPENSE THRILLER series, comprising three books (and counting).

An avid reader and lifelong fan of the mystery and thriller genres, Kate loves to hear from you, so please feel free to visit www.kateboldauthor.com to learn more and stay in touch.

BOOKS BY KATE BOLD

ALEXA CHASE SUSPENSE THRILLER
THE KILLING GAME (Book #1)
THE KILLING TIDE (Book #2)
THE KILLING HOUR (Book #3)

Printed in Great Britain
by Amazon

17715257R00120